A Well-Respected Dead Man

A Well-Respected Dead Man

Tricia Allen

Five Star • Waterville, Maine

First Edition, Second Printing

Published in 2003 in conjunction with Tekno Books and Ed Gorman.

Set in 11 pt. Plantin.

Printed in the United States on permanent paper.

Library of Congress Cataloging-in-Publication Data

Allen, Tricia.
    A well-respected dead man / Tricia Allen.—1st ed.
        p. cm.—(Five Star first edition mystery series)
    ISBN 0-7862-5441-6 (hc : alk. paper)
    1. Undercover operations—Fiction. 2. Women journalists—Fiction. 3. Organized crime—Fiction.
    4. Dallas (Tex.)—Fiction. I. Title. II. Series.
PS3601.L437W45 2003
    813′.6—dc21   2003052921

Acknowledgements

To Jill Hickman (who is *not* the model for
Wild Jill Cody in this book),
Bob, Hannah and Madison,
and to the Raven Mavens and the DFW Writers' Workshop
for their valuable critiques

Readers who recognize terrain around Dallas will also notice topographical "errors." To accommodate fictional needs, I took certain liberties which may be apparent to the city's history buffs. For instance, David Weather's apartment building, the Claypoole, sits approximately where the historic Lake Cliff Towers still overlooks Lake Cliff Park, although the Claypoole has balconies and fewer floors. Some days, I think the Claypoole stands in place of the Towers, other days I believe it sat next door. Likewise a motel at the corner of Sylvan and Fort Worth Avenue caught my fancy and underwent considerable fictional remodeling both in size and character. The Cliff Heights Hotel is a purely imaginary place, and is not intended to represent any existing business, past or present.

Resources

My gratitude goes to several people for their help in recreating Dallas and Texas in 1947.
Lorayne Genaro allowed me to give her late mother, Lou

Lattimore, a cameo in this story. I knew Lou and had wonderful conversations with her and her sister "Lobie" about life in Dallas after the war. These two wonderful ladies lived colorful lives among the city's champagne set at a time when style meant evening dresses, hats and gloves and following the exploits of gangsters like Lois Green and Herbert "the Cat" Noble. Their keen insight into the customs and taboos of the era added a dimension I couldn't have gotten simply from written records.

I am particularly grateful to Hugh W. Stephens, author of *The Texas City Disaster, 1947*, University of Texas Press, 1997. This fine book served as a valuable research aid and I recommend it to anyone interested in learning more about the *Grandcamp* explosion.

Ann Arnold's *Gamblers & Gangsters: Fort Worth's Jacksboro Highway in the 1940s & 1950s* (Eakin Press, Austin, TX, 1998), served as a valuable resource for general gambler behavior of the era. I hope my fictional gamblers are half as colorful as the real-life lowlifes Ann depicted in her book.

The *Times Herald* headline from April 16, 1947, was REPRINTED WITH PERMISSION OF THE DALLAS MORNING NEWS.

Additionally, Doug Jeanes of the Cavanaugh Flight Museum in Addison, Texas, helped me choose the right vintage plane for my fictional oil company of 1947; Tony Zoppi gave me valuable information about Dallas nightclubs of the era, and Larry Powell of *The Dallas Morning News* supplied interesting tidbits of Dallas history and directed me to other sources.

My good friend John P. Katsantonis provided invaluable information about Chicago's Little Italy in the forties.

And finally, special thanks to Jan Grape for passing my manuscript up the line at the publisher.

Other acknowledgements on page 319.

Prologue

Wednesday, April 16, 1947
Dallas, Texas

Willie Peabody lay belly down in the tall grass where they'd dumped him, cursing his killers for their inefficiency. Six bullets in him and all they'd managed to do was to paralyze him and leave him in the riverbottoms to rot. Incompetent idiots. Unless that's what they meant to happen—for him to die out here slow, decomposing all alone.

The bastards! Willie mustered up what little spit he could to give them that done this a sign of his contempt, but he couldn't get the lung power to spit it anywhere so it just dribbled out. They'd throwed him onto a little rise to where his head aimed downhill, so the spit ran up into his nose and tickled. Unless that was blood bubbles coming out of it; he couldn't be sure. Couldn't see his own lip or reach a hand up to wipe his face. Couldn't move his head to scratch his nose, but it wouldn't've done him any good anyway if he could, on account of the mud. Can't scratch with mud. A broke-off blade of grass was sticking him in the chin, but he couldn't move to get it over to where he needed it.

He let out a howl. Always swore he'd go out kicking and screaming, and here he was, couldn't even reach up to scratch his own face.

Six bullets and he was still alive, could even still think, if he tried real hard. Stayed awake all night last night after they left him, practicing thinking while he listened to snakes and bugs and what-all crawling around. Practiced remembering who done it, and why, so he could tell his boy who to go after when they found him.

It was getting hard to remember. Something to do with . . .

Six bullets. Six. All right, could still count and could still remember, just slower'n normal. Going to his car in that lot on Colorado Avenue. Paying a visit to . . . to . . . Could see the face but couldn't reach the name. Okay, skip that for now. Three men pull up from another car and come running at him. He'd knowed them and what they wanted. One, two, in the chest, hurt like hell, in like ice picks, blew like dynamite once they got inside. Not much noise for the neighbors because of the silencers. Took that third bullet when he turned tail to run, which he knew he shouldn't've, but he couldn't get in his car by then anyway. Musta hit the backbone, up high. It was on number three that he couldn't even reach out his hands to break the fall. Number three turned him into this carcass that he could still think out of and breathe out of but couldn't spit out of.

Them last ones he never felt at all, number fourfivesix, in the back, he didn't know where, but he knew they hit by the way his head snapped thisaway and thataway, three times, while he was falling face down onto the blacktop. Hit his chin hard and like to knocked him out. One of 'em let off a couple of shots into his car before the other told him to cut it the hell out, shots make too much noise hitting metal. He couldn't see nothing face down like that but then they turned him over and grabbed him by his arms and legs like a dead deer. He got a good view when they swung him. First it was them balconies on the building—the Claypoole Apartment Hotel, he remembered that clear now—and when they turned him to throw him in the trunk, the neon Flying Red Horse upside-down and way off, turning across the river downtown. Whole thing lasted six, maybe seven seconds.

They put him in Cab's trunk while the other one shot up the Packard. Wasn't no point in that. Idiots ought to've been picking up the cartridges and beating the hell out of there. Not professional at all.

Willie cursed aloud at the memory.

Now it was daylight, but the wind was cold on his head. Funny how he couldn't feel nothing, except his head, which felt like a block of ice. Must be eight, nine o'clock. They dumped him pointing west, so he couldn't see the sun to figure out the time, even if he'd a been face up.

Something was bad wrong. Ought to been a fisherman out here by now. You could always count on plenty of them colored fishermen, before dawn, near ever day. That's always who found the bodies. If one of them would just save him, he would make sure they got a big re-ward. His boy would pay it.

His boy would pay plenty. But first light was long past and there hadn't been a single colored boy out here with a single stinkin' pole.

Fourfivesix. Fourfivesix? Pick up sticks?

Now why in the hell was he saying them numbers? Couldn't rightly recollect. His boy would fix things. Would go after them that done it. Which was . . . ?

He couldn't rightly recollect. They brung him out here in a cab, though. He was dead sure of that.

There was a rustling in the grass. Might be them, coming back to finish him off. Never heard no car, though, so that meant it had to be a colored fisherman. A colored fisherman wouldn't have no car to come out in.

"You are late, boy," he called out. "What has got into you? Over here. Hey, boy, over here."

The rustling came closer. Wasn't no colored boy, though. White man in a Sunday-go-to-meeting suit. Old country suit, black, like for a funeral, with long tails flapping behind him like broken hawk wings in this wind. The man bent his knees and sank them fancy pants down in the muck, right in front of him. He had on a string tie with a little horseshoe for the slide. Thought he recognized him, only it couldn't be who he reckoned. Who it looked like had been dead fifteen years. Eyes had to been deceiving him.

Willie sat up for a better look.

It couldn't be, but it was. The devil himself, old Tom Weather, the District Attorney, with his coal black eyes and that dago-slick hair, parted down the middle like somebody'd shot a crease through it and couldn't no hair grow there; Tom Weather, kneeling down before him in the mud, ruining his suit pants to get a good, up-close look.

Old Tom chuckled, deep and satisfied.

Wasn't funny. That smart ass always thought he was better 'cause he was the D.A., but every man has his price. Even old Tom Weather.

The visitor grinned and grinned and finally spoke. "The devil is a busy man."

"You got no call to seek me out," Willie cried. "I done already took care of you."

"No statute of limitations on murder, Willie-boy. You made a real mess of yourself with that second chance I gave you."

"You gave me! Hell, mister highfaluting. It was th'other way around."

Tom Weather shook his head weary-like, the way them lawyer boys did when they thought they had you. Like they was even one hair better, with their devil's deals and plea bargains and shifty shenanigans. Wanting you to sell out your own kin.

"You had your chance, Willie, and look what you got to show for it."

"I done what I had to do. Never had me no rich wife or no lawyer diploma. Woulda been able to re-tire from my life of crime if I hadn't've of had to trade my oil leases."

Old sonabitch ought to understand what that meant.

The D.A. sat there and smiled and smiled, big as life.

Damn him, the old devil wouldn't take the bait.

"I'm taking you in," Tom Weather said, in that hoity-toit voice that used to make Willie so mad. He rose up out of the mud and made some kind of grand motion that Willie knew meant "get up." He didn't want to, but he figured he was obliged to, the man being the D.A. and all.

"I ain't going one God-damned place with you," he said, but there he was, standing up. Then there he was, following his summoner across the grass.

"Where the hell we going?"

Old Tom turned around and laid those coal black eyes on him and didn't say a word.

Willie felt a chill deep in his soul. "I ast you a civilized question, where the hell we going?"

"I expect you already know, Willie-boy," Tom Weather said, solemn-like. "Just think on it for a while. I know how you like to mull things over. But first I gotta see my son."

Chapter 1

David Weather did not believe in ghosts, Second Sight, visits from beyond the grave, or even very much in God, beyond the conviction that He was a Force to be reckoned with and that it wasn't wise to think you were Him, so he'd labeled this morning's dream a relic of last night's booze, influenced by Willie Peabody's surprise visit, with no deeper message to be divined, and vowed to shake it off. He stood in the shower and knew it wouldn't go peacefully.

It had been a doozy of a dream. His long-dead father and Willie Peabody appeared in his bedroom this morning, disturbing his sleep and arousing a vicious hangover. His father wore funereal attire, suitable for burial, while Willie jumped around and demanded to meet his Maker, the same way jailhouse scum holler for their lawyers.

You don't get to see Him, Tom Weather told Willie with a big grin.

Ever'body meets their Maker, Willie protested. *Gets a reckoning. A chance to explain.*

It don't work that way when you're condemned. The Old Tomcat fiddled with the horseshoe slide on his string tie and used his just-folks voice, the one he used to draw out witnesses on the stand who might be uncomfortable around all that courtroom pomp. This Tom spoke in the simple country style of his own daddy's people. *Ain't nobody interested in hearing your excuses. Judgment's already handed down.* Then his father tried to warn him about something but Willie kept tugging at the Tomcat's black coat sleeve like a hopped-up jackrabbit, distracting the messenger from his message.

Into that mix walked his father's old business partner, Red Holcomb, stately and elegant the way he'd been in life, red hair faded to gray, but still carrying a hint of fire.

You don't deserve her, Red said. Weather assumed Red meant his daughter, Leslie, Weather's fiancée until she caught him in an affair a few weeks ago, but he also knew, the way you know a lot more in dreams than anyone in them explains, that Red meant Jane Alder.

He'd started to argue but found himself in Jane's hospital room, looking at the empty bed that gave him the same message. That part was familiar. He'd had that part of the dream nearly every night since Jane checked out of Parkland and left town two weeks ago, leaving only a note at the nurse's station for him. A death in the family. Her father had come to fetch her home. She didn't know when she'd be back. He stood there in the dream like he'd stood there in real life, staring at the striped mattress ticking and feeling like someone had just shot a cannonball right through his gut. It didn't hurt, really, it was just awful to have that big a hole in you. And he hardly knew her, really. It wasn't like they'd spent their lives together. They'd shared an intense adventure that had solved several crimes and left them both bloodied, that had put her into the hospital and him in the hero's spotlight, but she'd been in town less than a month when she left again. You don't get attached to a woman that fast. Shouldn't, anyway.

Tom Weather floated back into the dream to interrupt his mourning. *Son, you've got to be careful. Roma can tell you. Help Belinda. You're the only hope she has.*

Who the hell's Belinda? He'd played ignorant, but the "he" who watched himself in the dream knew. His half-sister. The whore Roma's whore daughter. A dancer at the Star D.

13

Black-haired like him, like Tom, and sharing that same slight hump in the nose that he and their father had. Her mother, Roma Bain, had been prosecutor Tom Weather's snitch in some old, old case. Like plenty of powerful men, Tom Weather had his public face and his private thrills.

I can't carry your sins, he told the Old Tomcat. *I'm not you. I may look like you but I'm not you.*

The scene shifted to some fiery place. A burning man ran by. Dream symbolism, his watching self, who had spent too many evenings among Leslie's boring intellectual friends, surmised. The Tomcat burned up in a plane crash, and he should be in hell for his sins. Fire fit his character. Fire belonged in any dream about him.

Son, listen to me.

I don't want to listen to you, he'd replied, cold. *You betrayed your own family. You made it look like a normal thing to do. You made it look all right.*

Son, listen to me.

A ringing phone punched through his father's plea. He reached to answer it in the dream but couldn't locate the instrument. Then he understood that the sound was real and bolted out of bed to the phone in his den.

"Hello," he snapped at the receiver. The hangover waved over him, rubbering his knees and sending fists of nausea into his gut. He steadied himself.

"Turn on the radio! WFAA." His sister Resa's agitated voice implied nothing short of atomic war.

He clicked the knob on the little Philco.

". . . in the ship channel at Texas City," the breathless announcer was saying.

"Burning before it exploded, the *Grandcamp* had attracted hundreds of spectators dockside from the nearby Monsanto Chemical plant. The blast leveled the plant, engulfing the workers watching from the docks. Initial reports put the number of dead at seventy-five, but eyewitnesses say hundreds are still missing. This refinery town is reeling . . ."

Weather sank into his battered leather chair. Having Willie Peabody show up at your door entitled a man to at least one blackout bender. He looked over at his red sofa as if he expected the over-tailored hoodlum to be there.

"Troy just left Texas City yesterday," a subdued Resa whispered on the phone. Troy Porter was her fiancé. Troy Porter, with his rough-edged father's oil money and his mother's social graces, was a good catch. Charlotte Weather's, or rather Charlotte Hilyard's, influence had paid off in her daughter. Too bad Tom Weather's had done the same for his son.

The radio announcer brought on another witness, who recounted a tale of a burning man, running. Weather blinked and shook his head to wake up. Must have passed out last night with the bedroom radio on.

"We've got to do something," Resa said. "If only your arm weren't hurt, you could take a plane down there with supplies."

"Hmm, yeah. Yeah. But I can't even drive yet." A bullet through a shoulder, along with a busted wrist, had made his Chrysler Saratoga a widow before her time.

"Maybe I can get Troy to come in from the field," Resa said. The field in this case was in West Texas. Macauley Porter started out with the East Texas gushers of the '20s and '30s, but now had interests all over the state.

"The Red Cross has issued an urgent appeal for blood," the radio continued.

"That's it, we're giving blood," his sister declared. "I'll pick you up in twenty minutes."

"Whoa, girl. Can't I have breakfast first?"

"Breakfast! It's past ten o'clock in the morning. You didn't stay out all night in some trashy bar, did you?"

"Ask me no questions." He hung up and headed for the shower, where he reviewed his morning thus far and found it wearing. Through the connecting door he heard the bedroom radio, low. Well, that explained that. He finished his shower, shaved off the black stubble that required twice-daily removal to keep him presentable to women and children, dressed and went downstairs.

Resa was waiting in the lobby.

"You look like hell," she said.

Chapter 2

Little Mexico sat within spitting distance of the Red Cross on McKinney, and Weather ached for the cup of steaming menudo he knew he could get for his hangover at a tortilla shop over there. But the area was no place for a red-headed white woman, not even a classy auburn one like Resa, so he didn't ask her to drive him by before they went to the blood bank.

The Red Cross itself was crowded. Rows of blank eyes turned toward them, took them in, turned away. A blaring Admiral on the counter along the south wall gave updates on the Texas City fire. Weather felt like he was still inside the dream, watching himself, his mind a couple of paces behind his body. The long, too-thin body eased the door shut and removed its hat from its sorry head. Blood pounded through its ears. Black bags hung under its eyes. Its dark skin had a grayish pallor. All of its nerves vibrated. The mind didn't want to examine its own culpability in the body's sorry state, so it shut down.

In the Red Cross, no one spoke as the radio recounted the first moments of the explosion. Weather willed away the fog and listened. The explosion itself had flung ripped steel shards from the *Grandcamp* onto the dock. Panicked victims had scattered to avoid the hot missiles. The announcer urged medical personnel in the Galveston and Houston areas to go to Texas City immediately. Authorities also needed strong men willing to carry the dead and wounded. The rest of the state could help by giving blood at their local Red Cross.

Heads bobbed in affirmation around the lobby. Weather relaxed his vigil and the fog returned. Resa murmured something about a friend who volunteered here, or maybe she said she did. At any rate, she floated away down the narrow center aisle and through a door on the opposite wall.

Weather went to the counter along the back wall to get a donor form. He'd just picked up the paperwork when a fat man grabbed the injured arm and pumped, yapping congratulations and when you going back to the D.A.'s office 'cause this town needs more men like you in a stage whisper that would have carried in the Cotton Bowl.

He pulled away, not bothering to mask the pain.

His torturer gave a startled look at his own empty hand, as if he just that second remembered Weather's injuries, which every newspaper in town had described. The man stammered out an apology, followed by quick inquiries about the damage. "You all right, aren't ya? I didn't mean . . . Shame that happened on your right side."

Weather disengaged from the talking man and headed back to the front. Along the way he greeted several other well-wishers and two ex-cons he'd help make that way. Fred Atterly and Aesop Gance. Atterly nodded and looked away, but Aesop muttered something about Weather's courtroom style. He caught the words *shyster* and *railroad*.

"What did you say, Aesop?" He stared at the top of Gance's squashed bald head. Strands of greasy hair fanned across the shiny dome. The chinless little worm wouldn't look up, which made Weather mad.

He leaned in close where Gance could feel his breath in his ear. "I recollect you deserved your sentence for stupidity alone, bud. Beat a man half to death over a gambling debt he didn't even owe you personally? Boss Willie didn't order that, did he? If he did, he let you take the fall for it, didn't he? And where are you now? Selling your blood at the blood bank for pocket money? Willie cut you out of the operation because of your temper, didn't he?"

Gance tilted his head up. "It ain't like that," he said. "I'm back in. Getting back, anyways."

Weather caught a whiff of Gance-breath, sour and foul. He backed up a few inches and continued to stare down the little worm.

The ex-con developed some common sense and announced a need for a smoke. He produced a rumpled pack of Picayunes as proof and weaseled toward the exit.

Weather watched the shorter man's back 'til the door tinkled shut. Poor old Aesop. Willie himself beat a murder charge last year, but was known to cut his underlings loose in their hour of need.

Weather took Gance's seat and filled out paperwork. Across the aisle, two ladies eyed him with suspicion and whispered among themselves. He greeted them with his campaign face. The same incidents that had led the fat man to shake his hand in gleeful bonhomie led the more moral segments of Dallas to shake their heads in gleeful disgust. Yeah, he'd caught a killer, but in the process, he'd been fired from his job. "Leave of absence," D.A. Morson called it, because the newspapers made him out to be a hero, and the D.A.'s office needed one. Once the accolades died down, the leave of absence would become permanent. You don't get caught in an affair with a colleague's wife and expect to keep a job with Morson.

David Weather, Hero. David Weather, Rascal. Both shoes fit. Sometimes they both pinched.

He finished his donor form and took it back to the counter. The fat man was still there.

"Here's our injured hero now. The one I been telling you about." The fat man beamed at the gray-haired clerk.

"I heard about it, just like everybody else in town," she said, and informed Weather that his gunshot wound was too recent, and the Red Cross could not, therefore, take his blood.

"Fine," he said. "After last night, it's about eighty proof anyway."

She ignored the joke. "Then you can help others fill out paperwork." She showed Weather and the fat man how to help new arrivals fill out the donor forms. "Be sure to make them be honest about their medical history. If they've ever had TB, syphilis," she pointed out a number of other scourges on the list, "tell them thank you but no. You being from the D.A.'s, you ought to be able to tell who's lying."

"Now that I can, ma'am. You take the back wall," he told Gabby. "I'll send you half, so we won't have a bottleneck at the front." The fat man looked unhappy, but took the stack of forms Weather offered. The clerk winked. Sharp lady.

Two Negro orderlies brought a chipped enamel table and a gray folding chair to Weather's post. As soon as he sat, the hangover enveloped him again. He propped the door open to let the light breeze clear his head. Donors came, taking forms, asking for help, asking for the latest news. He sent the people who annoyed him over to Gabby and gave news updates to the ones who didn't. The governor had called in the Texas Guard. No, the rumor about poison gas drifting their way was not true. If such a cloud existed, the day's north wind would send it out into the Gulf.

A woman returning her completed form volunteered that she'd lost a niece in the New London schoolhouse blast ten years ago. He turned his best sympathetic attention to her, but could only focus on a gold brooch on her light coat.

Resa and her volunteer friend, a blonde he'd met once or twice, emerged from the back with an empty coffee can that they put on his table for donations.

"David, we've ordered lunch for everybody and we have to go pick it up at the Shamrock."

"For everybody?"

Resa grinned. "Troy's buying, only he doesn't know it yet."

"Already spending his money, and you're not even married yet."

"Practice makes perfect."

"Sure hope this explosion doesn't put you on a budget. Come on, I'll walk you to your car." He turned his desk over to the woman with the niece and walked out with the girls.

Aesop Gance leaned against the wall, smoking. Several crushed butts lay on the concrete near his feet. He didn't speak. Resa and the friend chatted gaily about who among their society friends they could bully the most money out of the fastest. Weather felt Aesop's appraising gaze as the trio passed the ex-con.

His headache and prosecutor's suspicion distorted the distance to the car, but finally the girls were installed in the butter-colored Buick, waving goodbye. Weather turned back. Gance had moved to the edge of the small parking lot, but kept his face toward the street. Side-winding little weasel! He wore a nonchalant pose that said he'd been watching and waiting for a chance at rebuttal. Let's go, then, Weather thought.

"*Good* looking sister you got there," the goon said. He made *good* sound dirty, and averted his eyes as Weather passed in front of him.

Weather gathered up the man's lapels. "Anything happens

to either one of those girls, they even hear foul language outta you, and I'll make sure you lose your parole."

"You got fired from the D.A.'s, you don't got no clout."

"The hell I don't. That girl is a D.A.'s daughter. You know Morson would protect the office."

Gance palmed at his captor's arms. "Sheesh, I just paid her a compliment, no need to get hot under the collar."

Weather let go, but stood toe-to-toe so Gance had to flatten himself against the building's brick wall to get past. Weather followed him to the corner, and watched the hood shamble off up McKinney.

After achieving a safe distance, Gance turned and yelled, "You got no clout no more, and soon as Morson finds out Willie was at your place last night, you're nobody."

Now how in the hell did he know that? Weather's blood did the same funny jolt that it had last night when he'd opened the door and found Willie Peabody there, hat in hand, asking to come in. Willie Peabody, who never stood trial for the half dozen murders (including Tom Weather's) attributed to him, said he wanted to clear the air between them. Last thing in the world Weather would have expected. Willie'd started out humble and polite, didn't taunt him about his downfall, acted more like a scared witness than the head of organized crime in these parts. Sitting on the edge of the red sofa, the gangster told him some things he already knew. Answered some questions he would never have asked. Told him a cockeyed tale about some stolen bank loot. Dumped a problem on him that he didn't want to solve. Almost earned his respect, in a twisted sort of way.

Weather looked up the street and thought about chasing after Gance and demanding to know what he'd meant, but he knew he wouldn't get anything out of him. The hoodlum disappeared around the side of a big square church. How *did*

Gance know about Willie's visit? Had to be the cab driver from last night. The only witness to Willie Peabody's visit, at least that he knew of. The news was probably all over town by now.

He swore aloud, enjoying the lack of audience that let him curse, and would have run through all the blue language he never could use as a public figure, except that a city bus pulled up and he had to behave.

The vehicle disgorged a group of women talking about blood donation. They eyed him with delight. *That Alder affair,* the tall one in the red hat whispered, and the other three gloated in his direction.

He sighed. At least half the city had him in bed with Jane, a goal he had not yet achieved. "Right this way, ladies." The Rascal, at your service.

Lunch arrived, along with two more Highland Park daughters who rousted the crowd for money and made everybody in the room feel equal to them and important as hell. The effects of last night's bad judgment receded to a pain the size of a baby's fist behind his left eye.

Close to three o'clock, most of the women disappeared, to be home for kids letting out of school. A factory shift came in, got sorted. Weather sat at his enamel table, bored. Resa and her friends did good deeds in the back. The Texas City fire raged a mile long and five hundred feet high, the radio said. The crisis area now had too many volunteers. The roads into town had to be closed. The public could send blood, medicine, and money, but should not show up in person. Weather's right shoulder and wrist ached without mercy from writing, and he'd begun to resent the disaster's interruption of his coming to terms with Willie Peabody's visit. An event of that magnitude needed no external stimulus.

Then a woman he didn't know slapped his face.

Before she did that, though, she came in and evil-eyed him, regarding him with the kind of contempt that could only mean he'd put her kin in prison. A blond boy of sixteen or seventeen fretted beside her.

"Can minors give blood?" She talked like any other donor, with donor-style questions, but her face radiated hate.

"No ma'am, I'm afraid they can't."

She pinched her lips together like she was trying not to say something, and took the form he held out.

"Give me one, too." The boy snatched a blank form from the stack. He viewed Weather with narrowed bleached-blue eyes. Weather viewed him back. Small and wiry, this boy might stay a runt all his life, or grow to be a strapping fellow. He had the impatient air of trapped adolescence, probably being force-fed a childhood at home that he likely tried to shed with his fists anytime he could get out of the house. Juvenile Hall, past and future, radiated off him, from the reddish stubble on his chin to the cocky tilt of his hip. "I ain't the minor she was talking about. She meant my little brother."

"You seventeen, that's a minor in all the books I know about," the woman snapped.

Weather made a mental note to reject the kid's file, and to make sure Gabby across the room didn't process him.

"This is so stupid, Bonnie," the boy said. "I ought to been on the train to Texas City hours ago."

The woman wrapped browned claws around the kid's arm and whispered, "*Aunt* Bonnie to you, young man. You know better than that." The accent was pure East Texas hardscrabble. Aunt Bonnie wasn't old, maybe late thirties, but she had the boozy, smoke-cured look of a decaying barfly. Gray face, gray-brown hair. Faded colorless dark eyes sat above dark circles. Sagging tits floundered in a ruby dress meant for the woman she might have been ten years ago. Sorry, lady, no honey left to attract the bees.

"Get over there, boy." She followed her nephew to seats near Weather. The kid stayed standing after she sat. Not out of manners, though, more like a still-wild pony champing at the bit. The boy scowled at Weather watching him.

New donors arrived, diverting Weather's attention. When he was free again, he realized the two were discussing him.

"All right, all right. You brung me and I seen him. Don't see no point." The kid was now slumped so far down in the chair his backbone might be touching the seat. Black pant legs rode up over bare ankles. His scuffed wingtips were too big for him. The runt in man's clothes, dressed for town as best he could.

"Now shush." She leaned down and whispered something to him.

The kid shook his head. "I don't care. I'm a man now and oughtta be on the train south, to fight that fire, not sitting in the stupid old Red Cross looking at a man or waiting for a poke in the arm."

She reminded him of what the judge said about how a young man on probation ought to've learnt when to keep his mouth shut.

Weather smiled. Bingo.

"I could be in a bucket brigade," the boy persisted.

"You gone do like you're told, and be grateful for it. Always up to no good anyway, sassing and complaining."

"Get off the boy's back, ma'am," Weather interjected. "He looks like he might be a handful, but he's talking about doing the right thing. I'd go down there myself if I could." The kid sat up a little and stared in amazement.

"This idn't none of your business, Mr. Junior D.A.," the aunt said. "He goes down there, we'll be getting a call to come get him out of jail. Come get him out of somebody's house he's broke in to. Come get him out of the hospital. Give him any inch, be ready to pay somebody a mile of hard-earned cash to fix it."

Weather nodded surrender. Of course she was right. What had gotten into him? Not even a month out of the D.A.'s office and starting to sound like a defense attorney. He hated that. He didn't want to talk like one, think like one, or be one, but that was all that was open to him now if he wanted to practice criminal law. Ought to go shoot himself.

The kid sat smirking like he'd just won a pennant. Weather wondered how to backtrack on this one. The woman snatched up the boy's donor form and approached the table.

"You don't know who we are, do you?" She stood on his right side waving their paperwork near his face. "You ought to. If you don't, this'll be a lot worse insult."

"Ma'am, I don't," he began. Then she slapped him in the face with the papers and let them drop. A couple of men nearby perked up at the entertainment.

"That is not called for, lady." Weather stood up so quickly his chair fell over.

"Car-Ray, come on, now, now." The woman looked a little scared, like she'd just realized what she'd done. She grabbed for the papers on the table but Weather beat her to them and held them behind his back with his good hand. She gave up and bolted outside without waiting for the kid. The young man strutted behind her, grinning, and gave Weather a big wave before he went out.

"Let it pass, gentlemen," Weather told his audience. He upended the folding chair and sat back down.

He looked at the now-crumpled donor forms he'd tossed onto the table.

Mrs. Bonnie B. Cartledge. The name meant nothing to

26

him. He read the boy's paper.

Carl Ray Bledsoe, Junior.

Oh.

Now he understood.

He was partly right about sending their kin to prison. The blame for that belonged to his father, though. One of Tom Weather's last acts as a prosecutor before he became acting D.A. was to send Carl Ray Bledsoe, Senior, to Death Row. Junior must have been a baby at the time. Maybe not even born. Senior had been Willie Peabody's third or fourth cousin, once or twice removed. The Bledsoes were oil field trash, country cousins not slick enough to ride Cousin Willie's gambling gravy train. Seventeen years ago, Carl Ray, Senior, came to the city. He hadn't even cleaned the tar out from under his fingernails good before he killed a guard and a city cop during a botched bank robbery. Carl Ray Bledsoe, Senior, had the distinction of being the last Death Row inmate to feel the hangman's noose before the state tore down the gallows and wired up Old Sparky. Assistant D.A. Tom Weather prosecuted the case before he became acting D.A. Willie had brought the case up last night.

More to that bank robbery than anybody ever knew, Willie had said in Weather's den.

What don't they know? Willie shifted the subject to Carl Ray, Junior, the punk who'd just pranced out of the Red Cross with his slap-happy aunt.

That boy needed a home. His mama was a dope fiend and a fortune teller and just plain trash. She kept him away from me 'cause she thought I was no good. Now what kind of mother was that?

The worst people sometimes show a core of decency, Weather thought, but did not share his opinion with Willie.

Now that his mama's dead, I got a second chance. He ain't got no kin on her side. I got his aunt named guardian, and I'm letting them stay out at this old farm I have.

Oh, Weather had replied without interest. The cab company called and said his ride would be late.

Gonna make it up to him, Willie said.

Willie, why are you here? Let's cut out the chat and you tell me.

Willie's face changed from the diffident visitor's to the one that gave him his reputation. *Don't tell me when to talk and when not to, Mr. Nobody. Them's my oil leases your daddy took from me. You didn't know about that, did you, big shot?*

Weather knew, but wasn't likely to admit it to Willie Peabody.

Resa and her friends brought him some lemonade and cookies. He yearned for a shot of Jack Daniel's to put in his cup, and vowed to get to bed early tonight. His shoulder ached so badly he wanted to go over to Parkland Hospital and beg for dope. Shouldn't have been writing right-handed, but every time he started with the left, he would automatically transfer the pencil over to his right.

The radio said that Texas City firefighters had run out of water, and were attempting to pump it out of the burning bay.

He decided he could grin and bear a little discomfort.

Chapter 3

Resa and her friend dropped him off at the Claypoole's circular drive and raced off to divest others of their money, or if not that, of their selfish pride. In the lobby, a ballroom compared to the Red Cross shoebox, he encountered several tenants draped on the three black leather sofas, huddled around evening newspapers.

Biedermeier's beaten-up portable sat on the front desk, giving news updates. The building manager himself was not around. Weather slipped behind the desk and retrieved his mail and newspaper from his pigeonhole, then walked around the mirrored Liberty etching at the back of the lobby to the elevators. He stepped inside one, wrestled the gate closed, and flipped the switch to Four.

The apartment felt cold and forbidding, but he didn't bother lighting space heaters. He left the mail in the kitchen, took the paper down the hall to his den, and spread it out on the desk. Dallas' only evening paper, the *Daily Times Herald*, had the first picture accounts from Texas City. Not atomic war, but nonetheless, a refinery town provides quite a combustion.

Texas City Blast Kills 350
Explosion Razes Gulf Coast City

Pictures showed the drama in a way the radio could not. Twisted heaps of metal poured smoke where rail lines once stood. Sheet-covered bodies filled an open-air morgue on the lawn of a clinic. Aerial shots showed a mile-long fire line. The paper had pages and pages of pictures.

He poured himself a shot of J.D. and continued reading. The drink quelled the last of the hangover and made him sleepy. Aesop Gance and Willie and Bonnie Bledsoe Cartledge and Carl Ray, Junior and Senior, could all go to hell. After a second drink, he'd almost consigned them there for good, when a small headline leaped at him from the bottom of page twenty-eight. He sat up sharply.

Body Found in Trinity Bottoms
Willie Peabody Shot Elsewhere, Dumped to Die

Two boys playing hooky after the school lunch break made a gruesome discovery along the Trinity riverbanks this afternoon, according to Sheriff Odell Orton . . .

Weather scanned the article quickly. The story was less than two inches long, with the briefest mention that Willie had been acquitted of murder last year and that the gangster had dodged indictments for years. Not a word about Willie being Tom Weather's unpunished killer. That had always been rumor, anyway.

Poor Willie! The gangster's death should be bigger news. Well, the old boy shouldn't have gotten himself killed on the same day the *Grandcamp* blew up down in the ship channel.

Weather stopped, remembering his dream.

Ever'body meets their Maker, Willie had proclaimed to Tom Weather. *Ever'body gets a reckoning. A chance to explain.*

The Old Tomcat's voice spoke from beyond the grave. *It don't work that way when you're condemned.*

30

Willie was dead in the dream.

Weather shook his head, disbelieving. When did Willie get that way? Last night, he'd been alive and slippery, dropping broad hints of dire events to come, sucking on a Cuban cigar Weather made him put out. Where did he go when he left? They'd ridden the elevator downstairs together, after Weather's taxi driver telephoned him from the lobby. The cabbie did a double-take at ol' Willie, and looked like he wanted to take off running. Must have owed the gangster a gambling debt. Many did, and perhaps would react just as strongly at coming upon the crime boss unawares. Willie gave the young driver a scary smile, said goodbye to Weather, and stepped into the phone booth.

"Gotta make a call," Willie had said.

Weather left Willie there and followed his driver outside. During the ride, the driver missed a turn and nearly hit a pedestrian. He excused himself by claiming he was new to town and didn't know the streets.

"You know what a pedestrian is," Weather had replied dryly, noting the guy's name and picture from the license. Clancy Burrows. He would be sure to tell them not to send Clancy the next time he called a cab.

Poor ol' Clancy almost forgot to collect Weather's fare when he let him out.

Weather re-read the news story and thought about Willie's visit.

Don't worry, I parked around back, Willie had said, after Weather came out of the bathroom and found Willie digging in the sofa cushions for his lost lighter. The gambling king-pin settled his big rump on the sofa and nodded toward the balcony, which overlooked the east parking lot four floors below.

Weather flung the *Herald* aside and walked out the French

doors to the balcony's edge.

In the twilight, the bright purple had dulled to black, but even viewed from above, a Packard's coffin-shaped hood identified it anywhere. Willie's '37 monstrosity sat three rows back from the building, not twenty feet from Weather's own neglected Chrysler. Willie loved that outdated relic and wouldn't trade up to a more fashionable car, even though he had enough money for a fleet of Cadillacs.

Weather swore and went inside to call the police.

Chapter 4

Weather shivered out on the Claypoole's loading dock, only partly because the mild day had given way to a chill evening, and the night promised to be even chillier.

"You said on the phone Willie Peabody came to see you?" Detective Prescott Hadley spoke in the affable, equable voice that Weather privately labeled modulated fury. The scuttlebutt among the city's vermin said nobody ever better try to put anything over Had-You Hadley because he Had-You, Had-Your-Number, Had-Your-Mother, Had-Your-Balls. Having all of those, and any number of inventive variations that cropped up among jailhouse wits, Hadley had no need to start out shouting, bullying, or even doing much emphasizing in an interrogation. He might haul off and knock a suspect's teeth out, but he wouldn't necessarily raise his voice before he did it. Newcomers who didn't know his reputation but who listened with even half an ear could feel the danger. It was like the low pressure before a bad storm. Those who disregarded it deserved what they got. If the suspect had any sense at all, he would admit he'd had fair warning. Hadley asked you a question, you better answer it. Truthfully, and before the shouting started.

Weather dreaded making a statement to this man, because he knew he would have to lie.

"Yes, Willie came to see me." Practicing the fine art of poker-facedness, Weather looked Hadley straight in the eye and said, "I'd just gotten out of the shower. Bell rang. I figured it was the building manager, who tends to show up at the wrong times. I was in my boxers and nothing else. It's Willie Peabody. We both get a big grin out of me being in my skivvies, then I park him in my den while I get dressed. I come out, and he's smoking a cigar and rooting around in the sofa cushions. Said he dropped his lighter."

"How long was he at your place?"

"Ten, maybe fifteen minutes. I had to cut the visit short. I'd called a cab earlier to take me downtown, and my driver phoned me from the lobby. I can't handle a car right now because of my shoulder."

"Your cabbie can verify the time he picked you up?"

"Yeah, he should be able to. It was around eight-fifteen. He saw Willie in the lobby. Willie was getting into the phone booth when we left."

"What cab company?"

"Starlight." He gave Hadley the driver's name and described the man's reaction to Willie. "We should talk later. The press have arrived." This last he said with a slight nod toward the back of the property, where his ol' pal Jemison from the *Beacon* was worming his way up through parked cars. Must have come up from the woods north of the building.

Hadley turned and pointed twice with his bullhorn: once to a uniformed cop standing on the loading platform, once to the intruder. The cop leaped off the ramp and hustled off toward Jemison. Weather watched, grinning, as the uniform re-routed the reporter to the throng of bystanders on the eastern periphery of the crime scene.

"Hey, Weather, help me out here," Jemison yelled.

"Sorry, this is not my show," Weather yelled back.

It was Hadley's, and would stay that way.

"We'll talk later. Do not speak to him—" Hadley jerked

his head in the direction of Jemison's banishment "—or to anyone else about any of this."

Yes, sir. Weather settled into the role of spectator. Seeing a crime scene develop was a fascinating show. He'd been to some before, but always after the police had arrived. This was his first Hadley production. Nice to be in there from the beginning.

The detective set up a squad car blockade at the east entrance to the parking area at the far end of the T-shaped building. At his direction, another police car nosed into view from the back of the T and blocked the dirt path some impatient drivers had carved behind the building. A cluster of watchers gathered behind the black and whites at the *de facto* entrance. A spotlight slammed on from 202's balcony. Tenants gathered on the loading dock. With one threat from the bullhorn, Hadley culled possible witnesses out of the herd and retained them by the freight elevator, with orders for them not to talk to each other. A cop stood guard to enforce these orders. No one spoke.

Get back, go on home, Hadley horned to the extras. Obedient to the letter, if not the spirit of the law, they disappeared, only to reassemble in greater numbers along the dark balconies up the Claypoole's facade. They had box seats in a bizarre silent theater where the overhead light turned Hadley's sharp, handsome face into a chiaroscuro devil's and cast his shadow, larger than life, across the crime scene. The stage was set, the Packard an important prop, that police detective—what's his name? Hadley, yeah, Hadley, you know the one—the dangerous cop who's always in the paper. The star. Look, isn't that that prosecutor who lives in the building, David Weather? If he's involved, too, you know this is gonna be big. Whatever this is, is history, and here we are with the best seats in the house. Better than that reporter with the camera, better than all those folks outside, being sent out of view around front.

Someone overhead flicked a cigarette lighter. Another someone tossed a burning butt off a balcony. Its little orange trail fell into the spotlight near the detective.

"Rogers, find out who did that."

"Yes, sir." A uniformed cop scurried up the loading ramp into the building.

Hadley, behind the Packard, hoisted the bullhorn. "Now, this is a crime scene, folks. Anybody messing it up could be charged with tampering with evidence. Taken to jail! Ha-a-ate to see that happen." Hadley spoke with the fiery rising inflections of a tent show evangelist. He loved on the words *jail* and *crime* the way the preacher would love on *Jay-sus*. The crowd froze.

The star never moved his gaze off the balconies, and Weather knew without seeing that the people up there hadn't taken their eyes off him, either.

"A crime scene must be protected, people," the cop bullhorned, the threat of brimstone in his voice.

The bullhorn dropped. There was no further speech, no indication of how real the threat had been. Imaginations could supply the dread, according to each owner's guilt or knowledge of the guilty party.

During the next scene, the bullhorn remained silent. Onstage, technicians drew tiny chalk circles around spent shells. Hadley's assistant, his partner in actuality, but only for show, muttered cop-talk to his boss. A photographer shot up film. The techs tweezed up shells and dropped them into three brown paper bags.

Careless of the killer to leave so much evidence, Weather thought.

"Find the other three," Hadley snapped.

So Willie took six bullets. The paper didn't say.

The second cop ventured that they could have landed in the shooter's coat pocket or loose shoe. Or in the getaway car. Then again, they might have gone to the riverbank on Willie's person.

Hadley flashed fire and growled a single word. *Orton.* The sheriff. Weather remembered the *Herald* article. *Shot elsewhere, dumped to die.* A quote from Sheriff Odell Orton. The body belonged to County, not City.

Weather reassessed his opinion of the bungling killers. Throwing the investigation into the arms of the sheriff had its inherent dangers, but putting it out of Hadley's reach spoke of self-preservation at a mastermind's best.

The Hadley-Orton feud was a long, old hate. To some, the sheriff seemed a bit soft on gambling. Maybe he was. Maybe he viewed local gambling operations like forest rangers viewed a back fire. Keep a dozen little ones going and big ones, like the Chicago mob, can't spread.

On a more practical note, much of the voting public liked a card game now and then and Orton wanted to stay elected. Hadley, on the other hand, had a hired job, and could knock gangsters' heads in without worrying about votes.

If either lawman ever turned up with a bullet in the brain, the other would be the prime suspect. Maybe knowing that kept each from turning their fight into a blood feud. Weather turned his thoughts off and suppressed the smile he felt forming, concerned that Hadley of the preternatural antennae would pick it up.

Too late. Hadley whipped around to Weather. "Let's go upstairs now and have a look at your place." El Diablo as host. Friendly, personable. Weather led the police entourage up to his apartment. He had an image of himself as the thief in a passion play, where the weeping crowd follows the rugged cross up Calvary. Hadley drove them all.

In 402, Hadley made Weather wait in his own hall while the men combed through the den where Willie Peabody had been. On some cue not visible to Weather, Hadley's men removed the two long cushions and dug around in the upholstery. One man held up some lint and pocket change for the detective's inspection. Hadley's unspeaking partner stood by, scribbling into a notebook. The partner, a short balding man with glasses, looked like an accountant or a tired salesman demoted to bad territory. He was easy to overlook.

"You think Willie planted some evidence about his killer in my sofa?"

Hadley ignored Weather's joke. "From when you caught Willie rummaging in the cushions, tell me about the visit."

Weather sighed. "All right. He was smoking, and I made him put the cigar out. He seemed nervous, and he said he was having some trouble right now and he wanted me to know, in case something happened, that he didn't kill my father. I told him I never thought he did, and I asked him what kind of trouble."

"And?"

"He just said, 'trouble trouble.' Then he changed the subject. Classic Willie. Flamboyance and intrigue, but no clear answer. He started talking about an old bank robbery and murder one of his cousins got executed for. You remember the night Margie Lunn's burned down? A kid named Carl Ray Bledsoe, Senior, robbed a bank and shot a guard and a cop, then ran into Margie's with two bags of stolen loot. This was seventeen years ago. I don't know if you were around then."

"I was around." Hadley's expression had grown sharper, more intense. Any sharper and the cop could decapitate a person with his gaze.

"Okay. Well, Bledsoe supposedly set fire to the place, to divert capture, and he got out of the fire with only one bag, which was recovered when the police caught him. Margie got killed in the fire, and the other sack of loot supposedly burned up. Willie told me a cockamamie tale about the money, which is probably why he came to see me in the first place."

"Because your father prosecuted Bledsoe?"

"No, I don't think so. You see that sofa there?" Weather pointed to the red Victorian monstrosity against his den wall.

Hadley nodded.

"Well, Red Holcomb happened to be downtown the night of the fire, and he and some other men helped drag a bunch of furniture out before the place was engulfed. Since Margie was dead, Red took the sofa to his office, where it stayed until he died. I used to be engaged to Red's daughter, and her mother had the thing in her attic. Mrs. Holcomb had it re-stuffed and gave it to me when I moved in here."

"Willie knew you had the sofa and he thought the money was in it?"

"He must have, yeah. Seems Bledsoe's widow died recently, but before she died, she told her son something her husband supposedly told her about the other bag. The woman was a grifter and read palms for a living, and she claimed to have Second Sight, Willie wasn't sure if she got the message in person before Bledsoe's execution or from the great beyond, so take all this with a grain of salt, but however she got it, she passed it on to her son, who passed it to Willie, who brought it to me."

"She said the money was in your sofa?"

Weather shook his head. "Nope. She said the money is buried '*by* or *in* something red.' "

" '*By* or *in* something red.' " Hadley eyed the sofa. One of his men opened a pocketknife and made slicing motions.

"Oh, no you don't," Weather protested. "Like I said, Mrs. Holcomb had the thing re-stuffed before she gave it to me. She thought it was too busted in from the time it spent in Red's office. If the money was ever in there, Red got it, or the upholsterer got it, or Lettie Holcomb got it. If she got it, then Neiman Marcus has it now."

Hadley blinked and his men pulled the couch away from the wall despite Weather's objections. The detective rolled his fingers once and the men upended the heavy piece and balanced it onto its big camel hump. Then, without any discernible instructions from their boss, they stepped back. Weather marveled at the unspoken communication between them. The detective stood there, looking the thing over. Even with an upside-down sofa in the room, Hadley dominated. Weather looked, too, but saw nothing but usual furniture underbelly crud, spider webs and dustballs clinging to a crisscross of thick grayed pine. There were no slits where anyone could have stuffed a bag of money.

Hadley stared at it for a long time, then signaled and the men flipped the sofa back on its ball and claw feet. Carved mahogany, needing some polish. Weather had never noticed them before. One of the men unzipped the cushions and felt around inside, then shook his head.

"I need the name of the upholsterer," Hadley said as his men pushed the sofa into its spot against the wall.

"I don't have it. Lettie Holcomb could tell you, but she and her daughter are in Europe."

Hadley swore, then swore louder at a ruckus up the hall at Weather's front door.

"You can't come in now. There's an investigation in progress," said the cop standing guard.

"The hell you say," a voice boomed. Weather watched from the hall as his apartment door swung open. The cop on guard rode it like a man hanging on in a tornado. The newcomer slammed the door and its cargo against the wall, then stomped toward the den.

"What in the hell is going on here?" he thundered. "Why wasn't I called right away?" He shoved Weather out of his way and stood toe to toe with Hadley.

El Diablo stood his ground.

"Hello, Odell."

Sheriff Odell Orton glared, beet-faced and apoplectic.

Hadley's anger sucked the air out of the room, but Orton was a creature from some other world anyway, taller and bigger than mere mortals, a creature that needed no oxygen but fed on indignation and raw power and bystanders' blood, and he wasn't having any of Hadley's dish.

"Willie Peabody died in the County and it's my investigation, no matter what," he thundered.

"What else did Willie say?" Hadley asked Weather, ignoring Orton as if some underling had crashed the interview and needed to be put in his place.

Orton turned the color of Willie's purple Packard.

"Hey, hey, fellas. Cool it," Weather said. "Just let me get the sheriff caught up." He repeated the story of the missing bank money, and of Lettie Holcomb and the upholsterer. "And you better not tear up my sofa, Odell. You do and I'll have to campaign for your opponent, next election." Weather said it cocky, to take the edge off, but he meant it, too. The Weather name had more than a little political clout and he would use it when necessary. He didn't want cotton stuffing all over the room.

"Don't nobody run against me," Orton said, giving back cockiness. El Diablo assessed them both, as if he were gearing up to throw a lightning bolt and knock them into the lake of fire.

"What else did Willie say?" Hadley asked again. "You didn't spend the whole time talking about the damned sofa, did you?"

"We pretty much did," Weather said, aware of his lie. "Before I made him leave, though, Willie said something big was going to happen around town—which I now figure was his murder—and it had to do with someone who was 'a prominent businessman, but not exactly a businessman.' "

"What?" Orton moved closer and gathered up Weather's shirtfront like he was some petty hustler.

"Hey, don't shoot the messenger."

Orton scowled, but eased up.

"Tell us what Willie said," Hadley demanded.

"Okay, okay." Weather spread his hands, and backed up from Orton. "Willie said, and this is a direct quote, 'Someone will be risen, as if from the dead, not exactly a businessman, not exactly not a businessman, and when he comes, this town will never be the same.' I figure he was describing his killer, his enemy."

" 'Not a businessman, not exactly not a businessman,' " Hadley said, as if examining the mystery of the ages.

Orton snorted. "This is time-wasting bull-larkey," he said. "Willie Peabody was always saying stuff like that. I'll tell you why Willie's dead. Somebody that owed him some money didn't want to pay. Or Martin Hubert had him killed. Or somebody thought killing Willie would clear a path for him to get the bank money. I'm going to talk to this Carl Ray, Junior kid. Maybe his mama told him some more about that old bank robbery."

Hadley looked from Weather to Orton, deciding. "I need to talk to the kid first," he growled.

"It's my investigation," Orton said.

"You'll never solve it," Hadley said.

Orton and Hadley left together, both glowering, and Weather thanked providence for the feud that diverted Hadley's attention and kept him from asking about the rest of Willie's visit. It didn't matter anyway, the law had plenty to go on. The rest of what Willie said, it didn't have a damn thing to do with his murder. Besides, some things just didn't need to be made public.

As he crawled into bed, he heard the radio murmuring on the nightstand. Something had the announcer excited. He turned up the volume.

A second ship had just blown up at Texas City. It got damaged in port during the first explosion and couldn't be towed away from the dock fires. Sometime during the day, flying embers ignited the cargo of the *High Flyer*. Weather lay awake with the news accounts for a long time, and finally drifted off into a light sleep, in which he dreamed that Willie and his father sat on Margie Lunn's old sofa, arguing about oil leases and betrayal and bank robbery loot, while the city burned.

Chapter 5

Thursday, April 17

Weather found Jemison camped in the hall when he went out to get his two morning papers, the *Morning News* and the *Beacon*, which building manager Biedermeier delivered directly to his doorstep every morning.

"You look a mess," Weather said, and invited Jemison in for coffee, after establishing that he would absolutely throw the reporter out the minute he asked the first question about Willie Peabody's visit or what he'd said to Hadley and Orton.

"Agreed. I could use a gallon or two of coffee, to clear my head." The tall reporter fixed bloodshot blue eyes on his host. Black circles rimmed pinkened eyeballs. Deep ridges cut into his long face. Jemison was the same age as Weather, thirty-two, but Weather, with his prematurely graying temples and world-weariness, usually looked older. Now, Jemison looked older.

"Coffee, but no questions." Weather ushered him into the kitchen, looking forward to kicking him out. After last night, he needed to fight somebody, and it might as well be Jemison. What were buddies for? Especially when one was after your woman. He'd run into Jemison at Jane's hospital bed a few times too many to think the reporter's interest ran merely along professional lines. After visiting hours, the two men had often shared a table at the Star D, drinking beer and practicing civility with each other, talking up a storm about the city, about how it had changed since before the war, about what it might become, but avoiding the subject most important to them both. Weather liked Jemison, and wanted him to move away to Timbuktu.

"You hear from Jane?" Jemison settled into his chair with a cup of steaming black brew and eyed Weather.

So now Jane was the neutral topic. Weather didn't know if this was better or worse. "Not since she left. A death in the family, in Chicago. A distant cousin. You?"

"Uh-huh." Jemison looked almost apologetic. "It was a first cousin. After the funeral, Jane decided to stay up there with her father for a while, do some visiting, recuperate there."

"I see. Well, she probably wanted to get away from both of us," Weather said flippantly. Ought to just kick Jemison out and be done with it. But then who would give him news of Jane? He wished he didn't like the guy so much.

Jemison peered into his cup with the air of a dying man praying over a charlatan's elixir. He gulped it down.

"She probably could use a rest from Francy as well," Weather added to fill the silence, referring to Jane's sassy boss. Although Francy wouldn't admit it, as a cub reporter she had been one of Tom Weather's mistresses.

Jemison shrugged. "Francy's the least of . . . Look, there's something I need to tell you."

"About Jane?"

"Yeah. No. No," the newsman said firmly. "About Willie. About this business. Now hold on. I'm not asking questions, I'm telling."

"All right, tell then."

Jemison shifted in his chair a few times. He had all the air of a reluctant witness about to stop the hem-hawing and give the court something of substance. The prosecutor knew to wait.

"You remember Deke Lascalle? The reporter? Did mob investigations at the *Beacon* 'til a few weeks ago? The one who found the missing witness from last year's debacle with Willie? Before the witness went missing again, I mean."

"Lascalle, yeah. I heard he inherited some money from an old uncle in California, and left the country. Which is why you've got his job now instead of covering the courts. Lucky guy. But lucky for you, too, if you wanted his spot."

"He didn't inherit any money or go to California." The usually talkative Jemison didn't add his customary column of background to the story.

"Why'd he leave, then? Trouble with Francy?" Weather put the question out to give his visitor room to collect his thoughts, but he thought he already where Jemison was heading.

The newsman looked around warily. "This can't go out of this room, Weather, not to Morson, not to the cops, nowhere. I know it's odd me asking you this but . . ."

"Deal. What happened?"

"He got a phone call."

"And?"

"The caller said Deke had a cute little boy, and it sure would be a shame if that child were to fall into a rock quarry. Said, 'kids can be so careless, never thinking anything can happen to 'em.' "

"Threatening children."

"He quoted the boy's birthday, Deke's address, and the location of the quarry the kid might wind up in."

"Damn." It had gotten cold in the room. The hot coffee didn't help.

"A paper in Tucson had been trying to hire Deke away

anyway," Jemison continued. "So he packed up his family that same day and sent them on, then cleared out the house himself over the weekend. Never even told Francy why, just resigned and took off. He was worried that Tucson wasn't far enough away, and thought about leaving the country."

"He told you all this?"

"Yeah. He forgot they'd invited me over for dinner that Saturday. I drive up and find a moving van there, the family already on the train. And Deke in the back yard with the lighter fluid, burning his files. He wouldn't have told me anything, if I hadn't happened by."

"You manage to rescue any of his notes?"

Jemison gave out a brittle laugh. "Burnt my fingers trying, but he'd already raked through them and was on the second or third burn when I came on the scene."

"The mob wouldn't have gone after kids," Weather said. "They called his bluff and he did exactly what they wanted."

Jemison shook his head. "I don't think so, son."

"I know Willie and sonny-boy Laidlaw Peabody, and Falvey and all the other two-bit hoods around these parts. Not a one of them would resort to that. Not even Martin Hubert, who'll likely get the blame, and if you quote me on that, I'll never speak to you again. No, these boys will kill each other, but they would never start up on innocent families. It would put their own in danger."

"You don't understand."

"What, then?"

"The caller didn't have a local accent. You know how there've been so many hoods from Chicago down here lately, trying to muscle in on Willie and Martin Hubert?"

"Yeah."

"Their families are a thousand miles away."

47

Chapter 6

"Family!" Carl Ray spat the word like it was dirty. Nobody was fooling him. Bonnie let him stay home from school, all nicey nice, but he knew she was keeping an eye on him on account of all those cops from last night, cops and sheriffs and deputies roaming all over the farm, even down to the cabin, asking questions about Willie on account of that David Weather guy. Now Burr and Bonnie were both furious that he talked to them, him being a juvenile, and family business not being cops' business. Well, Burr shoulda been home. Bonnie shoulda not been knocked out from them pills she took every night.

As punishment, they kept him out of school, which wasn't bad except the probation said he had to go; then they make him work the farm all day, what little land they actually worked. He didn't mind the horses, but didn't like that damn garden of Bonnie's. Had to make fertilizer for it out of horse-shit and this other stuff she had out in the barn. Ammonia nitric. Sure did stink when it all got mixed together.

He leaned on his hoe. Ammonia nitric was the same stuff that blew up that ship down in Texas City.

He had to go to the bathroom. Could just go out here, but he needed to track a little of this fertilizer stink into Bonnie's house. She could yell if she wanted to. Let her order him to use the old outhouse when Willie'd done dug a cistern and put running water in the house.

He got up to the back porch steps and heard the yelling.

Burr was on the phone. The kitchen door was open and he could hear just fine.

"The cops ain't after me. It's just that damned boy, running his mouth. Now look, Laidlaw, don't cut me out on account of him."

Laidlaw must have said a lot, 'cause Burr shut up for a while.

Then Burr said, "I'll dig up every inch if I have to, to find that bank money, even if it's the last thing I ever do."

Then Bonnie came out on the porch and saw him listening in. She shut the door, and later made Carl Ray eat supper out there, like he was some colored field hand.

Burr came out on the porch after supper and put on his muddy old boots and took off in the car somewhere. He was mad, mad as Carl Ray had ever seen. That vein was sticking out on his forehead, and his silver crew cut stood up wild like he'd been electrocuted.

Chapter 7

That bastard sister of yours is about to get herself killed, Willie said. *I try to take care of her and her mama, but I can't always do it.*

What do you mean?

She's running with a rough crowd. She don't know how rough. She's making some folks mad. This from the chief contributor to the body count in Dallas County.

Willie, if you want me to help Belinda Bain—here Weather made a point not to acknowledge her as his half-sister—*you've got to tell me what she's doing. Who has she been running with? Who's mad at her?*

Me! Willie dissolved into his wheezing laughter.

Weather mentally reviewed a part of Willie's visit that he had not reported to Odell Orton or Prescott Hadley, wondering how long it would take before one of them came back for the rest of the story. Who in hell wanted to admit to the cops that he had a half-sister who danced at the Star D? Who in hell wanted to save her sorry, in-trouble carcass from the mob?

Maybe he did. Why in hell else was he sitting in the strip joint on Industrial Boulevard in the middle of Thursday afternoon, drinking beer, pretending to be getting an early start on his self-destruction? At least his presence was believable, since he'd hid out there more than a few afternoons since Jane left town.

The Star D catered to a mix of railroad and factory

workers by day and added in businessmen at night. For some reason, criminal court lawyers drank there, maybe because of the association with owner Willie Peabody. The place was a local men's enclave that didn't distract with noisy tourists or the flashier dancers from New Orleans who slung tits at the nicer clubs on Elm.

Weather headed for a booth next to a greasy art deco mirror in the left table nook. The mirror featured a busty saloon girl, painted on the glass. She held up a draught beer. The light bulbs that chased around the mirror edge seemed to wink back, advertising the whole thing's need for a good cleaning, but that was part of the Star D's charm.

"Cheers," he said to the painted tart as he sat.

Three men at a nearby table snickered at his antic. "You kill Willie Peabody?" one was bold enough to ask.

Weather held up a mocking fist and shook his head. They grinned back and dropped their voices. *Aesop said . . .* one of them whispered, and nodded toward Weather.

Damned Gance belonged in a rock quarry, Weather thought. Of course, by now everybody in town knew about the Packard in the parking lot.

The whisperers moved on to other suspects, Falvey among them. Weather nursed the beer a while, then got up. He was wasting time and needed to do something toward the Belinda problem. He would take a look around.

As he passed the empty stage where Wild Jill Cody and her Six Gunns, Belinda Bain among them, strutted their stuff at night, he imagined he heard Willie speaking to him again.

Help that little gal. She's your flesh and blood.

Son, you got to listen, Tom Weather chimed in.

He shook them both off. Titty bars in the daytime were no place to dwell on one's bad dreams.

In the back hall, he passed a frosted door marked Office on

the left, and the backstage door on the right. The men's was at the back of the building, behind backstage, opposite the kitchen. No one was in the men's. He pushed open the kitchen's dented metal flap doors. The room was empty. The backstage door was locked. He stopped at Falvey's office. He didn't know what he wanted from there other than Belinda's address. Plenty of easier ways to get that, but they involved asking somebody, and he didn't want anyone to know he was looking for her. He turned the knob and pushed on the frosted glass. The door swung open without a sound.

"Falvey?" If anyone came out, he could chat about Willie's demise. If no one came, he would search the place.

No one answered. He stepped in and pulled the door inward, leaving it ajar for a quick exit. The place was wainscoted like the hall, but far cleaner. The room he stood in turned out to be the center room of three. A quick glance in the two adjoining rooms revealed no Falvey or anyone else. He slipped into the front one for a closer look. It held two messy desks and a surprise. A one-way mirror, covered in places by the busty beer girl, looked out onto the nook where he'd sat earlier. A couple of new arrivals now occupied his table. He stepped closer. A toggle switch in the down position stuck out of the wall under the glass. Obeying a hunch, he flicked it. Conversation crackled into the room. The men were talking about the Texas City explosion. One of them gave a curious look straight at Weather—at the mirror, of course—but shrugged it off and turned back to his companion.

So old Falvey had his office rigged. Probably to help bouncers keep order, but damn! Weather wondered how many times prosecutors from the D.A.'s had "private" conversations after work in that nook. He would be sure to let someone from his old job know. He flicked the switch off and passed through the central room into the back one. No mirrors here, just a battered desk and green office chair by the door and a row of filing cabinets against the back wall, nearest the kitchen.

He went over to the cabinets and eased a drawer open. It whined and screeched like a train with bad brakes, but brought no bouncers. In the drawer bottom, a pad of coffee-stained blank checks had long since adhered to the rust. Pacific Avenue State Bank. The same bank Carl Ray Bledsoe, Senior, robbed seventeen years ago, but so what if Falvey kept an account there? Weather kept an account there. So did his mother. He ran a finger into a folder, fumbling a little because of the cast on his wrist. Ought to do this left-handed, but habits of a lifetime were hard to break. He had no idea what he was looking for besides Belinda's address.

He read the file labels. Alvin, Cody, Cabs/Taxis, Vendor Receipts, Marten, Atterly. Somebody with bad handwriting who didn't know his alphabet had been here. No Bain.

From the other side of the wall, he could hear the Negro kitchen help arriving. They greeted each other loudly amid banging pots and running water. He caught a few snippets about the Texas City fire and Willie. In the distance he heard the muffled flush of a toilet. Weather checked his watch. The club was gearing up for the cocktail hour. He should have searched these rooms before now.

"What in God's name are you doing?" a female voice hissed behind him. He banged the plaster cast on the inside of the metal drawer and turned to face his accuser.

Jane Alder—*Beacon* reporter, love, or at least current strong interest, of his life—stood in the doorway. She balanced a stack of office supplies on her arm cast. Her curly, dark hair was cut short and her bruises had faded since he saw her last. Her narrowed eyes widened when she recognized him. He opened his mouth to greet her but she shook her head in warning. Two uglier heads than hers popped into the door space behind her. One had a Marine headshave so short the scalp had a five o'clock shadow. The body attached to it must have been an MP in the war. The other head sported curly brown hair, pomaded into a duck's ass, and was attached to a shorter man. Burly stood large, but Curly looked twice as mean. They filled the doorway and cut off his escape route.

"The hell is this?" Burly had a Yankee accent. Something Midwestern. Chicago, Weather guessed, wondering if he was part of the northern mob infiltration so feared down here. Falvey should have better sense than to use a Chicago foot soldier. He could get run out of town by the other locals.

"Mister, this is private property back here," Curly said with a happy growl, a bear that knew he'd cornered some tasty prey.

"Ha, ha, just looking for my long-lost sister." The men advanced. Each hooked a hand under Weather's armpit and they lifted him off his feet. Something roared in his injured shoulder. He yelped as they dragged him away from the files.

"Oh, don't," Jane's voice quavered within the confines of the wires that held her busted jaw together. "I don't want to see anyone get beat up. Just get Falvey, I mean, Mr. Johnson."

"Honey, you don't have to concern yourself with this." The jarhead gave her an almost loving look.

She's too classy for you, Weather wanted to blurt out.

"No really, I hate people getting beat up. Just call the police."

"The police!" Curly emitted a dangerous laugh, and together the two goons walked Weather to the adjacent wall, where they unceremoniously slammed him into the plaster, then pinched his arms behind his back. A hot flame ran from his collarbone to his fingers. Burly backed him up and smashed him forward again, inches from a rusty nail in the wall. The curly goon punched his kidney. Jane screamed. The curly goon told Jane to get out.

"What's going on? Connie? Albert?" Falvey Johnson's reasonable tones echoed from the middle office.

"Ohhh, don't let them hurt him," Jane said, in some breathy vamped voice Weather didn't recognize.

His captors spun him around to face the club owner, now sharing the doorway with Jane, who'd put a beseeching hand on the lapel of Falvey Johnson's lightweight gray linen jacket.

Falvey's puzzled expression gave way to amusement. "Let him go."

Both thugs took their time hearing Falvey, making sure they each got a couple more punches in before they slung him toward their boss. They'd permanently ruined something in the shoulder. Weather massaged it awkwardly with his left hand. Jane watched dispassionately from the door.

"I believe I can handle Mr. Weather myself." Falvey hooked a thumb toward the exit and the two men stomped out.

Falvey Johnson shooed Jane out of the opening and closed the door. He turned and shook his head, grinning.

"Have a seat, Mr. Weather." He indicated the green office chair. Weather sat. The club owner leaned against the desk and smiled, as if he had affable chats with burglars caught riffling his records every day. With his kindly face, Falvey could pass for a Sunday school teacher at any of the blander churches in town, although he lacked the firebrand zeal to appeal to the more hell-bent ones. Falvey looked like a philanthropist, or a railroad tycoon, or the mayor. Falvey had never been indicted, or even tied to Willie beyond the Star D, and had withstood plenty of Willie-inspired investigations. Yet he always came up clean. Everybody at the D.A.'s office figured Falvey for some underworld role. The guy was just too slick to get caught. Slicker than Willie even, because some actually believed in his innocence.

"You'll have to forgive Ronnie and Albert. They're new, and they are trying to impress me. The boys do have my interests at heart, I should think. But what with my partner in this nightclub getting murdered just yesterday, one can't be too careful. Now how is it someone from the D.A.'s office—late of the D.A.'s office, I should say—happens to be going through my files? You fellows, or the police at least, drop in too often as it is. Looking for a hidden gambling room, which we don't have. Looking for liquor law violations, which you don't find. Looking for parole violators, which unfortunately you do occasionally find. The Revenue Department has looked into my taxes. The police had a look-see yesterday afternoon, after Willie turned up in the riverbottoms, although from all indications, he was shot at your building." Falvey put his palms out in exasperation. "So what are you doing now, planting evidence?"

"No, I wasn't planting anything. I want to find Willie's killers as much as you do. I'm off to a stupid start, that's all."

Falvey reached into his breast pocket and pulled out a pack of cigarettes. Another dip into the jacket produced a gold lighter. "If those old files indicate who killed him, I do hope you will take your information to the authorities. But I suspect they won't. I'm afraid they're outdated and in disarray. I haven't had any on-premise clerical help since before the war. I do use a bookkeeper, but he's in an office downtown. That's why I've hired a girl Friday to sort things out." He lit up and offered the pack to Weather.

Weather waved it away. "A girl Friday? The one with her

arm in a cast? Don't expect she can do much typing."

"Well, she can sort through the mail and so forth. As you can see from her bruises, she's in a jam and needs some help. Husband's been beating her up." Falvey looked wistfully at the door to the center room. "I like to help young ladies who are down on their luck. And that one will make a fine dancer once she's healed. She's got the grace. Watch her walk sometime."

Weather had watched her walk many times, and had felt the same thrill. No way she was going to dance at the Star D, no matter what kind of undercover gig she had going.

Willie's partner leaned over and opened the door. "Connie, darlin'? Would you be so kind as to bring my friend here and me a couple of glasses?"

"Why of course," Jane murmured from the central room. She appeared a little later and lowered a tray onto the desk.

Even with the cast on her arm, Jane—Connie—did a fine job of pouring the Jack Daniel's, Weather had to admit. He watched Falvey watching her, and hoped all that grace would protect her life if the club owner found out she was a reporter from the *Beacon*. Falvey patted her on the rump as she left. She gave a little tut-tut, the way decent women who know the story do when that happened. Not prudish or angry, but still telling the guy to keep his mitts to himself. Falvey laughed.

Weather passed the next half hour in the small room, dodging Falvey's questions about Willie's visit and listening to Falvey blame the Chicago mob and Martin Hubert for Willie's murder.

Eventually he rose to leave.

Falvey put a hand on his wrist, the one with the cast. "Speaking of Willie, his funeral's Saturday. You are welcome to come as my guest."

"That would be salt in the wound for his son," Weather

replied. "Laidlaw Peabody should be able to bury his daddy in peace. You think your graceful girl Friday could call me a cab?"

Falvey checked a gold pocket watch. "No, she gets off at five. I'll have one of the bodyguards run you home. Or into town, if that's where you want to go."

"Er, no, I think I'll find my way home. Thanks, anyway."

Falvey shrugged and waved a hand expansively. Be my guest. Do as you please.

Weather left the offices. The curly goon, Ronnie, stood smoking on the bare stage, and watched him all the way past the bar until he got out of sight in the little foyer. Weather fiddled with the knobs on the cigarette machine, just to buy the chance to look back inside for Jane, in case she was waiting for him, but he met Ronnie's hostile gaze instead. Maybe Jane did go home. Where was home?

He walked outside and headed for downtown. It took five minutes to go up Industrial to Commerce, through the Triple Underpass, and over to the *Beacon* on Wood Street. The newspaper's front doors were unlocked. He went to the newsroom. He didn't expect to find Jane's boss, Francy Cotton, and wasn't disappointed. Bradley Murph, a pimply faced college intern who harbored delusions of a worldliness that he would never possess, told him Francy had gone to Texas City. Been there since yesterday. Most of the Texas press was down there.

"Figures," Weather said, and sent up a silent wish that Francy would get blown up with the next refinery, but only after she told him how Jane Alder had come to be Connie, working for Falvey. Bradley Murph had started into a reminiscence about their last adventure when Weather spotted Jemison looking at him from a typewriter at the back of the room. He did not want to fend off questions, so he beat it out of there.

Chapter 8

"With that busted jaw of yours, I know it's hard to get enough to eat, but you gotta."

Jane sat at the kitchenette table and watched as Albert Florentine put the ice chunk into the little icebox, and unloaded milk and eggs from a grocery sack. He plugged in the new hotplate, poured oil into the new skillet, let it get hot, broke eggs into a bowl, and added the milk. What a generous man. He'd paid for the room. He'd found the icebox and bought the groceries. If he found out she was Jane Alder, *Beacon* reporter, instead of Connie Petro from Cincinnati, he would find her a nice unmarked grave.

She shivered. The beating she'd taken last month should have taught her caution, but here she was in a more dangerous spot than before. And last time she'd had David looking out for her.

"Baby, you cold?" He set the skillet aside and went over to the bed where he removed the knobby spread and brought it to her, draping the thing around her with such care it made her want to cry.

"Thank you."

He gave her a sad look, like he was going to say something personal, but then shrugged it off and went back to the eggs. Scrambled, like she liked them.

Amazing. After two days undercover, she had Falvey Johnson doting on her like a movie producer cultivating a new starlet, and this Chicago goon cooking for her.

★ ★ ★ ★ ★

"Troy and his daddy turned up," Weather's mother, Charlotte Craft Weather Hilyard—whose calling card actually read *Charlotte Craft Hilyard*, but Weather took a perverse satisfaction in keeping his father's name in the pedigree—warbled in her fine Highland Park voice over the phone. Weather had called from his den to talk to Resa, but his sister was out with her fiancé. Troy and Mac Porter had been in the Permian Basin when the Texas City fires started, his mother said. They had flown right down to Galveston Bay, but were currently back in Dallas because Resa had pledged Portex Oil's company plane to deliver medical supplies and fresh Red Cross workers to the devastated area. Resa tended to have both Porter men wrapped around her heart.

"She wants to go with them but I don't think she should, not without a chaperone," Charlotte said. "Mac gets into those all-night poker games and Sylvia can't make the trip because of a bridge party. That would leave Resa alone with Troy in a hotel."

"I'll go," Weather said dryly from the desk in his den. He'd been wondering how to get down to Texas City to talk to Jane's boss at the paper about Jane, and here was a free ride on a private plane.

"Oh, I would feel so much better if you did."

Weather marveled at his mother and her protocols. In the public opinion poll of David Weather, Hero or Rascal, she had her vote firmly in the Rascal camp. The same woman who had chastised him heavily for losing Leslie Holcomb as a fiancée now felt he was suitable for protecting Resa's virginity—which he suspected was long gone—or at least her reputation on an overnight trip. Mothers.

"I'll call the Porters now and let them know." She gave

Weather explicit instructions about how alone Resa could be with Troy—" in the lobby only, or in your suite, but not in the bedroom, not even to look out the window, David, and I'm serious. I'll go ahead and call the *Houston Post*, too—" Weather knew she meant the society columnist "—so you'd better not let anyone drink too much in public. Especially Mac, you know how he gets." She would make the reservations at the Rice.

"What should we have for dinner, Mother?"

"Why, whatever you want, you silly . . . Oh, for gosh sake! All right. I'm being an old wet hen. You eat what you want, but I don't want any drunken shenanigans in the paper when you're all supposed to be doing charity work. That wouldn't look good at all, and we don't want any clouds on Resa's wedding."

"No, ma'am." No babies born less than nine months after the wedding.

After she hung up, Weather felt like he'd been battered by a hurricane.

Charlotte called back a few minutes later with the news that Troy would pick him up at eight the next morning and drive him to Love Field. She started into another list of Resa-shalt-nots, but Weather cut the conversation short. Packing to do.

He sat at his desk for a little while, thinking about Jane. The shoulder, re-injured by Falvey's blue-headed thug, nagged at him. Visions of the club owner patting Jane's rear end bothered him. Margie Lunn's red sofa across the room irked him. He swiveled his chair to the den's outer wall so he wouldn't have to look at it. If it kept bugging him, he would get rid of the thing. Then Belinda Bain, the dancer who might be his sister, entered his mental fray.

Help that little gal, Willie had said from the sofa. Weather hazarded a look over there and placed Willie back on it, chomping on his cigar. This was getting strange.

What's Belinda done?

Might a done, Willie corrected, waving the wet cigar stump. *What I'm telling you is all alleged, since you won't let me hire you for my lawyer and get client privilege, but there's some that say she's skimming money off a well-known gambler at a game she might be dealing cards for. Can't quite recollect who, but there's some say that kind of behavior deserves a shot in the head. Not me, I don't want that to happen, but I don't know if I have the power to stop it.* Willie frowned. That last sentence told of big trouble in gangland.

She's your blood kin, Tom Weather had said in the dream. He'd known it for a while but had filed the knowledge away as part of Tom Weather's excesses, not to be examined.

You might give her a friendly warning to get on out of town, Willie said from the sofa.

Weather had kept this part of Willie's visit from Hadley and Orton, and now thought maybe he should not have. Tuesday night, after he left Willie in the Claypoole phone booth, he had gone to the Star D to get drunk, but also to find Belinda. She wasn't there. Last night he'd had cops all over the Claypoole 'til late, and had been so caught up in the discovery of Willie's Packard that he hadn't given Belinda a second thought. Now Willie was back, in a manner of speaking, warning him again.

Weather planned to be in Houston and Texas City tomorrow night, so it would be Saturday before he could get back to Belinda. If the young woman's trouble was as bad as Willie said, and Willie had been her chief protector, she could be dead before he got back. She could be dead already.

He needed to find her tonight.

Dammit. He had to go back to the Star D. He didn't know

how late the dancers stayed on Thursdays, but figured they left earlier than on weekends. He slipped on his jacket, locked up, and went down to the Claypoole's east parking lot. To hell with waiting on cabs. He was driving.

To hell with you, Willie, he said, deliberately sauntering across the spot that had briefly contained the gangster's bleeding carcass. It was a little like walking on a grave, except Willie didn't die here. Weather climbed behind the wheel of his Chrysler Saratoga.

The car cranked right up, thanks to occasional spins by Beady to keep the battery going. Weather backed out and fought the wheel to get the car aimed. Even driving left-handed, it hurt like hell to make turns, but somehow he managed to get to the Star D without hitting any pedestrians, curbs, or light poles.

Belinda had better be there.

Chapter 9

A wreath hung on the glass door of the Star D, and two smaller ones draped the gumball and cigarette machines in the foyer. In memory of Willie.

The place was slow. Onstage, Wild Jill and her Six Gunns were down to No Jill and her Four Gunns, the lead Gunn being none other than Tom Weather's bastard daughter, Belinda Bain. Not dead, but her performance was. She cracked a child's toy whip and rode horse to an off-key piano rendition of a bawdy song about a honky-tonk, and displayed an appalling boredom with her art.

He took a seat near the stage, away from the private nook with Falvey's mirror. A waitress took his beer order fast and brought it out fast. Weather watched his sister work. Every jerk of her leg showed her contempt for her audience, her defiance and shame at her position in the world. Maybe she had their father's desire to rise, and stealing was her ticket out.

The girls began their patrol for tips.

He wrote a hasty note on a napkin and folded a five into it. Another Gunn spotted the green in the darkened room and sashayed over, but he shook his head and pointed to Belinda. The girl pranced toward Belinda and pointed him out.

Belinda came over and took it without so much as a thank you. She read the note while jostling her jugs, then dropped it back on his table.

"Midnight," she said, and galloped away.

The set ended and the girls disappeared backstage. He figured they all had to change, so he waited, wondering how he would handle the encounter. Maybe she thought he'd bought her favors for the evening, since his note said he wanted to take her home after work. He realized he was as nervous as a kid meeting his first whore.

She didn't show at midnight.

She didn't show a half hour later either, and he was as mad as a kid who'd been duped by his first whore.

He went to the stage door. A bouncer stopped him, but delivered a message.

"Wait in your car. She'll find you."

He made a stop at the men's, then waited outside in the Saratoga. She still did not come, and he thought she'd duped him but good.

At twelve forty-five, a car door slammed, and gravel scrunched nearby. Belinda slipped into the Saratoga's passenger side and gave him a West Dallas address. She gave no greeting, made no demand to know what he wanted. She eyed him with sunken, wary eyes. On the ride over, she nibbled her hair and stole glances at him. When he struggled to turn the big Chrysler onto the narrow roads, she gave a snort.

In West Dallas, the streetlights disappeared. This section of the city was factories and poor whites, and bad roads.

"Turn here, take a right," was all she said as she guided him past derelict buildings and ice houses and machine shops.

"Here," she said finally, pointing a lacquered fingernail at an unlikely home—a concrete rectangle that fronted the broken fence of the old Krueger Pants factory. He knew the place. The company expanded so much during the war, Biedermeier once told him, that it moved to a better site up on Lemmon. The old site needed the wrecking ball. Iron fencing sprang off either side of the small building. An automobile gate hung open to the right. Directly behind the main building, low-lying corrugated roofs suggested a drop in terrain not visible in the darkness. To the right of the gate, woods and brush dominated.

The building had two doors opening directly onto a sidewalk slab and had maybe been the front office and a night watchman's quarters. A place to stay, maybe, but not a place to live. Weather parked next to a black Ford with Illinois plates.

He and Belinda got out. Without speaking, she used a key on the right door and led him into a single room. A lamp on a bedside table by the door cast twenty-five-watt shadows. Perhaps to disguise the utilitarian nature of the building, she'd done the room up in Turkish slut. Gauzy red and purple veils hung off the ceiling. More of them covered the headboard on the left and the dresser against the back wall. At the open window in the back, black lace curtains flapped in the breeze. Belinda shut the door and the wind died down. A wicker chair took up a far corner, next to a dresser. Other than in adolescence on Tom Weather's nickel, Weather had spent little time in rooms like this, preferring as he grew older married mistresses and the occasional free-spirited tart who would visit his own austere digs. He couldn't judge, but he figured she didn't take on beginners. If she did, she shouldn't. This place was too Mata Hari for inexperienced youth. Hell, all this gauze hanging off the ceiling bothered him and he was no beginner.

Next door, a headboard launched repeated assaults against an innocent wall. His *sister* lived in a two-whore brothel. His sister. This was about as private and dignified as a twin outhouse.

She lit a candle and opened the back window further.

Dark Medusa curls flung themselves around as she moved. Her black eyes held an anger he should have expected. No, something more sinister, almost evil. Drugs. Of course. That was why she'd been so late, why she'd come from a car instead of the Star D. He grabbed her arms and looked for needle marks. In the dark he couldn't tell. She misread his intent. "All right, let's go, then." She grabbed him by the necktie and pulled him onto the bed, rough. She got above him and pinned him between her knees with strong thighs. The mattress was too soft and they sank deep into the bed. She leaned her face toward his. Her hair smelled of some kind of rose-water dressing. Her breath stank of whisky and too many cigarettes. She locked her lips onto his and ground her pelvis into his groin. He twisted her off him.

"No! I just want to talk to you. Willie said you're in danger. For skimming. You've got to get out of town. They're going to kill you." He didn't know where to begin, but not in her bed.

Car doors slammed outside. Like some jungle animal she sprang on her haunches and lifted the blinds on the front window.

"Oh, God." She dropped the blinds.

"What?"

Belinda looked from the door to the back window, and made some instinctive, creature decision. "Stay down. Go along." She covered him again and began writhing.

Someone kicked the door in.

"Get out while I'm working, dammit," she growled at the intruder. Her hair tickled his face. Her tits smashed into his chest. Weather looked toward the door. Two men in stocking masks held Tommy guns in gloved hands.

"Git on out," Belinda yelled again.

To his surprise, one of the gunmen grunted acquiescence.

He signaled the other and they backed out of the room and pulled the door shut. Their heavy footsteps thudded along the sidewalk and the second door gave in to kicks. This time the Tommy guns rattled.

With one mind, he and Belinda rolled off the bed. The gauze veils jerked overhead as stray bullets came through the common wall. A car door slammed. Tires screeched.

Silence fell.

His logic said it all took ten seconds. His nerves said ten hours. He tried to push up off his good arm but found it wouldn't obey. No adrenaline.

He looked at Belinda, crouched beside him, panting heavily, eyes dark and guarded.

"Who's next door?"

"Martel," she said in a tiny, cracked voice. "Oh, my God, Martel." She sprang up with a grace that rivaled Jane's and ran outside. His bad shoulder screaming, Weather sat. He used the bed to pull himself up the rest of the way.

An animal howl came from next door. He ran toward the howling, and wanted to join it when he got there.

Two naked, bullet-riddled bodies lay in the bed. Martel's staring eyes held the terror of her last moments. Blood still ran from her dark hair. The man's face wasn't there to tell any tales.

Martel. The woman's staring eyes took the center spot in his grim imagination. He hadn't recognized her in death, but he knew her. Martel Gines. The sister of Willie's tire-iron victim. She was the non-witness in Willie's trial last year. The poor woman said from the start she didn't see a thing, even though it was her own brother's brains that got flung all over the parked cars when Willie killed him. Now hers were flung all over the bed where she worked.

Belinda continued her shriek, in waxing and waning

whoops that mimicked police sirens. Weather put his free hand over her mouth to shush her and hugged her as best he could. Her skin was clammy. She shuddered a few times but then got hold of herself and shook him off.

Finally she said, "I'm sorry, Martel honey," in a choked whisper, and walked purposefully toward her room. He followed.

In the gauzy room, she dug under the bed and came out with a cigar box. She blew out the candle on the dresser and climbed into the open back window.

"You better get out of here before the cops come." Her voice held steady, but with the resigned timbre of the tough street girl, facing the realities of her life one more time. At that moment, he was terribly proud of her. She straddled the sill and ducked her head through the opening.

"Wait." He lunged for her, and managed to grab the box before she got all the way out.

She pulled, but he got it away from her before she dropped.

"Give it to me," she whispered from outside. The drop was lower than he expected and he was looking at the top of her head.

"Meet me around front and I will," he whispered back. Talking out loud did not seem appropriate. It might disturb the dead. Off somewhere, car tires squealed.

"Go to hell," she hissed. She shook a fist at him and took off toward the woods.

Weather went outside. Hands shaking, he got into the Saratoga and cranked up. Before he put it in gear, he flipped the lid on the box. It was full of photos and letters and cash. Belinda's life, and her life savings. He stowed the box under the seat.

In his rear view mirror, the Ford with the Illinois plates

stood sentinel over the death scene. He tried to drive past the woods where Belinda had run, so he could pick her up and help her escape, but the road curved away from them.

He drove down the street and took a left, seeking access to the woods, but hit a dead end. Belinda would be deep in the trees by now anyway. It occurred to him he should get out of this area, so he drove into the country and took another route into town to avoid any cops coming on the scene. Where were the sirens? He hadn't heard any after the shooting. He would have to call the police himself.

Chapter 10

District Attorney Franklin Morson eyed Weather with the contempt any man deserved for showing up uninvited on one's doorstep past one a.m., but got down to business quickly enough when Weather told him there'd been a shooting. Morson sent Mrs. Morson back to bed and beckoned his guest into his den. After getting Weather's hurried story, the D.A. telephoned Hadley at home. Morson knew about Belinda's parentage, so Weather could at least bypass explaining all that.

The D.A. handed him the phone. Weather told Hadley his story, not naming Belinda or how he happened to be in the neighborhood, and indicated his desire to keep his involvement out of the papers.

"Stay there," Hadley commanded.

"Stay here," Morson also commanded. The D.A. dressed and went out to the crime scene himself. Two hours later, Morson and Hadley arrived together. Weather had fallen asleep on the D.A.'s leather sofa, and Morson sent razoring pains into the shoulder as he shook him awake.

Weather repeated his story, leaving out Belinda until Morson barked, "Oh, for chrissakes, I told him she's your sister. Stop trying to protect yourself."

Weather told them about Willie's concern for Belinda.

"I oughtta put you in jail for not giving me that last night," Hadley said. His voice had that low pressure warning in it.

"I didn't deem it pertinent to Willie's murder."

71

"I'll be the judge of what's pertinent to my investigations," Hadley said flatly.

"Okay," Weather said, too tired to argue. "What about the man with Martel? Who was he?"

"No I.D. on his body."

"But his car? The registration, the Illinois plates?"

"Now here's a spot where your story just doesn't pan out," Hadley said. "There wasn't any black Ford there."

Chapter 11

Listen my children and ye shall hear,
Of the Midnight Ride of Big Carl Ray.

Carl Ray swore and turned off the flashlight. Didn't rhyme, and he knew it. Been thinking for a while about doing a poem like "Paul Revere's Ride," only it would be Carl Ray's Last Ride, to leave for Burr and Bonnie to puzzle over, and then running away. With Burr treating him so bad, it was high time, but he could barely think, he was so mad. Damn, damn, damn. He had to not wake Stevie up either and he had to be careful Burr didn't catch him up when he came home. If Burr came home. The son of a bitch must be out digging for that bank money, trying to get in good with Laidlaw now Willie was dead. Plain mean of Laidlaw to make him do that when all's Burr wanted was to deal cards and skim like the rest of the dealers.

Grown-ups! Willie tells that David Weather about the bank money and cops swarm all over the farm. Carl Ray knew he shouldn't of ever told Willie about it.

Little Ray, if Big Ray told your mama where that money was before they hung him, why didn't she go get it? Willie had asked.

She tried to find it, but she said he didn't say exactly where it was. "Buried under something red." Or "by or next to something red" was what he said.

Which was it, Willie asked, *"under" or "by" or "next to"?*

I just don't remember. All's I truly remember was the "something red" part. Willie loved riddles and puzzles, and that one was enough to get him and Stevie taken into the family after their mama died. Whilst she was alive, Burr and Bonnie thought they were too good to claim kin, because Mama was just a palm-reader with a few loser boyfriends and Willie let Burr run some card games out in Tyler, which made Burr a big shot. Carl Ray grinned. After Mama died and he told Willie that "something red" story, the entire Peabody operation wanted to take the poor orphan kinfolk in. The poor *ungrateful* orphans, he corrected. Especially him, with his juvenile record and sassing Bonnie all the time.

I think you made that story up to get you and your brother a meal ticket, Burr said about once a week.

No, I didn't, he'd answer back every time, and it was the truth. Mama really said it to him, but whether Big Ray ever really said it to her, he didn't know. Maybe he did, maybe she thought he did. Her with the Sight and the booze both, she was always seeing things.

Including his future. Mama foresaw that he would "prevail over all," in spite of his difficulties, but he wouldn't unless he took care of his little brother as long as he could. Mama said she'd read it in his palm, and the prevailing over depended on the taking care of. She told most of her customers they would prevail over something or other, so he couldn't put much stock in her prophecy. Probably she hadn't seen nothing, but just made up the prophecy to make sure Stevie had somebody better than Burr and Bonnie to look out for him.

It sounded good though, and he could believe it if he wanted to.

He looked over at Stevie, in the other bed. Twelve years

old and the fat brat still sucked his thumb in his sleep. At least he didn't wet the bed.

Take care of him, ha! Carl Ray didn't even like him.

He thought about the prophecy again. Mama did say, "as long as he could," not "until Stevie was grown," so that did kind of leave him some leeway.

He ran a hand under his undershirt and slid it behind his back as far as he could and felt along the welt. The time on "as long as he could" was getting short. Taking a whipping from Burr for talking to the cops was a sure sign.

Carl Ray did some thinking. Four things he had to do before Carl Ray's Last Ride. Or as part of it.

One. Write the poem.

Two. Get revenge for Big Ray's hanging.

Three. Make Burr pay.

Four. Find the bank money.

All of that had to be part of the Last Ride. The four didn't necessarily have to happen at the same instant, but they had to happen before he could leave. And when he did Ride, there had to be no doubt in his mind that he'd taken care of things and made his mark on this town.

Listen my children for I shall say,
Of the Midnight Ride of old Carl Ray.

It wasn't as good as "you shall hear" but he repeated it under his breath until he liked it. What he needed was a copy of the real poem. He couldn't remember what came next, and it would help to know. "One if by land and two if by sea" was in there somewhere, but that wouldn't work too good for Dallas.

Thinking so much made him want a cigarette. He pulled on dungarees and a work shirt and took his loafers out on the porch. Couldn't walk in the house with shoes on or Stevie would wake up, but it was too chilly to be out here barefoot. He slipped into the shoes and ducked under the house to where he kept his stuff, being careful not to slip and get any mud on him anywhere.

That old hound dog that stayed under here raised its head.

"Shut up and go back to sleep," he told it, and laid a hand on its rump. Thing was supposed to be a watchdog but didn't bark at him anymore, it was so used to him coming under here. Old dog didn't bark at much of anything, but Burr didn't realize that. It didn't like Burr either.

The dog went back to snoring. Carl Ray eased over to the trench he'd dug by the chimney and lifted up the plank over it. Dug it out when he first got here because the bricks were red, but wasn't no bank money by it. Couldn't be under it, or Big Ray would have had to build the house, which was already there when he came to Dallas.

Carl Ray popped the lid on the saltine tin and pulled out a cigarette and a box of matches. He managed to get everything put back and himself back up on the porch without getting any mud anywhere except his shoes, which he scraped off with a stick. He threw the stick off into a bush and fired up that cig. It tasted good.

Lucky this old farmhouse of Willie's was set so far back off the road, and facing sort of sideways, and had that winding dirt road coming up to it. He could smoke off the porch edge and let the smoke float off, and see the headlight beam bounce out in the field before Burr got up here and around the side and parked.

Dammit! There was headlights coming now, coming hell for leather. He jumped off the porch without making a sound and stubbed out the cigarette and then tiptoed up on the porch and got inside the screen door. If Burr was taking a woman or a card game down to the cabin, Carl Ray could finish the smoke. If Burr was coming into the house, Carl Ray could get back to the bed in time. Whatever Burr was up to, Carl Ray wished he'd slow down so the smoke outside could drift off some more.

It was after three a.m. by the time Weather left Morson's. Good thing he was going to Texas City later that morning—it might be a good idea to get out of town for a day. Whoever killed Martel and her boyfriend had returned for the boyfriend's car. The killers might be having more afterthoughts, such as disposing of all the witnesses. They might not have recognized him in the darkness of Belinda's room, but they might have. Belinda knew them. When she yelled at them, they left her and him alone. She'd sounded scared, but had a hint of irritation in her voice, like she knew them and figured what was going to happen.

Would they remember the Saratoga and look for it? Were they looking for it now? If they had any brains, they would be.

He had to hide it. But where? He thought for a few seconds and then a place came to him. A quiet, well-kept neighborhood. A big garage around back, and the owners out of town. He still had keys, by God.

He drove into Highland Park to his ex-fiancée's house on Arcady, hoping no neighborhood insomniacs were up. Or police, cruising for burglars, but he could talk his way out of that.

Carl Ray stood behind the kitchen screen door, watching Burr. What in hell was the son of a bitch doing? Burr stopped out back, cut off the lights but left the engine running, then went over to the garden and started pulling up them concrete blocks Bonnie had put out there to build a little wall for pot plants. One by one he put a bunch of 'em in the trunk, then he got back in the car and drove down towards the lake with the headlights off. Burr did that when he had a woman with him, in case Bonnie woke up and looked out the window, she wouldn't see no lights through the trees.

Bonnie didn't know about who all Burr brought out to that cabin when she was asleep on her pills. She didn't know he brought one of them dancers into their bed one day when she was with Stevie downtown shopping. The dancer-woman had black hair. Burr called her dancing girl and made her dance for him. Carl Ray had been in the barn when they drove up, and Burr musta thought he was with Bonnie and Stevie in town. He'd snuck up under the house to listen, once they got inside. He could hear them talking and hear her feet move on the plank floor.

He had to see what Burr was up to down at the lake. He slipped out of the screen door and ran through the woods. The footpath went straight to the cabin, and the road out there curved, so maybe he could get there before Burr.

Carl Ray reached the edge of the woods by the lake but was breathing too loud to move any closer. Burr had beat him there and parked past the cabin, right up by the lake. Burr was shining a flashlight down in the trunk. From up high like he was, Carl Ray could see down inside it a little.

There was some bad business in that trunk.

Burr took out all the concrete blocks first, and then he reached in and got the bad thing out. It was a white canvas roll, like a tarpaulin or a painter's drop cloth, tied up like a rug. Something in it was kicking and whimpering like a dog.

Burr threw the thing down on the ground and smashed at it with a concrete block. After four or five whacks, it just jerked and twitched a little bit. After a little while, it quit that, too. Carl Ray didn't take a breath the whole time, but finally made himself.

Out of the blue Burr spun that flashlight around and shone it out in the woods. Carl Ray stepped behind a tree and prayed to God, and to the spirit of his mama, and to Willie, and to the Devil, although Mama told him never, ever do that, and one of 'em must have answered, he didn't care which, because Burr took the light off the woods and put it on the cabin. Carl Ray stuck his head out from behind the tree just enough to see. Burr walked all around the cabin, and looked under it, and went inside. The door was on the lake side, not the woods side, but Carl Ray could see the flashlight flare up on each window from inside the cabin. Then Burr came out and shone the light on the blocks and the canvas roll and the boat dock and back in the trunk. He dug some rope out of the trunk.

Carl Ray watched his court-appointed legal guardian run the rope through the holes in the concrete blocks and truss that canvas up good. Then Burr drug all of it around the car and over to the dock. Idiot. Should've carried everything separate to the dock and done his tying there, but Burr didn't have near as much brains as he thought he did.

It took him a good ten minutes before he got it all in the rowboat. Then the stupid dumb-ass had to squat kind of straddled over that canvas the whole way out to the middle. Carl Ray prayed again.

God, Willie, Lucifer, let that boat tip over when Burr tries to heave the thing in the water.

It didn't tip over. Carl Ray sighed. He never had much use for prayer anyway.

That idiot Burr did manage to drop the flashlight overboard, though, and had to start back in the dark. Maybe that was as answered as Carl Ray's prayers would ever get.

He didn't wait for Burr to get back to shore, but slipped through the woods up to the main house and got undressed. He put his dungarees under his pillow, and got in the bed, and Burr still hadn't got back.

Would have been perfect, if only Stevie hadn't been awake.

Lettie Holcomb hadn't changed the locks, but then, Weather's sins against her family never included property crimes. He used his garage key and rolled the Saratoga into the darkened structure. There was plenty of room. A single car, Leslie's tan roadster, took up less than half of the cavernous space. Lucky for him Mother Lettie was too neurotic to handle an automobile.

He used another key to get in the house, where he phoned for a cab.

"I need to go to Union Station," he told the dispatcher. "And tell the cabbie there's a big tip if he doesn't honk. I don't want to wake up the neighborhood."

He waited outside behind a big hackberry until the cab came. It wasn't his regular cab company, and he didn't recognize the driver. He hoped the man didn't recognize him from the newspapers. At Union Station, he paid, waited inside a few minutes, then went out onto the street and walked across the viaduct to the Claypoole. Should have gone to a hotel in case Martel's killers had recognized him, but he had to be home for Troy to pick him up for the flight south.

"I'll tell," Stevie taunted from his bed. "You been down at the lake house, smoking. Stole Bonnie's cigarettes again and went down there, when Burr told you not to."

"Stevie, you can't. Not this time."

"Can."

"Can't. I mean it. He, he'll kill us both. He's mean drunk this time."

"How do you know that?" Stevie must not know Burr was back.

"I seen it with the Sight. With our mama's Sight."

Stevie made a raspberry, and kept it razzing and razzing 'til Carl Ray was about to hit him.

"What do you want? Anything, and I do mean anything."

"All your money."

Carl Ray got it from the dungarees pocket, and handed it over. Fifteen dollars, to that fat brat.

"All your cigarettes."

"They're under the house, next to the chimney." Which was safe enough, 'cause the fat brat was too lazy to climb up under there to get them.

"Your pocketknife."

"Hey! That was my daddy's. Not yours."

"I want it."

Outside, Burr's car drove up.

Carl Ray fished Big Ray's knife out of the pants and handed it over.

Stevie stood up in the bed and looked out the window. "Hey, he had his lights off. He came from down at the lake."

"Lie down!"

"What was he doing down there?"

"Shut up, Stevie, I mean it."

They heard Burr's foot up on the back porch. Stevie shut up.

When Burr got in the house, he stood in their doorway for a long time, looking at them. Stevie didn't pipe up, not once.

Chapter 12

Friday, April 18

On the Claypoole's circular drive, Troy Porter put Weather's bag in the Portex company limo and inquired after his health as the two men shook hands. Weather grunted amenities and climbed in the back of the big car beside Troy. His future brother-in-law was a dark-haired, square-faced, muscular young man, barrel-legged and swift. A good match for athletic Resa.

The driver took them to Love Field, where Resa and Troy's father and three Red Cross volunteers waited. To Weather's surprise, Mac Porter gave him a cold stare while Resa made introductions. The two disaster coordinators were Doyle and Irene—call us Doyle and Irene—Wimberly of Dallas. They'd been doing this since they retired; this was their second trip to Texas City, and they would direct the unloading and the delivery. The nurse volunteer, Vicky Broom—Nurse Broom, please—was there to see that the donated blood stayed refrigerated. Those other canisters were embalming fluid, which needed no refrigeration—or explanation. The three of them would relieve other exhausted volunteers, Doyle Wimberly said, but civilians such as themselves should not expect to get near the fire.

Mac Porter took a long gulp from a silver flask. "I got a half interest in a refinery down there and I'll go where I damn

82

well please." Macauley Porter was a burly man, muscle going to flab, face going to jowl. His aftershave didn't cover the bourbon on his breath.

Doyle and Irene grinned approval of the big Texan's display of individualism. Nurse Broom pasted on the kind of smile that said she could easily hook Mac to an I.V. of embalming fluid without a second thought. Weather took a liking to her. Rich people, generous though they could be when it came to charities, made him tired at times. Especially family.

Troy put a hand on his father's shoulder and, in a good-son sort of way, told him to calm down. Mac grumped a bit but shut up.

"Be sure to take a good look from the air when we get near Houston," Doyle said, apparently smoothing the storm by diverting attention from it. "You can see the smoke for miles."

"Kind of smoky here, too." Weather sniffed the air.

"Huh! You know, you're right." Doyle licked a finger and held it up to the wind. "Coming out of the south. I bet it's from Texas City."

Troy and Nurse Broom pronounced the plane loaded, and they all climbed aboard.

"Everybody find a seat," pilot Troy said, then spoke via his radio to the control tower.

Weather sat beside Resa, behind Troy. Mac sat up front next to Troy.

"Go sit in the back for a few minutes, won't you, Resa honey," Mac Porter said to her once they were airborne. "I need to talk to your brother, man to man."

Resa went to the back row and Mac took Resa's seat next to Weather.

"C'mere," he beckoned.

Weather leaned in. Tiny capillaries traversed Mac's bagging cheeks and reddened his nose. Without the mystique of his millions and the "better" trench coat from Neiman Marcus, he was just another puffy-faced guy in late middle age, one who ate too much and probably paid with a bad stomach. Take away the trench, the good barbering, outfit him in a Salvation Army coat, and he could pass for a rail-riding hobo.

"I want to tell you I don't appreciate you giving out my name to the po-lice in relation to Willie Peabody."

"What?"

Mac Porter's face flared red. "Now I enjoy a card game now and then, but that doesn't mean I'm in any trouble with any gangsters. I didn't have anything to do with Willie Peabody's killing."

"Mac, what are you—"

Porter's jowls shook. "My son is about to marry your sister, man, don't you have any sense of family honor? For you to be telling the cops that Willie named me is about the lowest, dirtiest, shiftiest—"

"I didn't." Weather stared at Mac Porter, amazed. "Hadley told you this?"

"Questioned me this morning. Don't you know a scandal like this could ruin both our families?"

"Hold on. Your name never came up from Willie. Oh, he dropped a lot of hints that someone big, someone known locally, was unhappy with him, but he never named you."

"Who do you think he meant, then?"

"I don't know. It never occurred to me that Hadley would think this man was you." Now Weather wondered if he were. That would definitely put a cloud on Resa's wedding.

"It's a murder investigation, son, don't you understand?

Now you been a hotshot D.A., but some things are out of your league."

Like you killing Willie to end a gambling debt, Weather thought. He would hate to testify against Mac Porter, but if the man confessed to the killing, he would. Then move to California.

"Now I do owe the man some money," Mac said.

"Mac, you'd better not say another word."

"And this Texas City fire has hurt Portex," the older man's voice dipped so low Weather could barely pick up his words over the engine drone. "But you understand, I pay my debts. Cards are a vice, but a vice paid by money, not murder. It's not like the clap or something that can make you crazy if you don't treat it. I would never resort to murder."

"Mac, stop it. Your name never came up from Willie. Nor did I send Hadley your way. He called your bluff, that's all. He listed up all the high rollers who might owe Willie and your name was on the top of his list. He turned you upside down and rattled you to see what would fall out of your pockets. I bet he scared a few other names out of you, didn't he?"

"Not a one. Threatened me with withholding evidence, though, and I got no evidence. I ain't played cards in months." Porter's chin rose, bulldoggish, bottom teeth showing. "I don't run with that crowd no more."

Weather doubted that, although he knew Sylvia Porter was running a no-cards 'til the wedding campaign, probably with as much success as Charlotte's plan to preserve Resa's chastity. Some impulses just couldn't be controlled.

"I think you can relax. Hadley's just looking for information. I guess I'm going to be getting visits from a lot of scared gamblers, huh?"

Mac Porter grabbed his left arm and gave it a squeeze. "Can you use your influence to get this detective to leave me

85

out of it? I don't know a thing about this murder and it won't help the family any if the newspapers thought I did."

"Now, Mac."

"Please, son." Mac squeezed the arm again.

Weather shook his head. "I tell Hadley to back off anyone, he's going to get more interested, not less."

"You think so?" Mac put a palm up in exasperation. "Why in the hell isn't he talking to Martin Hubert? For chrissakes. Those two have been rivals for years."

"I expect he is talking to Marty. I expect he's talking to everybody. Look, just stay away from any card games, don't discuss this with anybody, and roll with the punches. Hadley, or Orton, will figure it out soon enough, and nobody will be bothering you."

"Orton?"

"Yeah. Willie died out in the riverbottoms, not in town. The murder investigation actually belongs to Orton. Technically, Hadley has only the shooting and the kidnapping."

Mac's face broke into a smile. "I didn't realize that. Well, hell! Odell's a good friend of mine. I'll just have a little talk with him and take care of this myself. Thank you for your offer, though." He let go of Weather's arm and gave it a few pats. Then he stood up and leaned between the pilot and co-pilot's seat and patted Troy on the shoulder.

"Watch it, Dad, I got a plane to fly."

> *Listen my children and you shall hear,*
> *Of the Midnight ride of Paul Revere.*
> *On the eighteenth of April in Seventy-five;*
> *Hardly a man is now alive*
> *Who remembers that famous day and year.*

Carl Ray sat at his desk in Dallas High School, feeling

heartsick. Paul Revere's Midnight Ride was *today*, April eigh-teenth, so he should've had Carl Ray's Last Ride all planned out already, for today. Damn poem was in his schoolbook all along, and he didn't know it until today when he asked Mrs. East about it. Well, he didn't have his poem done and he didn't have enough money saved up and he didn't have his vengeance for Big Ray figured out. He knew exactly what he *could* do about Burr—call the cops and tell them about that canvas roll in the lake—but what if whoever came out to have a look was on the Peabody payroll? Lots of them cops and deputies and D.A.'s were. He'd wind up rolled up in a tar-paulin himself, and that would be that.

"Carl Ray," the teacher said. "I asked you a question. Are you daydreaming?"

Everybody stared. His face got hot. "Er, no ma'am, I wasn't. I was thinking about this poem. Did you realize that it took place on April eighteenth and that's today?"

She came over to the desk and read over his shoulder. "Why, I do believe you're right. And it's so nice you're finally taking an interest in your schoolwork, even if that's not the assignment. Why don't you get up and read the first verse to the class?"

Everybody started giggling at that, but he got up and did it, and it turned out okay, and then she made the others read some more of it, and then they talked about the founding of the country and about performing heroic acts in the face of danger. It took up the entire period. First time he ever liked school. Mama would have called it a sign. So did he, and it meant he had to do something big today. He just didn't know what.

"Holy Moses. Look out there." Resa shook Weather awake. Troy pointed to his left, where black smoke joined a

87

gray mass over Galveston Bay.

Texas City looked like wartime newsreels. A partly submerged ship lay on its side at the pier. Other piers were burned skeletons. A fireboat sprayed water onto a smoldering pile on land. Blackened steel skeletons lined the mile-long shoreline. As a pilot himself during the war, Weather had done this kind of damage to Japanese ports. Only he'd never seen the destruction. All his raids were at night.

"Zeroes, twelve o'clock," Troy cried out, laughing. He made machine gun noises— "atta tat-tat. At-at-at-at-at."

"Stop that," Resa said from the co-pilot's seat. She'd moved up front not long after Weather's talk with Mac. She couldn't stay away from her man for even a couple of hours.

They touched down at Houston Hobby. Doyle and Irene had a number to call for the Red Cross truck, but Porter Oil, Senior said he would take care of it. Porter Oil, Junior stayed on the tarmac and played handsies and footsies with his intended. He was a good-looking boy, Weather acknowledged. He seemed devoted to Resa. He looked to be the backbone of the family.

Doyle and Irene beamed at the display of young love. Nurse Broom frowned.

Mac's calls produced transport in a Texas Guard troop truck.

"The governor owes me," he said with a grin. They let the Red Cross people and supplies off at a hospital, then continued at Mac Porter's direction to the outskirts of the ruined town. It took a couple of hours to get there, even though the town was only about twenty-five miles from Houston. The closer they got, the worse the traffic and the blacker the air. The truck stopped at an army drab tent, the kind with no sides, just poles and big top. It contained lots of folding tables and more than a few people typing. Most of the relief effort had moved to area hospitals by then, but this tent housed the media and the Guard command. Weather and Resa found a table. Mac and Troy Porter went off together into the rubble to meet with the executives of their destroyed property.

"I'm going to play Jane and get a story. Maybe her paper will print it," Resa said. She produced a little spiral notebook out of her purse and found a flock of guardsman willing to talk to a vivacious redhead.

Jane. Weather would play Jane and find Francy and, he hoped, get a clue as to how to pull her out of her secret life.

"I'm looking for Francy Cotton," he told several people at typewriters. These were journalists from all over the state, who lost interest in him quickly enough when they found out his cast and sling were not the result of injuries from the explosions. He found a kid, an adolescent boy who seemed to have the run of the area, and asked him for help.

"What's this lady look like?"

"About this high." Weather chopped the air at the five-foot mark. "Frizzy white hair." And she's not a lady.

"I've seen her," the boy said. "Not today, but she'll probably come around."

"Tell her I want to talk to her about Willie. Tell everybody you see who might see her that I want to talk about Willie. She'll understand." If any bait could flush Francy Cotton out of the brush, Willie was it. He gave the kid a buck.

The kid saluted—something about burning ports brought out one's military instincts—and ran off to spread the word.

Weather struck up a conversation with a weary young woman who sat at a table near his. She lived in Texas City and had come over to the tent to have something to do, although her mother would kill her if she knew. Her father had worked the day shift at Monsanto. She didn't reveal his fate, but Weather figured he knew. The Monsanto plant had been directly across from the *Grandcamp* when it caught fire. Day shift plant workers had crowded the docks, watching the fire when the blast occurred. The running man of Wednesday's radio broadcast likely came from the Monsanto day shift.

The girl, hollow-eyed and a little off-kilter, kept talking about Monsanto, and pointing to various steel ruins in the distance. Cotton warehouses. Fuel tanks.

"I'm sorry."

"Daddy's funeral's tomorrow."

"I'm sorry." He fetched Resa, who was better at these things.

"Yoo hoo," Francy Cotton yelled from outside the tent. At her height, she didn't have to stoop much to get inside. She popped up beside him, grinning big. "Helluva mess here, huh, David?"

It took a couple of hundred dead men to put the bloom in the *Beacon* publisher's cheeks, Weather thought sardonically. And less than half an hour for him to name-drop Willie Peabody and have her appear at his side. If he ever wanted to lure her to an isolated spot and kill her, he could just say, *Willie!*

"Let's walk."

Jane's boss followed him to a clearing. White hair flew around her round head. Bulldog jowls flanked Clara Bow lips. Tiny eyes peered out of too much face. Gah. She'd been one of Tom Weather's mistresses, and thank God she wouldn't admit it. Francy never admitted to any of her lovers, which was probably the only way she could get them. He was being uncharitable, he knew, but he couldn't help it. He'd spend his entire life living down Tom Weather's diverse taste in women. Francy did have a nice enough figure, though.

"Willie Peabody," Francy said breathlessly over the

metallic screeching of a bulldozer on the distant rubble.

"Jane Alder."

Francy's eyes narrowed. "Ha! I figured there was some trick here. You wouldn't come down all this way to give me any exclusive, now would you?"

"The Porters have business here and I tagged along. What in the hell is Jane doing working at the Star D?"

"Is she now?" Francy gave an exaggerated surprised look, a sure sign she knew already and didn't care if Weather knew she knew. "I thought she was in Chicago at her cousin's funeral. She said she needed to stay for a while and get over her beating. And of course be with family."

"Francy, don't toy with me."

"Don't toy with me. Willie."

"All right. Off the record, he came to visit me. Said he did not kill my father. He said something big was going to happen around town, and it had to do with someone who was a prominent businessman, but not exactly a businessman."

"What?"

"He wouldn't elucidate. 'Someone will be risen, as if from the dead, not exactly a businessman, not exactly not a businessman,' was his direct quote."

"A lawman on the take, then. Doing business on the side."

"I won't speculate. This businessman is going to bring about a big event, and when it happens, we shouldn't say we weren't warned."

"What big event?"

"He didn't say. His own murder, I think. I don't know."

"You think that's enough to get me talking about Jane?" Her voice took on the ranch-gravel toughness that always lurked beneath the Highland Park upbringing.

"I expected you'd at least want to brag about how your girl slipped into the mob. You're dying to tell me how the D.A.'s office never could get Willie, and here your young protégée is undercover after two days. I wonder if any of the other papers know she's going to scoop them."

"You wouldn't."

"I don't know what I would do. It just strikes me as a bad thing for her to be in there. Are you trying to get her killed?"

Francy sighed. "Let's go sit down." He followed her to a table just inside the tent, away from Resa and her new friend, away from clacking typewriters and listening ears.

"You know how there's been this influx of Chicago mobsters in the last six months or so? Really since the war, but more and more lately," she said.

"Now I'm off the record, but yeah. They want to take over the rackets Willie and Martin Hubert and others of his kind deny running," Weather said.

"Well, Jane's cousin was mixed up with one of them."

"The dead cousin? Did he get on the wrong side of a capo?"

"*She,* not he," Francy said. "And no, it wasn't mob-related, at least not directly. Christina Bianca was older than Jane, around thirty-five, maybe older. Wilder, by far. Jane came from rough trade, you know. Got her class from a Catholic boarding school."

"I knew that. She doesn't talk much about her background, but I knew that."

"Well, the cousin dropped out of school early. Christina has been, or rather was, a mob girl for years. Went from man to man, every few years. You know the type, cheap-pretty, not quite marriage material."

"The mistress, not the wife, type."

"Yeah. Starts out young with some rising star in the organization, loses her looks, and winds up with a bottom-rung man. In Christina's case, one Robert Verdi."

"What's this got to do with Jane being at the Star D?"

"I'm getting there. Christina went out a hotel window. That's how she died. Maybe suicide, maybe Verdi tossed her. Witnesses reported a big fight. Her yelling he didn't love her anymore. The cousin had been with this one guy for ten years, and he was about to dump her. Maybe he did, literally."

"Jane and the Star D," Weather said impatiently.

"Okay. The Chicago cops think the death might be a suicide, but would like to have a word with Verdi. Only he skipped town. Jane decided to track him and turn him in. She picked up a lead that says he's here. I mean in Dallas."

"Odd coincidence, don't you think?"

"No, I don't. Dallas is crawling with Chicago mobsters. One reason I hired Jane is she knows them, her being from Chicago."

"Then they could know her."

"They don't. She's been out of that neighborhood too long. She knows them the way most Dallasites know Willie and Martin Hubert. By reputation. By cocktail conversation. Maybe by face. Now, I don't know what story she gave to get in the Star D, maybe she showed Falvey a little leg. In fact, she was in before Willie got killed. Her cover is she's running from a wife-beater."

"Not too far off there, since her real husband used to beat her. Good thing the son-of-a-gun is already dead."

"Yeah, she can draw from personal experience. And with her arm in a cast and her face all beaten up, she figures she won't be expected to go onstage or turn tricks, so she decided to stay in."

"I'm pulling her out."

"Don't. She'll find out who killed Willie. Odell won't. Or can't. Mob insiders aren't going to tell him anything that'll get themselves killed. You know that. Opportunity like this only knocks once in a lifetime."

"She's going to get killed."

"She won't. That girl is charmed."

"Cats have only nine lives. How do you know which life she's on?"

"Let her alone, David."

"Jemison knows, doesn't he?" Jealousy pinched at a nerve under his eye as Weather remembered Jemison's hesitation yesterday morning when he asked about Jane.

"Yeah. Jemison and I are the only ones. Now you."

Chapter 13

"Damn, damn, damn," Carl Ray said low in Bonnie's barn. Making fertilizer out of horseshit and ammonia nitric on a historic day such as April eighteenth! Ought to be off doing something big about the Last Ride. Damn Bonnie and her stupid garden. Damn Willie, too, although that was probably already taken care of, Carl Ray thought with a smirk. Had to put this slop on the vegetable patch out there and get cleaned up and dressed up and go with Burr and Bonnie over to Willie's house tonight and be polite all evening, so Burr could impress "Cousin" Laidlaw.

If he didn't think of something fast to do to honor the Ride on the very day of it, he was going to run out of time. Carl Ray swore and pulled a cigarette and a match out of his overall bib. The smoke ought to be okay, didn't nobody from the house ever come out here when there was any work to be done anyway.

He sat down on the dirt-packed floor and lit up.

Listen my children for I shall say
Of the Midnight Ride of Old Carl Ray.
On the eighteenth of April in forty-seven.
Twas a night old Willie didn't go to heaven.

Carl Ray dissolved into a laughing and coughing fit so loud he didn't hear anybody coming until almost too late. He did notice the barn door moving, though, and he twisted that

95

cigarette around so it lined up with his arm and there was Burr, standing there. Carl Ray jumped up.

"I smell smoke," Burr said. His blue eyes were about to pop out of his head, and he had his teeth bared in that mean smile of his, and his eyebrows were up high on his head and pointy, like devil's horns he couldn't tamp down.

"Must be from that fire, Burr. I heard on the radio the wind done shifted. That's Texas City itself you smell burning, all the way up here." Carl Ray backed up to the barrel that had that ammonia stuff in it. If he could only push the cigarette down in the hole . . .

Burr gave a mean little snicker. "Whatcha got hid behind your back, son?"

Carl Ray backed up some more and tried to get his arm over to that hole to drop that cigarette in, but Burr was too fast for him. Nearly wrenched his arm off, and got the lit cigarette out of his hand.

Burr's face went all deadly and he slapped him upside the head. "You idiot. You are even dumber than your daddy! Don't you know what that is?" He pointed to the barrel.

"Fertilizer."

"You bet it is. It's ammonium nitrate, the same stuff that blew up that ship down in Texas City. You drop a lit cigarette down in that hole, let it burn awhile, you got a explosion that'll take down this barn, probably that house out there, and all of us with it." Burr held onto him with one arm and dropped the cigarette on the barn floor. He ground his shoe all over it 'til there wasn't nothing left but shredded paper and tobacco flakes.

"Willie left this property to your Aunt Bonnie, and here you are about to destroy it. From stole cigarettes, no less." Burr dug around in Carl Ray's overalls until he found the pack—lucky wasn't but two in it, the rest was in a fresh pack under the house—then he slung Carl Ray up against an empty stall. Burr went for his belt, of course. Carl Ray looked around for an escape.

"There isn't time for that," Bonnie said from outside the barn. "We got to all get cleaned up and dressed and drop Stevie off down the road and get on over to Laidlaw's."

"You know what he almost done?" Burr's neck muscles flared up like they would strangle him or anybody that got near them.

"I don't care what he done! It's always something, even when he didn't do it, or whatever it was, wasn't that bad. Let's just say you've already got him for it beforehand, and just be family for once? Just for a little while?"

Carl Ray felt his mouth drop open. Bonnie didn't ever stand up to Burr, but there she was, doing it. Must be because she owned the place now. Willie left it to her in his will. Laidlaw done come out and told her earlier that day.

Thank you, Willie.

Before dusk, Troy maneuvered the Twin Beech onto the postage stamp of an airport that was Love Field, where a company limo waited. No overnight stay in Houston after all. Macauley Porter had stayed behind to look into his ruins and talk to his people. Resa and Troy had an engagement party to attend in Dallas. It must be their tenth one. Weather had been invited, but had declined. His mid-air snooze in the cramped cabin made him want to get in bed and get some real sleep. And maybe find Jemison to talk about Jane.

The entourage had traded this morning's fresh Red Cross volunteers for four weary ones, and at Resa's command, the driver dropped them off first. Then they went into Highland Park where Resa and Troy held a long goodbye smooch in the privacy of the back seat before they separated for the couple of hours it would likely take Resa to get ready for their evening. After she was gone, the driver let Troy off at the Porter mansion.

A few minutes later, Weather got out at the Claypoole. It was past five, too late to drag Jane out of her gal Friday niche at the Star D.

In his apartment, he showered until the water ran cold, then shaved for the second time that day. After Texas City, he wanted to feel clean. He put on old clothes, intending to take a cab to the Shamrock for dinner, when someone knocked at his door.

Laidlaw Peabody, a younger, slimmer version of Willie, stood in the main hall, flanked by two bull-chested thugs. One of them Weather didn't know at all. The other was Shorty Lamont, a Fort Worth gambler who switched allegiance between Willie and Martin Hubert about every other year. Shorty was as tall as Weather, but most of his height was in his legs. Shorty had a good twenty pounds on Weather.

"Get dressed," Laidlaw commanded. The son shared his father's general ugliness, but lacked the style to give it mystique. The suit he had on looked too big for him, not intentionally too big like the zoot suits the Mexicans wore, just too big like his new role as the head of Willie's empire was too big for him.

"Get dressed, I said."

"I am dressed."

"I want you to come to Willie's—my—house. For the visitation. You can't go like that."

"No disrespect, but I wasn't planning to go, period."

"You're going," Shorty said, opening his suit coat to flash a pistol in the waistband.

"I guess I am," Weather said, wondering how to get out of this. No way to get to the den to make a phone call, or slip out the den's French doors onto the balcony. Nor could he, with his injuries, expect to successfully span the three-foot gap between the balcony edge and the old fire escape, if he could have gotten out there. Laidlaw and the stranger took off down the hall and went in the den. As Shorty shoved him into his bedroom to change, he saw Laidlaw pulling out the cushions on the red sofa.

"What is it about that damn couch?" Weather asked from the hall before he went into his bedroom. The tall thug hefted his gun toward Weather and did not reply.

When they were all together again in the front room, Weather said, "I don't guess you found the missing bank money in my sofa cushions, did you?"

"Shut up," Laidlaw said.

They ushered him down the back stairs to the east parking lot. Hadley's stage was deserted. Not a nosy neighbor in sight, not a soul smoking on a balcony. It was the loneliest place on earth. Did Laidlaw, seeking some kind of poetic justice for Willie, intend to shoot him in the same spot where Willie had fallen?

Shorty opened the back door of a black Cadillac and motioned Weather in. The gambler got in beside him. The third man drove, and Laidlaw sat in the front passenger seat.

"I bet you want to see the spot in the riverbottoms where Willie died." Laidlaw looked expectantly from the front.

"No, I don't."

"Maybe you don't want to go because you've already seen it?" The gangster laid an arm across the seat and nudged the leather with the barrel of a .38.

Chapter 14

Jane sat in the back of Falvey's roomy Buick with Albert, who stroked her neck. Wild Jill Cody sat between driver Ronnie Vincent and Falvey up front. Jill was whispering to Falvey. The car was so big it was like being in a separate room, and Jane couldn't hear much over the engine and the road bumps, but she still believed the conversation was about her. Wild Jill just wasn't wild about Jane being in the inner circle.

They pulled around the back of Willie Peabody's house and Ronnie eased the big car into the carport. Willie's funeral was tomorrow, but the viewing was tonight. Somebody would have to sit up tonight with the body. It was not going to be her.

"Be nice," Falvey told Jill as they stepped out of the car.

To whom, Jane wondered. To Laidlaw, she assumed, but heard a "she-devil" among the few words she could make out.

Probably Willie's widow, who, according to Belinda, gave herself airs.

The back of the house had two doors, one leading to a kitchen and one to a screened porch. The porch led to a parlor visible through the back windows. Wild Jill Cody and Jane took the kitchen steps. The men went in through the porch.

A ham baking in the oven made Jane's eyes water, partly from the cloves, partly from nostalgia for solid food. Willie's widow, a middle-aged dragon with lots of undergarment support, came in from the parlor, swept her eyes over Jane's figure and told her to get a maid's uniform. The hostess turned to Jill, presumably to utter a similar command, but Jill arched her back high and went into the parlor. For once Jane felt a twinge of admiration for the dancer, a sentiment she knew would not be reciprocated.

A frizzy-haired fat woman who seemed to be the chief cook handed Jane a black and white uniform and told her to change in the pantry. She pointed to a room at the end of the narrow kitchen.

The uniform was a couple of sizes too big. Maybe Mrs. Peabody's cook had orders to make any younger, prettier servant look dowdy. House rules. Her own in-laws had objected often to her figure, as if she'd developed her curves to annoy them. At least they were back in Illinois and she would never run into them again. Jane tied the apron tight at the waist, and went back into the kitchen.

Mrs. Peabody had already left.

The fat cook dictated kitchen procedures from a folding chair in front of a door opposite the sink. "You! Yeah, new girl. Stir the gravy and don't spill anything on that uniform. It's a rental." She handed Jane a wooden spoon.

Four other women besides Jane and the fat one worked the kitchen. Two Star D dancers chopped vegetables at the counter next to the cook; a woman she didn't know applied tinfoil to a casserole. The fourth, a tiny woman with a thin nose who looked about twelve, climbed above the sink and opened a window to cool the room.

After introductions, which included discussion of Jane's bruises and her fictional husband's probable destination in the afterlife, they fell into muted speculations about who killed Willie while one of the dancers served as lookout over the parlor door. Martin Hubert and/or the Chicago mob seemed to be favorites.

"It could be Laidlaw himself, wanting to take control," the girl-woman whispered eagerly.

"You shut your mouth." The fleshy cook pointed a rough finger at her.

The conversation moved to Martel Gines' shooting. Martel apparently commanded no sympathy in Peabody territory, since it was her brother's head that Willie had bashed in a couple of years ago for holding back some money. Besides Martel's family ties, being stupid enough to get herself killed seemed to be the chief complaint against the dead woman.

"Didn't Belinda live in the same place as her?" Jane asked as she scrubbed a pot one-handed, feeling sufficiently part of the group to venture into the chat.

A silence enveloped the room, broken only by boiling sounds and the clinking of cutlery.

"What if she did, it ain't none of your business," Belle, the redheaded dancer, snapped.

"I like her, that's all." Jane shrugged. "She gonna be here? Seems like she would; she spoke well of Willie to me."

All cutlery stopped. Jane looked around at the women exchanging glances.

"I don't expect she'll be coming," the blonde dancer, Delilah, said. "Best not to mention her name in this house. If certain parties was to hear . . ." She let the threat go unspoken.

"I just . . ."

"For someone with her mouth wired shut, you sure are working yours an awful lot, honey." The cook flicked a wet dishcloth at a housefly. "Now how about pouring off those 'taters."

Chapter 15

Laidlaw's driver parked in a gravel turnaround in the riverbottoms near the Sylvan Avenue bridge. Willie's body had been found west of here, a fact that sent a bone-deep chill into Weather. This time of evening the remote stretch of road was isolated. Less than a mile down the length of the darkened greenbelt, headlights flowed to and from downtown in a silvery stream across the Oak Cliff viaduct. The Claypoole stood sentinel on the southern end, as familiar as everyday life, as unreachable as the moon.

"What did Willie tell you?" Laidlaw asked from the front passenger seat. "As the next of kin, I got a right to know. Don't be scared, I just want to talk to you."

"I'd feel better if you'd send him for a walk," Weather indicated the large thug on his left.

"Shorty, go stretch your legs."

The gunman got out of the car. The legs went on for a good half-mile, then the rest of him unfolded and pushed out.

Laidlaw flicked a gold cigarette lighter with one hand and used the barrel of the pistol he had in his other hand to push his hat up higher on his forehead. The lighter flame gave his features a menace that the pistol suggested wasn't just theatrics.

Weather's ears roared and his thoughts fragmented, then froze on the idea of a bullet in the head. Pop, it would go, and all of David Weather's thoughts, loves, expectations, wit, will, and education would splatter onto the back of the Cadillac's leather seat.

"I want to find out who killed your daddy as much as you do," he said with counterfeit assurance. "Maybe more than you. When I do, you'll want to have me as a witness at the trial. It would be good for Willie's legend to have Tom Weather's son as a prosecution witness." He hoped to God Laidlaw bought this line of bull.

Laidlaw Peabody laughed and balanced the open lighter on the seat back. The fire flickered during his expulsion of breath, then stood up again. "You think I'm gonna kill you, don't you? I ought to, but my daddy's funeral is tomorrow and I don't want to be sitting in jail. Big local hero like you, police would bust us all and take their time sorting us out. This ain't no time to be out of commission in the jailhouse. I got family business to tend to."

Weather relaxed a little.

"Course, theoretically," Laidlaw continued, "your body might not be not discovered for a while. Funny how some will lie out here six months and not get found, and some will get found right off. Like those kids playing hooky found Willie." He dropped his head down low before giving it a shake. Just like Willie. The motion sent a chill through Weather.

"You ain't gotta worry, Weather. I got this gun out for my own protection, in case whoever killed Willie might be coming after me." He flipped the lighter closed and scratched his chin with it. In the dark, the metal up against his beard stubble sounded like insects scrabbling at woodwork. Laidlaw handed the lighter off to his driver and told him to light it and keep it going so he could see. The guy took it and flicked it.

Laidlaw lit his cigarette off the steady flame and exhaled smoke before he spoke again. "I just wanted to invite you to

my daddy's gathering and let you pay your last respects.
Willie would like that. I would like it. And I'd like to know
beforehand what my daddy said to you, 'cause I would like to
know who killed him, and you might have some information
that is the key, only you might not know the significance of
it."

"I might not, but I can't be party to any vigilante action,"
lawyer Weather said. "Here's what your daddy said to me."
Weather gave him an edited version of Willie's visit.

" 'A prominent man, not exactly a businessman, not
exactly not a businessman'?" Laidlaw repeated. "That
sounds like ol' Willie. He liked to be mysterious. What else
did he say?"

"He said that Carl Ray's bank robbery money was still out
there somewhere, that it didn't burn up the night Margie
Lunn's burned down."

"Yeah, he's been saying that for a while. Ever since that
kid Carl Ray weaseled his way into a meal ticket with that
story about his mama on her deathbed. You think that
money's anywhere?"

"I think it burned up in the fire, the way it's always been
said."

Laidlaw pouted over this for a while, but then signaled his
driver to crank up. Shorty came running out of the darkness
and had to beat on the window to get the driver's attention.
Weather relaxed a little, even with the large goon beside him.
Laidlaw seemed satisfied, and Weather had not mentioned
Belinda Bain. The four of them rode to Willie's wake.

Weather followed Laidlaw into the house amid a cascade
of flashbulbs and shouts from reporters behind the police
barricade on the front lawn.

Too bad there weren't any cameras inside when Tom
Weather's son walked in with Willie's. The frozen expres-

sions on most of Dallas' gangster elite deserved photographic recording for posterity. Weather gave up his coat to a Negro maid and offered a small bow to the mourners while he surveyed the room.

A mahogany staircase divided the open double parlor—a small area on the left, a larger, deeper room on the right. The crowd formed a tight cluster on the right side around the family's receiving line. Behind them, pushed against windows opening onto a porch, a banquet table provided tempting aromas. Weather could flatter himself that his arrival had caused everyone to move to the rear, but the real reason lay in state in the smaller room, where Willie Peabody's hooked beak showed above the dark casket's satin sides. The casket sat on big sheets of plywood held up by sawhorses, an oddly informal support for such an ornate casket.

Weather resisted going in for a closer look, but knew his real work lay among the living, at least for the moment.

He headed toward the receiving line. Twenty people watched him cross the room. It was worse than approaching an irate judge's bench. He'd only met a few of these hoodlums in court, given Willie's silencing influence on witnesses. Powers greater than D.A. Morson's would be needed to break this gang.

"Evenin', boss," Fred Atterly said, respectful. Falvey Johnson eyed the transaction with amusement. The two goons who'd roughed him up at the Star D flanked Falvey. Jane herself was not around, which disappointed him a little, although he told himself to be glad she hadn't dug her way any deeper into the mob. No Belinda Bain, which was no surprise. No Aesop Gance, which was. Maybe the little weasel sat below the salt in the new organization. Maybe he killed Willie and that was why he had known the gangster's whereabouts the night of the shooting. Of course, a short fellow like

Aesop could still be here, tucked behind a coattail or two in this throng.

Weather arrived at Mrs. Willie in the line.

"My condolences, ma'am."

"Mr. Weather. You're the last person I would expect here," Mrs. Willie said, but gave him her hand, almost like she expected him to kiss it. Chunk diamonds dripped off long fingers finished in red lacquer. Black eyes fluttering false eyelashes inspected his face.

"I came at your stepson's request, not to ogle," he explained. She shrugged and held on to his hand, looking him over, so he looked right back. This was not the original Mrs. Willie. The first one, Laidlaw's mother, got sick and died back in the '30s. Willie had done what any self-respecting gangster with an empty bed would do—he'd gotten a better-looking wife. The new one had volumes of black hair and a golddigger's nipped and tucked figure no amount of funeral drapery would disguise. The marriage had produced no new little Willies, but he bet it generated some pretty hot sheets.

If Willie had been up to it, that is. Willie'd sure wanted the town to think he was.

Maybe sensing his judgment, Mrs. Willie let go of his hand with a sniff and grabbed onto Laidlaw, standing next to her. She threw herself onto her frowning stepson and squeezed out the best crocodile tears Weather had ever seen outside a courtroom. Laidlaw gave her perfunctory pats and looked irritated. Stepmama better have the deed to the house, Weather thought, or the next shoulder she got from that quarter would be the one shoving her out on the street.

"I think I'll give you folks some family time," Weather said and weaned himself off the line.

"Glad to see you changed your mind about coming,"

Falvey said, grinning. The owner of the Star D pulled two whiskeys off a fast moving tray and handed Weather one.

"It was a spur of the moment thing."

The dancer Jill, stage name Wild Jill Cody, watched from Falvey's side. She looked right nice in her black dress, and little older than she did onstage. A simple corsage of red poppies adorned her bosom, and a small black hat with a tiny veil topped her combed-down hair. Not Wild Jill, tonight, not cheap at all. She could have passed for class at a Highland Park funeral. You never could tell about women.

Falvey was saying something else Weather missed.

"Huh? Sorry."

"You're respected, even among this bunch, but showing up here might cost you a little."

"It almost cost me a lot. Laidlaw dropped by my place and brought me over. You could say against my will."

"I see." Falvey looked concerned. "He's got this idea you had something to do with that." He waved in the general direction of the coffin.

"I think we got it straightened out. He knows I want to catch Willie's killer as much as he does."

"Well," Falvey's mouth twitched against a smile. "I'm glad to know that, then."

Falvey's voice had the rehearsed sincerity of a politician and Weather knew he was lying.

The conversation moved to neutral ground.

"That fire down south is something else, isn't it?"

"Yeah, I was just down there today." Weather recounted his visit, minus his talk with Francy, and let others take over the conversation. Everybody had a Texas City story to top the last one.

Free of Falvey, he mingled his way to the edge of the cluster and slipped its borders to go have a look at the corpse.

★ ★ ★ ★ ★

"You better behave," Burr said. He had his finger in Carl Ray's face. It folded up into a fist that Carl Ray had no doubt Burr Cartledge would use if Bonnie hadn't been right there in the car. Then Burr shoved the big Ford's door open and headed toward Willie's house. He didn't wait for Bonnie or Carl Ray.

"Just don't say nothing smart," Bonnie pleaded as she pushed at her own door and looked up the street. Ol' Burr was out of sight, hot-footing it to kiss Laidlaw Peabody's ass.

" 'Nothing smart,' " Carl Ray said, making it sound halfway between smart-ass and agreeable. He didn't know why he was sassing her after she saved him. She was right, he was ungrateful. He could be nicer to her. If only she didn't expect him to be polite all evening with a dead body in the house.

Long fingernails dug into his arm. "Now you listen to me, young man. We took you in to help you because Willie wanted you helped. Him gone, Laidlaw might not be so kindly disposed. If your Uncle Burr can't get on in there, why, we'll have to go back to Tyler. That happens, we can't feed you or your little brother."

"I know."

"You want to go to that juvenile work farm? You want Stevie in the orphan home? Now, get on out and open this door for me. Your Uncle Burr should have done it. And close that other door."

Carl Ray got out, slammed Burr's door, and went around to let her out.

"Uncle Burr ought to learn better manners, Aunt Bonnie," he said while she was tugging her dress back down. "Not go off and leave you setting in the car."

That made her happy and she grabbed onto his arm like

they was at a wedding or something and made him walk her up to the house. There was a bunch of men out front with cameras, and she started primping at her hair like they ought to know to take her picture. None of 'em did.

"Well come on, slowpokes," Burr said from the front porch. That vein in his forehead was sticking out real big.

Weather wondered what bright-eyed idiot in Willie's house chose a banker's lamp for the viewing. The green glass hood gave the corpse an unearthly glow that a mortician had used a lot of cadaver paint to prevent. Possibly because of the ghastly lighting, he had Willie to himself.

Either death had not wiped the smirk off Willie's face or the mortician had deliberately preserved it. The corpse wore a new black suit, but had on the same pearl tie slide he'd worn the night he came to the Claypoole. Thanks to modern embalming techniques, the room smelled only of flowers and whiskey and lemon polish. Weather wondered inanely if the corpse wore shoes. He set his glass down and reached out to touch Willie's face, but couldn't quite put fingertips to it, so he made a fist of his good hand and touched knuckles onto cheekbone. It was cool and waxy, but a lot harder than he thought it would be. He half expected the eyes to fly open and Willie to rise up and laugh at him. He sensed someone watching. He pulled his hand away and looked left and right. Nobody.

With a growing sense of unease, he turned. Laidlaw Peabody stood in the arch, and a few hard faces stuck out around him. Atterly, the goons from the ride over, plus a couple more hoods. They all watched him without speaking.

"He looks so lifelike," Weather said, deadpan. Laidlaw eyed him with suspicion, apparently testing that statement against some inner list of what David Weather could say and not be taken back to the riverbottoms.

The heir nodded slowly. "You know, he does."

The entourage agreed heartily and for too long. Then some new arrivals at the front door caused a flurry and took the attention off Weather. It was Bonnie Bledsoe Cartledge, her delinquent nephew, and some large silver-blond, crew cut ugliness he guessed was Burr Cartledge. He wasn't in the mood for them yet, so he moved into the shadows at the head of the coffin, behind the lamp. He still had that sense of being watched, but there was nothing behind him except a bookcase and a window. Over in the main parlor, out of his line of vision, condolences and toasts were going around. Burr and Bonnie were so very, very sorry.

This bother you, Willie? Everybody in the other room, playing up to your son?

They'll pay.

He looked down at the smirking corpse beyond the lamp. It hadn't moved.

Heh, heh, heh, heh.

"Stop that," he growled. Willie was giving him the willies.

Chapter 16

Carl Ray stood on the edge of the adults, watching Bonnie and Burr trip all over themselves to stand next to Laidlaw. Them two poured out enough syrup to cover everybody's plate at a pancake supper. It wasn't gonna do any good. Willie'd already said Burr and Bonnie didn't have the class to work for him in Dallas. Willie said they had too much corn in their voice. Laidlaw probably would say the same thing.

He looked around, then backed up enough to get to the staircase. If he could grab that wood pineapple on the stairs and lean back a little, he could take a look in that other room, without having to go in it. He thought somebody was in there, somebody alive, that is, along with Willie, but he wasn't sure. He'd kept his eyes straight ahead when they come in so he didn't have to look in there, but he thought he saw a man standing in the dark. At least he hoped he did. What if he cut on a light and wasn't nobody in there but Willie? He shivered and pulled his suit jacket around him.

It wasn't good to be in the same house with a dead body. His mama would have said so.

A maid with a busted face and a cast on her arm was giving out drinks. When she came his way, he took one like he was old enough. If she said something, she said something, and he would put it back. But when he took it, she didn't say nothing, so he drank it down real fast. Didn't gag or nothing. Bonnie and Burr were too busy licking Laidlaw's boots to notice.

Just act like you belong, like it's all right, he told himself. He followed the maid into the corner and lifted another drink off her tray. She looked kinda scared, like she was worried whoever beat her up would pop up out of the blue and do it again. Or maybe she didn't like being around a dead body either. He took another drink off the tray, and poured it in with the other one. Nobody said anything.

Jane looked around for David but didn't see him. She'd spotted him from the kitchen door when he came in with Laidlaw and had stayed back there until the other helpers got snippy about her using that cast as an excuse for not working the main room.

"You think you're so much better than us because you work for Falvey, but he don't necessarily have no pull no more." The fat cook glowered from the folding chair. To get away from the sniping, Jane had grabbed up a drinks tray and gone out into a large parlor. If David blew her cover, she would probably not be murdered—too many witnesses —but she would never speak to him again either. That would be easy, since she would be laughed out of town by her newspaper colleagues for getting caught this early into her investigation. Luckily, David didn't notice her. Not even when Falvey took two glasses off her tray right beside him.

She'd made a few rounds with the trays and now didn't see him at all. Maybe he left. She told herself to relax.

You don't have no idea who's the real power in this town, Willie had said that night in Weather's den.

You're right, I don't. Everybody thinks it's you. Mighty big of you to admit it's not. I take it that's what you're admitting.

I ain't admitting *nothing. You too tied in with the D.A.'s office for me to talk to you. Don't go construing something to be something it's not.*

Oh, I don't do much construing at all, Willie. I deal in facts. Evidence. I don't even know what you're talking about, so it would be hard to "construe" anything.

I have no doubt you could do it, though. That wheezing laugh. A coughing fit. Maybe Willie had some disease, and had come to unburden himself before he died. For the sake of the unsolved crimes in town, Weather should control his irritation and find out what his visitor really wanted to tell him.

Willie patted the sofa arm, chewed on the cigar stump, and fingered a pack of matches up out of his shirt pocket.

You're not going to light that thing again in here. You want to talk, talk. You want to smoke, take it down to the lobby. Damn. He wondered what sort of crimeland revelation he'd just passed up.

Willie put the matches back in his pocket. *Now if you was my lawyer, say, or if I could hire you for tonight only, I could talk a lot freer. Say a hundred for privilege. Attorney-client privilege.* Willie looked up almost shyly.

Uh, Willie, I am still officially with the D.A. He leaned against his desk, but bent forward just a tad. Reject, but show interest just the same. The art of persuasion. Come on, out with it, Willie.

Carl Ray chuckled to himself. Burr's nose was so brown, it matched Bonnie's dress. Laidlaw, Cousin Laidlaw, Burr'd made a point of saying when he finally got up to him, looked like he was tired of the both of them already. Also like he wanted to smash somebody. Maybe old Cousin Diamondback, Carl Ray's secret name for the new wife. Burr was talking about catching whoever done it to Willie and taking care of them personally. All the men agreed and nodded.

The whiskey spread to Carl Ray's chest and made him feel taller, like a man. A special man, since he'd been Willie's favorite. Maybe whatever thing he needed to do for the Last Ride was something he needed to do here. Where'd that girl with the tray go?

"I'm gonna strangle whoever killed Willie with my bare hands, and feed him to the alligators," Burr was saying over by Laidlaw. Carl Ray watched Burr put his fingers in a circle and squinch up his arms like he was choking somebody. Stupid bastard.

"I know who killed him," Carl Ray exclaimed, sick of Burr's bootlicking. "Saw it in a dream." That got their attention. Willie had always believed Carl Ray had the Sight, like his mama, and kind of treated him with respect for it, and made everybody else, too. He didn't actually have no Sight, except he had funny feelings sometimes, and some things he knew would happen, did happen. But if other people believed he had the Gift, he might as well take advantage of it.

Burr and Laidlaw and the others spread out from their circle. About time they paid him some mind. He stepped up to the group, but stumbled on his own feet doing it. Damn hand-me-down shoes.

"You been drinking," Bonnie said, like some Highland Park priss-pot.

"So what? I know who killed Willie!" His head spun a little bit.

"Now, son." Falvey Johnson put a hand on his shoulder. "This is not the time for that sort of talk." Ol' Falv gave him a little squeeze, like he was telling him to shut up. Well, not this time. He was tired of all these grown-ups always telling him what to do. He shook Falvey off. He would Ride out of here soon and they would know he was a man. He tugged at his collar. Hot in here.

＊ ＊ ＊ ＊ ＊

You living off my oil leases, boy. I traded 'em to your daddy for Carl Ray, Senior's life, then he betrayed his own word and let that boy hang.

You say you bribed Tom Weather?

Willie got pouty. *Ain't saying that. Ain't saying that at all.*

Yes, you were. Did you expect a lesser conviction? Or was Carl Ray supposed to go free?

Willie lowered heavy lids over those pop eyes. *You imaging things. I didn't say nothing like that. Now forget what you think I said about your daddy. He was a devil, yes he was, but there's worse ones than Old Tom. Someone will be risen, as if from the dead, not exactly a businessman, not exactly not a businessman, and he'll turn this town upside down!*

"That person who killed Cousin Willie is in this house," Carl Ray intoned, trying to sound scary, like his mama when she told people's fortunes. He wished he hadn't ever opened his mouth, but he had to keep going now. Everybody was watching. Some guy next to him with a hawk face stared straight through to his soul and it gave him the worst feeling.

"If he is here, you oughtta keep your mouth shut, or you might find yourself in serious trouble," Burr said. "Maybe dumped in a field."

"Or at the bottom of a lake—" Carl Ray shut his mouth in a hurry. Burr wouldn't catch on to what that meant, would he?

"Now, now, now." Falvey waved his hands and made all these calming noises.

Burr stared. That vein in his forehead popped up.

"—Or under a bridge. Or down in a rock quarry," Carl Ray continued, hoping he didn't sound like he was rushing or covering up. The hawk-face man kept staring, like he was deciding something.

"Or out in the woodshed," Burr growled, grabbing him by one arm.

"Folks, please." Falvey threw a look over to Burr and Burr let go. "He doesn't anymore have any idea who killed Willie than anybody else in this room. This is a seventeen-year-old boy. A boy, I repeat, that's got hold of some whiskey and is big-dogging it."

"Now isn't that so, son?" Falvey ran his hand under Carl Ray's arm and pinched hard. He had a warning, pleading look in his eye.

Carl Ray hung his head. "It's true, I was just big-dogging it."

"I got a cure for that," Burr said. A lot of the men laughed.

"No, no, let's not mar this evening with any of that. Let me talk to the boy in private," Falvey said. Most everybody was laughing by then and talking about young folks not having a lick of sense.

Falvey kept that pinch going and pushed him round the staircase and over to the other side, where Willie was. Carl Ray closed his eyes, but had to raise one open when they stopped. They was right in front of old Willie. Falvey let go, but stood close behind him to where he was jammed up next to the coffin.

"Falvey, Carl Ray," a voice said. Carl Ray just about jumped out of his skin.

"Mr. Weather," Falvey said, all calm.

Carl Ray squinted over the glare of some old green lamp.

"You stay put," Falvey told him, then he went around to the left a little bit and shook hands with Mr. Weather. It was that guy from the Red Cross. He had a cast on his wrist, though, and couldn't do a normal shake. Had his arm in a sling, too, because something was messed up about his shoulder. Carl Ray had read that in the paper. Falvey and him started talking about the Star D and whether or not it was open tonight. Carl Ray slipped off a ways and would have made a run for the front door if the bell hadn't rung just then.

It was them cops that had come out to the farm that night and asked all the questions about Willie. Hadley. That other one, the one that didn't talk, was with him. The ones that didn't talk could be as scary as the ones that did, because you never knew what they was thinking. The sheriff came in too, looking mad that Hadley was there. He'd looked mad that night at the place, too.

Laidlaw and a bunch of them, Falvey and Burr included, came over and stood around all them lawmen. Now everybody was being polite and careful. It was worse than church. Burr kept looking over every now and then, but he didn't come over. Must be scared of Willie, too. Carl Ray caught that Mr. Weather looking at him.

"Son, if you have some idea about who killed Willie, it'd be best to get him locked up," Mr. Weather said.

"I wouldn't tell you if I did know. You sent cops out to my house and got me a beating from Burr. Your daddy killed my daddy." Carl Ray had to get out of here, fast. Burr was watching, and if he thought he was telling this guy anything now, he would kill him for sure. Might anyway, on account of that slip about the lake.

There was too many people at the front. There was a door right here that went into the kitchen, but the foot-end of the coffin was blocking most of it.

"I know kids like you," Mr. Weather said. "They come through the juvenile courts all the time. Twisted up and angry and don't know what to do. Sometimes they get beaten by parents for no good reason. Then they wind up hurting somebody else, and they hurt themselves, too."

Carl Ray didn't answer. There was a little space between the foot of the coffin and the door to the kitchen. He could skinny up through there and maybe get out that way. He edged over to it.

"I remember you at the blood bank," Mr. Weather said. Why wouldn't he just shut up?

"You wanted to go down to Texas City and fight the fire. You can't decide for yourself right now, being on probation, and released to your aunt and uncle, but that time will pass. Think about the kind of man you want to be, the kind that could go fight that fire. If he knew who killed Willie, he'd want it told. I could help you . . ."

Carl Ray stiffened. This guy was the son of that bastard D.A., Tom Weather, and he was supposed to hate him. "I don't know anything, I was just talking. Besides, I don't need no help from anybody named Weather. Your daddy killed my daddy and got away with it. He traded for our oil leases and broke his word." Hell, he shouldn't have said that. Now the guy would want to shut him up. He just wanted to get out of here. Carl Ray sucked in real tight and slipped in between the coffin and the kitchen door. The door was the swinging kind and ought to just open backwards when he pressed on it, only it didn't.

Mr. Weather stepped closer to him. He had some concerned look on his face the way adults do when they're gonna try to stop you talking. "Son . . ."

Carl Ray gave that door a shove. It swung open a little ways and bumped hard into a fat woman, sitting on a chair. She turned around, mad, and pushed back. Pushed so hard it knocked him off balance and he grabbed out at a corner of that plywood table holding up the coffin. From this angle he could see up Willie's nose. The idea of it stirred that whiskey in his stomach. He put his hands out to get straightened up, but his foot got caught on the sawhorse leg and when he jerked it out, the leg slipped down. With one sawhorse leg doing the splits, he knew that coffin was coming down—didn't need no Sight for that—so he just got his leg untangled and ran. Past Burr and all them people toward the front door.

Behind him he heard a big crash and a lot of people screaming, mad, not scared. He got outside good, where there was some cops standing guard. He slowed to a just-taking-some-air walk.

"They need your help inside," he told the cops with his best innocent child voice. Lot of noise in Willie's house now. The cops ran inside. Carl Ray hurried down the front steps. There was some guys with cameras out by the barricades. He cussed at them and ran.

Heh, heh, heh. Told you they would pay. Willie's corpse lay cheek to floor and half out of its mahogany box.

Weather's face ached from restraint, but he managed not to laugh. Some of the less disciplined gangsters in the place failed; Weather wondered at their future with Laidlaw now. The young crime boss, faced with this breach of funeral protocol, sputtered curses and indignation at the laughter while Hadley, the sheriff, Weather, and Burr Cartledge stuffed the stiff back in its container and righted the coffin on the floor. Throughout the effort, Cartledge's blue-gray eyes remained as frozen and expressionless as a blind man's. Weather looked up to see Laidlaw glaring at him.

"You. Out."

"What? I didn't knock it down, it was . . ." He pictured that seventeen-year-old kid against this mob. "It was a wobbly sawhorse leg. Look over there."

The leg in question had broken under the weight of the shifting coffin, so there was no proving him a liar.

Laidlaw let out a stream of profanity.

"Watch your language in my house," Mrs. Willie yelled. Weather seized the opportunity to pull Hadley aside.

"I need to talk to you." Behind Hadley, Weather caught a glimpse of Jane Alder in a maid's uniform. She met his eye and ducked out of sight. He started to follow but had a better idea.

"Come on," Hadley said to Weather. "We need our coats."

"It was Martin Hubert that done it, snuck somebody in to tamper with that leg," Ronnie Vincent ventured while maids brought out the coats.

"Naw, it was that Bledsoe kid," somebody else said. Burr Cartledge muttered to himself and looked a lot like a man whose career had just gone down the flush toilet.

Chapter 17

"Let's get this straight," Hadley said half an hour later. "Laidlaw kidnapped you, and nearly shot you down at the river, but you don't want to press charges. And your reporter girlfriend is doing some undercover gig as a maid in the organization to find some goon who may have killed her cousin?" This conversation took place in Hadley's car after the three of them—Hadley's partner Keller being the third—had a lengthy laughing fit over Willie Peabody hanging out of the tipped-over casket.

"She was a secretary yesterday," Weather said. "And now she's moving around like a mob insider. You've got to pull her out without blowing her cover."

"Let me give it some thought. Meanwhile, show me where Laidlaw took you."

"Sure." Weather gave directions and soon the car stopped in the gravel turnaround on Sylvan. The driver, Keller, cranked down his window and lit a cigarette while Hadley went out with a flashlight into the tall grass. A light breeze came off the river, carrying with it the faint odor of some other smoke, not tobacco.

Maybe it was from Texas City.

Hadley returned after a long time.

Weather stuck his head out his window and asked, "Did you walk out to where they threw Willie?"

"No, that was further down. The killers parked here, though, to drag the body. Their footprints in the mud started up from about this same spot. I came out yesterday." Hadley punched the air. "Of course Orton's men tromped through here like they were on a Sunday school picnic, and tore up the evidence. After they destroyed the crime scene, I couldn't even get a count of how many men drug Willie out there." Swearing, Hadley brought a fist down on the Ford's hood. But just once. Modulated fury.

"Okay. Let's go," Hadley growled at Keller, who thumped his fifth cigarette out the window and cranked up the car. "Now we gotta do something about that girlfriend."

Chapter 18

It took Carl Ray a solid hour to get back to the house, and by then most of the whiskey had worn off. Not all of it, he still felt pretty warm, but he also knew how close he'd come to getting himself killed and that had knocked the silliness out of him fast. Or maybe he was like his mama and had a high tolerance for drink, he didn't know. Any which way, he got back to the house expecting to say goodbye to Stevie, get his stuff, and take off. When he got there, though, he remembered the kid was staying down at the Rinkers so he wouldn't have to go to Willie's, so wasn't nothing to do but pack his stuff and go.

It wasn't what he wanted for Carl Ray's Last Ride, but he wasn't going to stick around and wait for Burr or somebody else to put him in the lake, either. He would have to come back and contact Stevie somehow, and get that poem written, and call somebody about that canvas roll. He took his things into the kitchen and laid them up on the table. He put everything he had in a grocery bag and counted the money he'd stole back from Stevie, plus some more he'd stole from Bonnie. Eighteen dollars and eighty-three cents. A pack, hell, the whole carton, of Bonnie's cigarettes went into the sack. He felt his pockets one last time. Glad he thought about pockets, because that reminded him of the pocketknife.

He went back to his room and felt around under the brat's mattress. Little punk better not have the knife with him.

It wasn't under there. Carl Ray swore and looked around in the dark. He heard cars up on the main road and hoped it wasn't Burr and Bonnie, but it could be them any minute, on account of how long it took him to get back here. It also depended on how much time Burr had put into kissing Laidlaw's rosy red butt, and how much of it Laidlaw could stand.

He eased open the dresser drawer on Stevie's side, and felt up in there. He wished he had a flashlight. Remembering the one Burr dropped in the lake made his knees go wobbly.

Where was that damn knife? He looked in all three drawers and didn't find it, but then thought to take out that last drawer and feel around on the floor. The cold metal almost shocked him. That little sonabitch! It was Big Ray's knife, anyway. It never belonged to that muttonhead that was Stevie's daddy. He slid the knife into his pocket and grabbed the paper sack off the floor.

That's when he heard Burr's car out on the road. Not the main road, either. Coming up to the house.

All he could manage was to get out the back door and under the house good before the car came around the side and flung gravel almost in his face. Lucky that old hound dog avoided Burr, too, or it would've been barking like crazy and Burr might look under there to tell it to shut up, and catch him.

Car doors slammed and Stevie got out yelling for him. Damn dog didn't even go out and wag his tail or anything, but he guessed it didn't much expect a pat on the head anyway.

They all yelled out his name a few times and the dog shifted like he wanted them to shut up, and then they went up the steps to the back porch, Bonnie's little feet in them high heels, Stevie's clomp, clomping into the house—too damn fat, but he couldn't help it, he had a fat daddy—and Burr's heavier steps, careful, like he was looking between the porch slats. Carl Ray didn't move or breathe.

"You go in to bed," Bonnie said to Stevie, and the kid whined some about it but did it quick enough when Burr yelled at him. Bonnie stayed on the porch and pulled the kitchen door shut and then eased the screen door shut, too.

"Hon, I was planning on going inside," Burr said.

"Aw, let's sit out here a spell, and have a cigarette. Been inside too much, could use a little night air." The skin on Carl Ray's back lurched up and crawled. If she was out of smokes and went in there for that cigarette carton . . .

Burr snorted a little but then a lighter clicked on.

"Well, can I have one?" Bonnie sounded all indignant. Carl Ray wanted to laugh. There went old Burr, ignoring her as usual. Finally the lighter flicked again.

Bonnie's butt plopped itself onto the top step and her hand patted the spot next to her. Carl Ray could see her rump and her hand, and the backs of her legs. Burr was up on the porch now. After a while, Burr's legs came down and he sat, too. He left enough room for Stevie and a couple of house cats between them, but Bonnie scooted over. Carl Ray willed that old dog not to move.

"That damn boy," Burr said, meaning him. "He needs some straightening out, real fast. And I'm gonna be the one to do it."

"Let's just let him be for a little while," Bonnie said. She was patting Burr's leg. Cigarettes got smoked. Carl Ray could've used one himself. Real bad.

"It was him knocked that coffin over."

"Nuh, uh. It was Martin Hubert. Got in the house somehow, or sent somebody, and loosened up that leg." Bonnie defending him. Who woulda thought?

"I wish I could say it was, hon, but you know it was Carl Ray. Ought to beat the tar out of him and throw him in the riverbottoms next to Willie. Wherever that was, I mean."

"Now, Burr. He's my flesh and blood. You can't hurt him without hurting me, too." Bonnie had that sweetie-pie tone that meant she wanted Burr to do something.

"I don't want to hurt you. Just him. I want to teach him a lesson."

"But honey, we need him. We need him to find that bank money." She was rubbing up real good on Burr now. He couldn't see where, and wondered. Once he saw her do it right on Burr's pants, but Burr made her stop. Bet he let that dancing girl do it, though.

"Aw, sugar, he don't know where that money is, any more than he knows who killed Willie."

"He don't know he knows, but he does. The Sight is like a code, or a riddle. His mama liked to be mysterious. She wasn't just going to tell it straight out." Bonnie's voice was different now. Exasperated a little.

Stevie's clomping came up from inside the house. The back door flung open, then the screen hinges squeaked.

"His stuff is gone, and he took my money and my pocketknife," the kid yelled.

Mine, Carl Ray seethed silently from his hiding place.

"He better not of took anything of mine!" Burr and Bonnie went running into the house to see what else might be missing.

Carl Ray didn't know what time it was when they finally gave up and went to bed, but they finally did, and he crawled out from under the house, hoping it was still April eighteenth, like in the poem. He sneaked his stuff along into the barn and went over to the barrel of ammonia nitric.

Couldn't carry the whole thing. Needed something to put some of it in.

Carl Ray felt around in the dark barn, and finally put his hands on a big old burlap bag. He dumped some nitric in it.

Then he found a kerosene lantern, with some kerosene still in it. That would probably help it explode, but would it go off the minute you mixed in the nitric or did you have to put a match to it? He didn't know, and didn't want to blow himself up finding out. That was not the kind of Last Ride he was planning. Maybe Burr had lied about how it would blow anyway. No, he didn't; it burned first in that Texas City ship, and then it exploded. But only after it burned long enough for all them plant workers to line up and watch it.

He crept out into the back yard. He hated to do it, but he would have to boost Burr's car if the Last Ride was going to happen on the eighteenth. Wasn't no time to walk to town and he couldn't ride the bike carrying explosives.

Chapter 19

"How dare you have me dragged out like a common criminal," Jane sputtered. It was a difficult mouthful for someone with her jaw wired shut, but Weather still caught the bared-teeth challenge of her panther heart behind the strangled hiss.

"Your boyfriend would like to save your life, you lovely young idiot," Hadley said solemnly from the head of the table in the police interrogation room. The two detectives had met with Jane for a few minutes, then locked her in and left for a few minutes, then finally had allowed Weather in to see her.

Keller, standing along the tobacco-yellowed wall, snorted. Across from Weather at the table, Jane stared at Hadley, apparently taken aback by his cool delivery. Weather, the trained observer, watched them all.

"He's not my boyfriend."

"Whatever I am or am not to you, I am trying to protect you," Weather said, stepping in before Hadley, who'd paused to grin at Keller, could say anything else. "You're dealing with stone cold people. You think you want to find your cousin's killer—yeah, Francy told me—but this is not the way to do it. A month ago you and I both were all over the Dallas papers, with our injuries described in detail." Weather pointed to the cast and her battered face.

Jane draped a sweater across her cast. "No, nobody would suspect. I'd just moved here nine days before the beating. I spent two weeks in the hospital. I don't look like my pictures anymore. Nobody here knows me."

"Everybody knows your story. You think the crooks don't read the papers? That they won't notice coincidences? A brunette Dallas reporter gets her arm and her jaw broken and some brunette named 'Connie Petro' shows up with her arm and her jaw broken, just willing to cozy up to Falvey?"

"Well they wouldn't have taken 'Connie' in if they'd suspected, now would they?"

"They could be stringing 'Connie' along," Hadley interjected. He tilted his chair back against the wall, shoulders back, as languid as a photographer's model. The pose, the silver-streaked brown hair, the aquiline nose, the utter confidence of the man suggested a life of women pawing at that lap. Weather watched Jane's eyes travel over the package and sat a little straighter.

"They could be leading you on, to have a joke at your expense, to find out what you know, to find out what the cops know," Weather said. *Stop looking at him.*

"They don't suspect a thing," she protested, but there was doubt in her voice. She looked back and forth between the two men and finally settled on her cup of water as a neutral zone. She took a sip from it and gingerly touched her bruised face. A determined look settled in her eyes.

"One of them killed my cousin. I have to find him. He's supposed to be in Dallas or Fort Worth, but I haven't found him yet."

"The police will locate this Verdi fellow. His picture's all over the wires, they'll pick him up soon enough," Hadley said.

"They might not pick him up. A lot of them don't care about people like Christina."

"We do care, and we'll take care of him." Hadley brought the chair forward and leaned on one elbow on the table. Weather had to shift to the right to get Jane back into view.

130

"You might not. Suppose he looks different? Suppose he's dyed his hair?"

"Robert Verdi has an anchor tattoo with a buxom gal swinging in it on his right arm," Hadley said. "I checked the wire reports from Chicago. Someone will see it, and turn him in for the reward money."

"Most men wear shirts."

"And most men of his type see whores. And most whores will collect reward money if they don't see a danger to themselves. An out-of-towner like him will be fish bait in Dallas. Come out, Jane."

"I'm not coming out, David. They think I'm Connie Petro from Cincinnati, running from a wife-beater. I'm safe." Jane crossed her good arm over the cast.

"This woman is determined," Hadley turned to Weather, wide-eyed. Then to Jane, "I admire your courage, young lady." He shook his head as if to reinforce his admiration.

Jane beamed.

There was a knock on the door. Keller went out, and came back in almost immediately. He whispered something to Hadley.

"Ah," the lead detective said. "Well. That Star D dancer, Jill Cody, and one Albert Florentine are downstairs, offering bail and bribes for the release of our Miss Petro."

"Who's Albert Florentine?" Weather leaned across the table and took Jane's hand.

"New man in Falvey's operation. From Chicago." Hadley put all kinds of meaning into *Chicago*. "Did a little B & E time about ten years back. Been clean a while. Course we'll get him for something soon enough."

"If he's from Chicago, he could spot you as Jane Alder, then. Your story must have gotten a lot of attention back home. Local girl goes to Dallas, gets beat up." Weather squeezed Jane's hand. She pulled away.

"What I need to know," Hadley interrupted, "is what, if anything, you've found out while you've been at the Star D. If you're committed to doing this—"

"She's not gonna do this!"

"If you've gotta do this, for your cousin, or some kind of personal integrity reason," Hadley spoke over Weather's protests, "then it ought to be put to good use."

"It will be, when I get the story."

"But before the story's ready. Let's make a deal. We need to know who killed Willie Peabody. You want as much police protection as we can give you, offstage, of course, so you could stay undercover without getting yourself killed."

"Now wait a minute," Weather said.

Hadley gave Weather a stern look. "You can see how important her job is to her."

"I can see you manipulating her to do your bidding. You ought to be in the courtroom."

Hadley shook his head slowly. "I don't want to be. Too many rules. Too many judges. In police work you have to fly by the seat of your pants, and not be bogged down by some old man in a robe."

"I didn't say I would help you," Jane hissed. When she was upset, Weather noticed, she had trouble speaking through the small opening the wires offered.

"You know," Hadley said nonchalantly, "Connie Petro could get shipped back to Cincinnati for questioning on that little matter I brought her in on. She could be tied up for days in the jails up there."

"So you're blackmailing me!"

"Or Connie could go home to Cincinnati," Weather said, "and Jane Alder could come back to Dallas."

"With no story?" Jane gave out the panther gaze, glassy,

predatory eyes that seemed to size up a man prior to going after him, tooth and claw.

"Or she could sit in jail here while I arrange extradition," Hadley said.

"One call to my paper and I'm out of jail."

"True, but then the other papers would get the story of your undercover and you'd be Jane Alder again," Hadley said. "Now, the way I look at it is simple. We all three want the same thing. To find out who knows what about these shootings. Willie's and this couple's. You tell me what you know so far, I give you what little protection I can, and you do whatever you want to do at your paper. Foolhardy as it is," he said by way of concession to Weather.

Jane looked at Hadley, and at Weather. She didn't seem pleased with either one of them. "Oh, all right."

"So what do you know?"

Not much, it turned out. She hadn't found her cousin's killer, or Willie's. In her few days inside Falvey's operation, she had struck up an acquaintance with a dancer named Belinda Bain. Belinda was friendly, but had lots of secrets. She lived next door to that woman, Martel, who was killed last night. Jane thought Belinda Bain knew something about the killers. She relayed the kitchen helpers' warnings about Belinda.

"That's some fine detecting you're doing, Jane," Hadley deadpanned quite nicely.

Weather didn't tell her they knew all that, because he didn't want her to know he'd witnessed Martel's shooting. No point in getting himself in the *Beacon*.

"You might also look into the lead dancer, Wild Jill Cody."

Hadley leaned in again. "What do you know about Jill?"

"Very little. She won't talk much to me, and she treats me

like I'm a threat to her. She and Falvey have a lot of secrets. I think they're sleeping together."

Hadley crossed his arms and considered this. "I doubt there's anything much with Miss Cody. I busted her a few times, for soliciting, a long time ago. She's not a hooker anymore; she just loves intrigue. Finds drama on every street corner. If there isn't any, she'll make some up. I'd like to meet this Albert Florentine who's trying to post your bail. Keller can take you for a powder room break while I go see Albert." He stood in one graceful motion and held his hand out for her. Weather rose when Jane did and went around the table to claim her.

"Wait, Dave. You can't be seen coming out with her. I got snitches on the outside, the mob's got 'em on the inside." Hadley shook his head sadly at the very idea of it. "Give us a head start and, Keller, you check the halls and make sure nobody's around before you come out with him. We'll meet back here in, say, fifteen?"

"Don't go with him, Jane."

"David, please leave this alone."

"I won't."

Keller ushered Jane out and Hadley followed. Weather came up right behind, but before he could get out, Hadley spun around and shoved him hard, back into the room, and pulled the door shut.

A key turned.

"Son of a . . . !" Weather tried the knob. Locked.

"Sorry, old man, but it's gotta be this way," Hadley said from the other side of the door. The grillwork of iron bars outside the bubbled glass cut Hadley's silhouette into wavy two-inch rectangles. Then the shape disappeared. Weather was locked up alone on the fourth floor.

Chapter 20

It was a quarter past ten, a man in front of the Colony Club told Carl Ray.

That was earlier than he expected, but he still didn't have much time, since he really didn't know how to make this stuff explode. That ship, the *Grandcamp*, burned, just plain burned, for an hour or more before it blew up. Plus the ship had tons of ammonia nitric on it, not just this one burlap bag's worth.

The thing to do was leave Burr's car here and boost another one, and take it off somewhere else and see what he could do about a bomb. There was plenty of cars downtown. It was just a matter of picking one that the people wouldn't be coming back to for a while. It was a Friday night and everybody was in the clubs drinking and probably wouldn't come out 'til everything closed. He didn't even know when that was, him being a minor. Midnight, maybe two a.m.

He shifted the kerosene lantern under his jacket and almost dropped it out on the concrete. Carrying the grocery sack with his clothes and the bag of ammonia nitric was getting hard.

He picked out a gray Studebaker in a parking lot around the corner from the Colony Club. It took maybe two minutes to hot-wire the thing and have it out on the road. That was too long, he would have to practice some more somewhere.

What now? The whiskey had worn completely off and he needed to pee. He couldn't risk getting picked up for indecent exposure and have the cops check out the car, though, so he rode west, through the Triple Underpass and out Commerce. Plenty of places to stop, but too many people out milling around. He kept going west and down some side streets 'til he was lost. This was somewhere close to the river, he thought, all empty buildings and warehouses and welding shops. He stopped and put the Studebaker in neutral and set the brake, then he got out and peed on the side of it. Had to stay close by in case any cop came up and he had to jump back in, in a hurry. He wondered what time it was. The dashboard didn't have a clock, and it felt like an hour since he'd asked that man. Couldn't have been that long, but he still had to explode that bomb on April eighteenth, so he'd better just get on with it.

He got back in the car and drove around some more. He needed a little building, little enough for this little bit of ammonia nitric to do any good.

It was dark out here. Not too many streetlights.

There was a low white building over there, next to those woods.

The old Krueger Pants factory. Bonnie worked there after Falvey fired her for getting too fat, before she moved back to Tyler and met Burr. Poor old Burr, thought he'd married himself a ticket to a good job in Dallas, only Willie made them stay out in Tyler.

Carl Ray pulled into the drive. There was a gate chained shut to where he couldn't go in any further. He would have to make do with this little building out front. He hoped no cops drove by. He got out and looked for a likely place to set a fire or toss a bomb.

There was tape on the doors from the police. Oh, yeah. This was where some people got killed yesterday. It would be neat to blow up a place that had a murder. He peeped into

136

one of the windows. There was a bunch of fabric, like curtains, hanging down straight off the ceiling. Maybe if he soaked some of that in kerosene. He could siphon off some gas from that car, too.

Weather checked his watch. Eleven-fifteen, and nobody had come back for him. Hadley had snookered him but good. He was so busy thinking about his revenge that he didn't give much thought to a flurry of activity on the street below. A half dozen police cars raced west. In the distance, fire engines whined. Out the window, way off along the riverbanks, he saw a faint red glow.

Carl Ray laughed and laughed. Close enough to midnight to call it the Midnight Ride of Old Carl Ray, just like in the poem. He put the Studebaker back near the Colony Club, maybe in the same parking spot where he'd found it. Not in the same shape, though. The owner would have a time figuring out why it smelled burnt.

The Midnight Ride had worked.

> *Listen my children, for I shall say*
> *Of the Midnight Ride of Old Carl Ray.*
> *One if by the riverbanks, two if by sea.*

Well, that didn't work.

> *One if by Krueger Pants, two if by something.*

Hell. He still had some work to do on the poem.

Without even thinking about it, he walked back to where he'd left Burr's car. Somebody put a flashlight up on his face and told him to hold it right there.

★ ★ ★ ★ ★

At five a.m., a tall shadow appeared at the door of Weather's ad hoc cell. A key turned and Hadley stepped into the room. Weather had fallen asleep and now had a series of stiff muscles around the shoulder injury.

Hadley waved a dismissive hand around the room. "Keller and I had to go out on a call, so I locked her up for a couple of hours. We let her go when we got back. That's the life Connie Petro would lead—cop rousts, cooling her heels in the prossie lockup. Her goon and Wild Jill Cody took her home."

"Home where?"

He shrugged. "Not my concern at the moment. Your girlfriend hasn't done anything wrong, and I had some real police work to do. Seems somebody tried to blow up the old Krueger Pants place. Just the front building."

"Blow it up?"

"Yeah. With a kind of Molotov cocktail. We found traces of ammonium nitrate outside. They burned Belinda Bain's room pretty good, but not the other one. Somebody didn't want us to find something in there. Look, I need you to stay a while and go over everything you saw that night."

Hadley the bewitcher of on-the-fence girlfriends had disappeared. The cop Weather halfway respected was back. El Diablo in all his forked-tail charm.

"What did we miss that they'd want to destroy?" Hadley asked.

Weather remembered Belinda's cigar box, now under the Saratoga's seat, locked in Lettie Holcomb's garage.

He shrugged. He would keep the box under his hat for now.

Chapter 21

Saturday, April 19

Somehow the ubiquitous Jemison had managed to get the firebomb story onto the front page of the *Beacon*.

Weather read it in Biedermeier's ground floor apartment while the old man fed him breakfast and plied him with questions about Willie.

"Hey, Willie is yesterday's news. Somebody's going around setting fire to buildings with ammonium nitrate now."

"It ain't old news to most of the town. I bet that explosion has to do with Willie. Most everything criminal does in this town. Him or Martin Hubert." Biedermeier rubbed his neat white beard and shook his head.

"Well, I can't discuss it." Weather downed his second cup of coffee. It didn't do much to offset the bad sleep he'd had in Hadley's interrogation room or the bad sleep he'd had the night before on Morson's couch.

"Yeah, that place where that couple got murdered. They ever find out who the man was?"

"Not that I'm aware of." In fact, Hadley had told him at headquarters that the man was still unidentified, but that Weather's cabbie, Clancy Burrows, had come from Chicago and owned a black Ford. Burrows had finished out the evening shift the night he picked up Weather and had since disappeared. A search for him and his Ford was underway.

Weather thought about Belinda and wondered where she was. He hoped she left town. He had her life savings in the cigar box in the Saratoga, so she couldn't get far. No way he could go over to the Holcombs' in the daytime and pick up the car or the box without alerting the neighborhood.

He needed to look up Belinda Bain and he needed wheels.

"Say, Beady. Didn't you put a suicide knob on your truck, from the time you broke your elbow?"

"Yup."

"It still there?"

"Yup."

"I need a favor," Weather began, intending to wax eloquent until he was in the driver's seat. But Beady shook his head like Weather was a nitwit to have to explain, and handed over keys.

"Just don't wreck it, and if you tear your arm up driving, don't blame me."

"This is the last time," Bonnie said to Carl Ray as Burr drove them all home from the juvenile jail where Carl Ray had spent the night. Laid up most of it puking his head off, feeling dumb at getting caught, but also relieved. The judge would send him to the work farm and he wouldn't have to worry about Burr any more. Why his aunt and uncle bailed him out when this was a probation violation he didn't want to know. Both of 'em acted so concerned, almost loving toward him this morning, even Burr. Something was up. He wished he'd told the cops about that canvas roll when they booked him, but of course he couldn't know which cop he could trust and which one he couldn't. Kept his mouth shut this morning while Burr and Bonnie lied for him and told the cop they forgot they told him he could take the car to the picture show.

On the way back to the farm, Carl Ray said, "I didn't mean to tip old Willie over. I was just trying to get away from that Weather guy through the kitchen and there was this fat lady."

"Now shush, son. Don't none of that matter. We're gonna start this family over with a new leaf today. Me and you, we got off on the wrong foot but we're gonna put it right, from now on." Burr had on his open, honest face, which wouldn't fool any jury on earth.

Carl Ray sat in the back seat with his head down. He'd ruined the Last Ride, and now Burr was going to take him out to the lake and kill him. He wondered what Paul Revere would've done if the Redcoats had caught him. They would've shot him for sure, but how would he have acted? Brave, probably.

Burr pulled up to the barn. They all got out and Burr said, "Let's you and me go in here and have a little man-to-man talk." Burr had a newspaper with him. Probably had a tire iron rolled up inside it.

"Now Burr, we agreed." Bonnie patted them both on the back like they were her little boys and said she would stay out on the back porch and have a cigarette. Carl Ray looked back at her, grateful. Burr wouldn't kill him while she was there.

Burr shut the door and opened up the newspaper. It had the story about Krueger Pants on the cover.

"Now we're going to keep it between us, and not say a word about this to anybody. Not your Aunt Bonnie, not Stevie, not anybody. But I want you to tell me the truth. This was you." Burr pointed to the newspaper and then to the barn floor around the barrel. White chunks were all over the place where he'd spilled that nitric stuff last night.

"Naw."

"Was, too." Burr chuckled.

★ ★ ★ ★ ★

Beady's beat-up old pre-war Chevrolet jalopy cornered like Sonja Henie on ice with the suicide knob attached to the steering wheel. Weather drove around West Dallas for a few minutes, just for the joy of driving, before he buckled down to his detective work and found the street he wanted.

Downwind of a meat packing plant, crosswind of a lead smelter, adjacent to the river, the street Roma Bain reputedly lived on needed repairs a bulldozer could best perform. He'd gotten her address from Creevy, the D.A.'s chief investigator. Along with his tendency to marry among them, Creevy had a photographic memory of last known addresses of most of Dallas' gutter rats. Weather enjoyed Creevy, and was glad he'd managed to salvage his friendship with him after the fiasco at the D.A.'s office.

The problem with Creevy's information was, none of the houses had numbers. He parked the truck where he thought the house should be, blessed it, and hoped it still had tires when he came out.

From a rutted dirt yard, a group of teens in cheap thug attire stared at him in suspicious wonder. They'd probably never seen a business suit before, outside church or juvenile hall.

"Can one of you tell me which is Roma Bain's house?" It was time for a talk with his father's old mistress. Maybe she could connect him with Belinda and he could give Belinda her cigar box and help her leave town. Then he would be done with this piece of Tom Weather's legacy.

"I'll tell you fer a quarter," a pale-eyed kid said.

A boy in a black pompadour too long for school admission spat tobacco juice carefully onto the pale kid's shoes.

"Fer a dollar," the hoodlum said, with a growl toward the pale kid. A black-haired girl in a tight skirt and saddle shoes giggled.

142

Weather dug into his wallet and handed over the dollar, which purchased the information. He promised another dollar if the truck had all its parts and no tobacco streaks when he came out.

"Not a lot of point in going in, mister," the kid said. "You ain't gonna get any. That ol' whore's sick. Ain't working no more." He patted the jacket pocket where he'd stashed the dollar, to let Weather know he'd been taken. The others snickered at his cleverness.

"I'm not here on that kind of business anyway," Weather said, a reply that elicited universal disinterest. He walked past them on the dirt road and approached Roma's house.

More of a building than a house, the rambling tar-papered thing looked like a hodgepodge of sheds and lean-tos pulled together from so many wrecked Dust Bowl farms. The only house-like accoutrements, a chimney and a long porch along the front, peeled away from the rest as if they knew they didn't belong. Patches of corrugated tin served as the outer wall. Weather walked past the front porch. Nobody would answer up front, the kids had warned. Just go around to the side porch and go on in.

A white county services van stood on the packed-dirt yard. He'd missed it from the street. On the porch steps a tired-looking nurse sat, smoking a cigarette. Weather wondered if he needed shots before going inside.

"Are you the undertaker? You're about a week early, I'd say."

"No, ma'am, I'm a lawyer. What's she sick with?"

"Hah, wouldn't think she had anything to leave," the nurse said, ignoring his question. She stood and stretched. "But I 'spect that's none of my business. Her daughter quit coming around. Guess she couldn't take it." She shook her head. Strings of gray hair bobbed all around the barely

143

pinned cap. "Young people. It's just you and the neighbors and the charity lady, but that one's not 'til Monday. I guess you met the hospitality hosts."

"Yeah."

"Not as bad as they look. Juliet out there comes in and turns her twice a day and stays nights, although I'm pretty sure she's really entertaining Romeo. That's the one with the hair. He 'protects' Miz Lee's car when she's here and the lady pays up. That's the charity lady, I should've said. She pays the girl's mother to stay the nights. The lady don't know the mama sends the girl instead. I don't blame the mama, though. There's six other kids at home and the daddy got killed a couple years back at the quarry."

She took another drag off her cigarette and exhaled. "I don't pay nobody nothing," she said, waving the smoke away. "I told them kids I'd throw a vial of TB on 'em if they ever thought about extracting money from me or damaging county property. Idiots believed me." She chuckled and threw down the cigarette. After grinding at it with her foot, she gave a bored wave and said, "Long as you're here, then, I'll head on out." Her footsteps crunched some loose gravel as she went around the van.

"Hold on, ma'am. What disease does she have?"

The woman paused by the van door and looked over the hood at Weather. "Son, I can't discuss her business with you. You show me the paper says you have power of attorney, and I'll discuss her condition. Without that, I can't say a word, you understand."

"I understand," Weather replied, courtroom solemn, hiding a smile.

He watched her drive off, then he climbed over a missing step onto the lean-to that served as the side porch. The rusted screen door reminded him of lockjaw. He pulled the handle and went through. A second door led to a main room.

An overheated, mildewy fog failed to mask the stronger sickroom smell. Weather let his eyes and nose adjust and reminded himself to be tough, he was a veteran of a foreign war.

The inside was shabby, but with a few nice touches. Someone, maybe Juliet out there, had tidied it a while back but left it to collect dust. A vase of wilting flowers stood on a bowfront chest pushed beneath a beveled mirror in need of resilvering. Weather laughed. That chest once graced the Weather home. So old Tom gave his whore furniture right out of his wife's house. Long ago, when Resa was maybe five, she'd asked about the chest. Charlotte claimed she'd put it in storage, planning to refinish it one day. He entertained a twinge of pity and admiration for his mother. Always saving face when her husband spit in it. Poor woman had endured a lot, too much, with Tom Weather. No wonder she'd constructed such a tight facade.

A corrugated passage led to a small kitchen on the right and a bedroom on the left. He pushed curtains aside and stepped into a long compartment containing an iron bed and his father's old mistress.

She wouldn't get much older. The gray-blond wraith lay in the narrow metal bed, tubes from an IV bag going under the sheets. Another tube led out to a jar on the floor. It was about a quarter-full of black tar. On the bed, sunken pale eyes peered out of a skull covered with skin. Sometimes decomposition starts in before death.

She turned her head his way. Dull hair lay in neat waves on the pillow. Someone had brushed it for her.

"Belinda, honey?" She squinted to see who stood in the dark doorway.

Weather stayed near the curtained entrance, reluctant,

now, to step too far into Tom Weather's past. He cleared his throat.

"Roma?"

The muscles worked around those sockets until a panicked recognition came. "Not yet," she shrieked. The bones gathered up and flung themselves into a trembling heap along the far side of the bed. She pawed at the air, warding him off.

"Miss Bain, wait, you'll dislodge your IV," Weather ran to her and grabbed one of her arms, worried it might snap the way a dried reed would. His own wrist cast prevented him from getting a firm handle on her other arm. She clawed at his face until he managed to pin her down. He let her writhe underneath him until she wore herself out. It didn't take long.

"Not yet, Tom! I can't go, not while our girl's in trouble." She clasped her hands together in supplication and raised her taut face to him. "Dear God, send me to hell, but let me find out what's happened to my Belinda 'fore I go."

"I'm not Tom Weather, Miss Bain. I'm David, his son." He backed off into a sliver of daylight coming through battered window blinds. "See, I'm not Tom."

Roma Bain wrung the bunched sheet in her bony hands. She looked him over long enough for it to get awkward, then agreed. "No, you're not Tom, you're David." She cackled as if that amused her. "Not Tom. David."

"David."

"You should be about sixteen," she accused.

"I was, once. Time flies."

"Time! Where did it go?" She reached out a hand and beckoned him to come closer. He stepped in a couple of inches and stopped.

She waved him closer, c'mon, c'mon, the way one might coax a puppy in from a rainstorm.

"I remember you as a boy but I never expected to meet you as a grown man." She took his good hand into both of hers. He'd expected a cold death grip, but the gnarled fingers were warm. They kneaded at his palm and put him at ease, even among the tubes and the death smell.

"You hurt yourself," she said of the hand in the cast.

"It's nothing."

"Fall out of a tree house, did you, Tom Weather's boy?" He couldn't tell if she were mocking him or losing her senses again. Even sick, she should have heard about his recent exploits. But if she didn't read the papers, and Belinda didn't tell her, she might not know.

"I'm too old for tree houses, Roma."

"Course you are," she soothed. Her fingers traced the edges of the cast and kneaded his exposed skin on the injured hand. It felt strange and good, like mother love.

She settled her head in the pillow and kept working his hand. "Belinda's in trouble. They'll kill her if they catch her. You've got to find her and help her get away." Here she was dying, yet she was trying to take care of her daughter.

"So I've been told."

She looked at him curiously, not understanding.

"Who told you?"

"Willie."

"Willie," she spat. "He shouldn'ta never gave her that extra job. He knew she would be too much like her father, and see the opportunities, but not the dangers."

"Is that how you saw Tom?"

"Oh, yes. He went far in his day. He was good in seeing opportunities, taking them. He took care of me even when he knew I would get in his way."

By sending you out of town when his career rose? By letting you turn tricks for a living? No, that was unfair. He knew that Tom Weather had tried to get Roma Bain into a different line of work. He had paid for her typing school. He'd tried to raise her above her station. Some people just could not be raised. Maybe if he'd helped her to better herself within her own class . . .

As if she'd read his thoughts, she started to cry, or at least make crying sounds. He doubted there was enough fluid left in that body to produce tears.

"Ohhh, Tom! He never could see I was what I was. My daddy warned him. But at least I had our girl." She released him for a moment and wiped her face with the sheet. Then she went back to kneading his hand. "Smart like her daddy. Cunning. If only he could have gave her his class. I never had none of that to give."

Weather thought of Belinda's listless dancing onstage, and of her animal grace when she leaped out the door to see about her friend Martel.

"She has loyalty, though."

"She does." The bony head nodded. "She stole that money from those card games to take care of me. To pay the doctor. And now she has to hide because they're after her."

She began her keening again, but instead of letting go, pulled his hand to her face and held it. He wanted to cry with her, take care of her.

"I'll find her."

"I don't want to put her in danger, but I want to see her before I go. Don't you understand? She's my baby girl. My only living child."

"I'll bring her to you."

"Willie tried to save her, but they got him."

"Who got him?"

"Don't know." She lay back on the pillow, never releasing his hand as she resettled herself.

"His funeral's today." Weather checked his watch.
"About now."

Roma turned those awful sunken eyes on him and smiled.
"I know."

He was afraid to ask her how.

Carl Ray figured Willie's funeral went all right, for a
funeral, that is. Lots of people smiled at him, and whispered a
lot, but that was okay. At the cemetery, Laidlaw surprised
him by shaking his hand and patting his back. Back at the
house, Laidlaw gave this big talk about how important family
was. The only thing normal and natural about the whole day
was Cousin Diamondback, Willie's wife, scowling at him.

Carl Ray pulled Bonnie off into a corner—not where that
coffin had been, he didn't even want to look in there, even
with it gone. "Aunt Bonnie, I done it, and everybody was mad
enough to kill me last night and now they're being nice. Even
old Burr is being nice. What in the heck is going on?"

Bonnie started laughing. Her eyes had a sparkle he hadn't
seen in a long time. "Now don't act stupid if you don't understand this, but the whole town thinks it was Martin Hubert
that messed with that sawhorse and tipped Willie over. And
Martin heard about it, too, and heard Laidlaw was out to get
him. So he left town."

"Martin Hubert's gone?"

"Yeah, cleared all the way out. With that old man gone,
Laidlaw can run things the way he wants, and Burr got a big
job out of it."

Romeo and Juliet came in with broth and watched
Weather like he was a circus freak show.

"Who are you, anyway?" Romeo demanded.

Weather didn't like the cheek on the kid and told him it

was none of his business. He left without giving the kid the dollar. The truck was unharmed, so he drove around Roma's tired neighborhood and watched the tenants mill around their dirt yards, smoking and drinking shine and cursing their own children for whatever they hated about their lives. He drove west of town thinking about Tom and Roma and Belinda and whether or not blood made character. The sunset, full of smoke from Texas City, produced strong colors, reds and purples and blacks and greens. It reminded Weather of blood and death and rot and loneliness.

He wanted to help Belinda but hoped for her sake she'd skipped town. Remembering her hate for him the night Martel got shot, he wondered if she would even accept his help. He also wanted to rescue Jane, who'd made it clear she didn't want rescuing. Besides, he had no idea where she might be. The damnedest thing about saving Jane or Belinda, he couldn't ask anyone about either woman without drawing suspicion to her. He cursed his helplessness a few times, then his own stupidity.

Willie's funeral was today. Jane, at least, was probably back at the house, serving again.

He drove over to Willie's house in Oak Cliff. Like the night before, cars lined both sides of the streets for blocks. Weather parked and walked. The line of cops at the saw-horses let him through.

"Hope these things hold up," he said, kicking one. The cop laughed.

He walked across the lawn and around back, going in through the kitchen. Maybe Jane would be there and he could speak to her privately.

She wasn't there. He went on into the main parlor.

No one nudged anyone else about his presence. Mrs. Willie appeared irritated, but managed a civil nod. Laidlaw looked happy in general. Not happy, relieved.

Laidlaw shook his hand and thanked him and turned his attention to the next person. Burr and Bonnie Cartledge were there with the Bledsoe kid and a younger kid, a fat boy. Mrs. Willie made banal comments about the two families together at last, but loaded too much sarcasm into her voice.

Sans Willie, the small parlor held a table laden with food this time, but the fact that the space had housed a corpse the night before took Weather's appetite away.

He stayed for maybe half an hour, and never once spied Jane. Or Belinda. Or Aesop Gance, for that matter. The chinless little worm had claimed at the Red Cross that he was getting back into the mob's good graces. He should be at Willie's house right now.

He spotted Carl Ray, surrounded by a group of back-slapping people. Odd, the kid seemed to have some kind of minor celebrity today which didn't make a lot of sense, given last night's fiasco. He walked over to the group.

"Hello, Carl Ray."

The kid gave a snarl. "You here to celebrate? Or look down on my family?"

Several of Laidlaw's men laughed their approval. Carl Ray beamed. Weather saw the kid's future like it was branded on his forehead, and knew he couldn't do a damn thing to change it. The D.A. would be watching him in a few years. Bonnie Cartledge appeared at Weather's side.

"You really don't need to be here," she said.

He couldn't argue with that, so he left.

On Mrs. Willie's lawn, he breathed the night air and imagined he could pick out the Texas City smoke beneath the garden smells. He sniffed a gardenia and thought of the perfume Jane sometimes wore.

Jemison caught up to him while he walked to the truck.

"What's the atmosphere like inside?" the *Beacon* reporter asked.

"Funereal."

"Ha, ha. Is Laidlaw taking over Willie's empire, or will he be edged out by Falvey or Martin Hubert or some of the Chicago connections?"

"I don't know who's taking over what. I hear Martin Hubert's left town. You get one of them to tell you." He waved back toward the house. Getting kicked out had started to sting.

Jemison followed him all the way to Beady's truck. "Whose jalopy?"

"Borrowed from a friend because of the knob."

"Where's your car? You could have a knob put in it as well, and have a better ride."

"In the shop," Weather replied unhelpfully. He could hear the gears grinding in Jemison's head. *Please do not put me at the Martel Gines shooting. Please do not have a witness who saw the Saratoga in the neighborhood.* "I had it taken in for some routine repairs. I'll probably get a knob put on it."

"When? I mean, when did you put it into the shop?"

"Jemison, can it." *When did you know Jane was going undercover with this foolish assignment? Do you admire her for it? You're interested in her, too, yet you just let her step into that mess?* The questions went unasked, because there were other reporters around, and cops. Who knew who would carry Jane's secret back inside to Laidlaw?

He got in the truck and didn't invite his old drinking buddy to come along. As he drove off, he saw Jemison on the curb in the rear view mirror, taking down the plate number. Damn!

He had dinner at the Shamrock and then went to the Star D. No Jane. No Belinda. Five or six men sat at four or five tables. He didn't know the bartender. He staked out a spot, away from the two-way mirror, and drank in solitude while listening to two machinists at the next table. They were switching back and forth talking about Willie's murder and the Texas City fire.

"It was Martin Hubert that killed Willie," one said.

It was Red commies that done both, his companion insisted.

Disgusted, Weather went downtown and walked among the tourists until late.

Chapter 22

"We spent all night out here waiting for you, the least you could do is say thanks," Jill snapped as the desk sergeant had Connie Petro sign documents for her release at four o'clock Saturday morning.

"Thanks," Jane said without enthusiasm. All Connie Petro wanted now was to go home to the Claypoole and sleep in Jane Alder's bed, but since Albert and Jill were waiting at the front desk, she had little choice but to remain as Connie for the time being. Besides, Willie's funeral was this afternoon, and she wanted to go.

"What was that about, the cops picking you up? Detectives, too, not regular Joes." Albert applied a menacing squeeze to her arm as he helped her into the Hudson. He looked like he'd been working on a foul mood all night and had honed it to perfection by the time of her release.

"It was about nothing." She avoided looking at him as she shook his arm off and slid onto the seat. What was her cover story, exactly? Fatigue blurred the details.

"Well, let me in," Jill Cody demanded from behind Albert. He stepped out of the dancer's way and she climbed in beside Jane.

"The police want you for something, you better head on down the road," Jill said. "We don't need no heat because of the likes of you."

Albert, who had come around the car, got behind the wheel and cranked up.

"I'm not wanted for anything, I'm not."

"Ha," Jill said from her right.

"This ain't no baby's game," Albert said from her left. "I got no need to hang around no cop station in the middle of the night."

"Maybe you should find somewhere else to stay," Jill said.

"Now hush, dancer-woman, this is mine to handle." Albert grabbed Jane's chin and pulled her close. His breath smelled of whiskey covered by orange lozenges. "I took up with you 'cause I saw you needed help. But we can't have any cops, you understand? Now tell us what they wanted." He squeezed her face tight and held it.

"Okay, okay. I, my husband . . . oh, hell. I left my husband. Some guy got killed in Cincinnati, they thought maybe my husband did it and maybe I saw it. Or maybe I knew where he was. He, my husband, that is, he has a temper." She lifted her cast and pointed to her bruised face for proof.

"Did he kill the guy?" Albert relaxed his grip but kept his hand on her face.

"I don't know. I'd already left town when it happened. There's no problem. They let me go. Nobody's looking for me."

"What about your husband? He could come looking for you. He could come looking for a place to hide out, which would still bring police," Jill said.

"No. He doesn't know where I am. There's no way my husband will come looking for me."

"Ha! I bet you killed him," Jill said. "I'm a good judge, and you are not on the level, girl. In fact, I bet you made that whole story up about your husband killing some other fella. I think it was *you* that killed *him*. You put on this goody-goody Eye-Tie Catholic girl act, but you're no better'n anybody else."

"I don't, I'm not," Jane exclaimed.

"Both you ladies shut the hell up," Albert said. "Jill, you seen those bruises on her, and her with her damn mouth wired up. If she killed him, she had a reason. Now let's just go back to the hotel and get some shut-eye. Ain't nothing can't keep one more day, is there?" He shifted gears and pulled out into the street.

"Don't be an idiot," Jill hissed from Jane's right. "She is bad news, and those cops will come around looking for her and they'll find—"

"Shut *up*, woman." The deep growl in Albert's voice sent a chill through Jane.

"Sir Galahad, rescuing a damsel in distress. I never heard of such a thing." Jill let out a final snort, then shut up.

The Cliff Heights Hotel sat high on a limestone cliff so steep the hotel had a retaining wall around its north side. Jane's head fell back as Albert shifted into first to make the steep grade up the driveway through the Spanish arch into the enclosed courtyard. Jill bolted out the minute Albert parked and disappeared into her own room in the south wing. Jane slid across the wide seat and got out.

Albert met her at her door.

"Goodnight, Albert."

He kissed her on the top of her head. "Don't you worry about ol' Wild Jill. She don't mean nothing by it."

"All right," Jane said, unwilling to argue and wanting to get away from him. She went inside, undressed and crawled into her metal bed, then couldn't sleep.

How funny life was. Two men trying to protect her, David at the police station, and Albert, in spite of his fear of police. Albert had attached himself to her within minutes of their first meeting. He'd paid for her room, her food, most of Connie's earthly goods. He'd indicated they could set up house-keeping when she was up to it. Albert was just the sort of nice young Italian fellow her father wished she'd brought home instead of stepping above her class with Kenny Alder.

In spite of his good behavior, Albert might actually be Robert Verdi, the man who'd thrown her cousin Christina out that hotel window in Chicago.

If the Chicago police had done their job, she wouldn't be here at all. Her cousin's death hadn't seemed a priority to them when she inquired about it back home, so she'd launched her own investigation in Chicago. With little effort she'd picked up the trail of a man—Albert—who she thought might be Verdi using someone else's identity. The man got on a night train heading south, so she got on, too. She'd followed without packing a bag, without telling her father, and lay awake all night in the Pullman sleeper marveling at her own foolish behavior.

Early the next morning, her quarry got off in St. Louis. She watched him from a corner of the depot diner, then followed him via taxicab to a bank and then on foot to an office building. Over thirty businesses occupied the ten-story building. She hid behind a potted plant near the elevator banks, watching the traffic. A woman in black frame glasses, maybe a legal secretary, emerged from the elevator. A thick-necked man came out of another one. A skinny woman. A fat man. After a while, too many people to matter had passed by. Eventually, Albert and a tall, elderly man stepped out of the same elevator. Were they together or just coincidentally in the same lift? From her hiding place she watched them go out through the revolving doors. The old man shuffled away down the sidewalk. Albert hailed a cab.

She went out and flagged a cab of her own to follow him. Albert got out at a cheap hotel near Union Station.

Home in any city to her.

Lady, this ain't your kind of neighborhood, her driver had said, and recommended the Chase.

All right, take me back there, she'd answered in her Jane Alder voice, a cadence refined by nuns, charm classes, her own desire to rise in the world.

In the Chase coffee shop, she phoned her father, telling him she had been called back to Dallas, and would he send her luggage on to her apartment building? After she hung up, she went shopping, and invented her alter ego, Connie Petro. A Salvation Army thrift shop supplied Connie's clothes, pretty but slightly frumpy. (Poor Connie had a suspicious husband, so she wore simple skirts and blouses to avoid inflaming his jealousy.) At a Woolworth's, she bought a pair of scissors and two mouse brooches with herringbone chain tails.

In a luncheonette ladies' room, she cut her curls into a bad short haircut, changed clothes, pinned the mice to her blouse, and became Connie Petro.

The next taxi driver did not tell her the hotel was too shabby for her kind. She checked in and waited in the lobby, hoping the man was still there. What kind of wild streak had possessed her? It would take months to grow this hair out, if she lived that long. Perhaps despite her education, her manners, her Jane Alder clothes, she hadn't changed enough from the bold young girl she'd once been. Would natural instincts turn her into a Christina in another ten years? Or earn her the same fate as her cousin, only sooner?

"It makes me so sad to see those ugly bruises on such a pretty lady," a man said. It was the man she'd been following. He introduced himself as Albert Florentine.

"Uh, I'm Connie Petro. I'm on my way to Dallas. To get a job. To start a new life." She wouldn't look him in the eye, certain he'd spot the ruse, take her up to his room, and toss her out the window.

"Dallas. Well what do you know. I got a few contacts down there myself, hell, I got 'em everywhere, but I know somebody in particular might help you with a job. Likes to help young ladies, is his motto. Let's go down together and see what shakes out."

She hid her panic. Why did she say Dallas when she could have picked Houston—or Hollywood or Miami for that matter? Even though she'd lived in Dallas less than a month and spent two weeks of that time in the hospital, somebody might recognize her.

She shook off her fears and went with him. Albert rented two rooms at the Cliff Heights. He introduced her to Falvey, who gave her a job. That first night, he picked her up from work in a battered gray Hudson. She'd planned to expose Albert as Christina's killer and return to her life as Jane Alder, but then Willie Peabody got killed.

The reporter in her made her stay.

Jane awoke late Saturday afternoon, too late for Willie Peabody's funeral. A peek out her front curtains revealed that Albert's car was gone. Her black knight must be at the funeral with Jill and Falvey. She got up and headed for the shower.

It took an hour, what with the cast and the rib bandages and the pain she still felt from the beating. Finally she was clean, dressed and making an omelet, which she ate without enthusiasm. With her jaw wired shut, she'd dropped weight, and had begun to hate all the liquid or spongy foods she had to take for sustenance. She especially hated the frustrating ritual of brushing her teeth. The fronts were easy, but she had to run a baking soda rinse into her mouth to get at the inside because the wires were too tight for a toothbrush.

After dinner, she sat on her bed, wanting to talk to somebody who knew Jane Alder, not Connie Petro, but there was no one to call. Francy was probably still in Texas City. Jemison from the *Beacon* might steal her story if she called him. David would try to persuade her to come out, and right now he might succeed. She wished him to hell, then revised her curse to a year or two in purgatory. His interference did have the best of motives.

She ought to get over to the Peabody house and serve food again, but this might be the only chance she would ever get to look around the place in private. Last night Jill had slipped that "Connie" might find out something.

Which meant there was something to find.

Chapter 23

Jane put on her loafers and stepped out into the courtyard. Her room was the second of four on the north wing. She wanted to be sure she was alone in her snooping so she went to the first door and knocked. No answer. She stepped over to the window and through a gap in the curtains saw a bed with no sheets or pillow. It was a vacant room. She passed her own room and knocked on Albert's door. No answer. Nor at Ronnie's in the corner. Along the courtyard edge, pieces of red roof tiles lay among dead leaves and debris. Yesterday morning, she'd noticed a big sag in the roof on this wing of the building. The manager, a guy who only worked days, wouldn't rent Albert any of the second floor rooms because of it.

The west wing contained no rooms for rent but instead featured a ground floor door marked Boiler Room, and a single staircase to a padlocked door on the second floor. She walked past without giving them any thought and stopped at Jill's door on the south wing, directly opposite Ronnie's. No one answered her knocks, no curtains moved in the window. She tried the doorknob. Locked. Then the window. Latched.

She looked around, sensing someone watching. Nerves, she decided, or guilt at the idea of breaking in. The nuns at boarding school had taught guilt well.

"You better not let them catch you," an adolescent voice piped up from somewhere behind and above her. "They'll kill you for sure."

Jane turned, then scanned the upper floor of the opposite wing in the waning daylight.

"Up here."

She stepped out into the courtyard and looked left.

"Here."

A hand waved from a barred window upstairs above the boiler room. The window was three feet to the right of the padlocked door she'd ignored earlier. The bars prevented anyone from leaning out. A dark-haired boy of maybe fifteen looked down at her.

"Come up the stairs so we don't have to shout." He pointed to a spot halfway up the iron banister.

Jane went. From the window, four children, five, counting a baby in the boy's arms, looked out at her, two teenagers and two younger ones. The other teenager, a girl of even darker coloring than her brother, had the kind of head-turning looks that would become man-killing beauty in time. She gave Jane a sulky stare that said she would put her looks against any grown woman's, any time, just for sport. The younger children, a boy and a girl, curled their fingers around the bars near the bottom. They were both light-haired.

"Who are you?" Jane asked.

"Who are *you?*" the girl countered.

"I'm J—Connie. I stay over there." She nodded toward her room. "I'm from Cincinnati."

"Are you another one of those whores that work out of that room over there?" The girl pointed to a room in the south wing, two down from Wild Jill Cody's.

"No, I'm not. I'm a married woman." Jane had seen the two women the girl referred to taking men into the room two nights before. They'd worn evening gowns and gloves, a bit much, she'd thought. Back in Chicago, cheap cocktail dresses were costume enough to announce one's trade. But then, Dallas was a fashion city. Maybe a girl really had to compete here.

"Hmmph! You're too beat up to get any customers anyway," the girl said.

"Hush, Swan," the older boy said.

"At least I'm not locked inside," Jane retorted, regretting her words as soon as they were out of her mouth.

"That was mean!"

"Swan," the boy put a hand over his sister's mouth.

"Why are you padlocked inside?" Jane asked in a mollifying tone, remembering the frustration of being locked in at their age.

"Our daddy works graveyard at Cement City," the boy said. "We don't have a mother anymore. Ours died, Swan's and mine. Then theirs left." He touched the heads of the little ones. "We all have the same daddy."

"He's trying to protect us from the ghost," the little boy said.

"There ain't no ghost, he's just trying to keep us in prison," the brunette—Swan—said.

"He has a girlfriend that doesn't like us, and he goes over to her house before work," the blonde girl added.

"She's got three kids of her own, Becky," big brother said impatiently, as if that explained their father's neglect. So the boy was the head of the household.

"He likes her kids better than he likes us," the younger boy said.

"Worse than that. The old witch wants to put us in the orphanage." Big sister narrowed her eyes at Jane. Women, her natural enemy.

"She will not put us in that home, because we're not going to give her reason," the boy said sternly to his siblings.

Jane would have bet big sis had already given old dad

plenty of reason for suspicion, but she held her tongue this time. "My daddy did the same to me when I was your age. He tried to keep me locked away from the bad elements." As a child home for the summer from her charity spot at parochial school, she had perched in her father's second floor window-sill above the Little Italy bar he managed and watched the men and women meet and go off together. She'd yearned for adult life, whatever it was, dirty as it must be.

"Did you hate him?" The older girl's tone made it clear how she felt.

"No, I didn't. He was a very kind man. Poor but good-hearted." This elicited a snort from the bombshell.

"Did you ever sneak out?"

"Yeah, I did, but . . ." Jane stopped, unsure where to go with this conversation. A "grown" man of nineteen had given her knowledge beyond her years but, fortunately, nothing contagious or in need of diapers. Somehow she knew young Swan would not fare so well. "What I learned didn't necessarily give me any sort of happiness."

Swan muttered something quite adult and left the window in a flounce that made it clear she thought Jane too old and dowdy to teach her a thing about life.

"What's this about a ghost?" she asked the older boy.

"There's a bunch of cabins and an old empty swimming pool down there. And some big building, a warehouse or an old factory or something by the cliff. I seen all of it before that stup—before Swan got us locked in. But it ain't no ghost. It's a man with a crew cut and staring eyes. He goes in through the back gate." The boy hooked a thumb behind him. "And he takes a shovel and a big laundry bag down there. He chased me out the little gate—the one on Sylvan—one day when I was down there exploring."

"He's burying dead bodies," the younger boy said.

The little girl started to cry.

"Calvin, hush! Don't get her to squalling. He's not burying any dead bodies. If he was, he'd have something in that bag he carries. And it's always empty, coming and going down into that bowl."

"Bowl?"

"The hill scoops out way down there where the cabins are. My daddy called it a bowl."

"Who is the man? Is he down there now, or can you tell, being locked in?"

"He's not there. We got a back window where we can see the gate, and hasn't nobody been in there tonight. I don't know who he is. Daddy says it's none of our business."

"You won't tell on us talking to you, will you?" Calvin asked. "We're not supposed to talk to strangers."

"I won't tell."

Night had fallen. Jane didn't want to go explore the property and its ghost in the dark but knew this could be her only chance. She excused herself from the children and went back to her room for her flashlight and black sweater.

Later, tomorrow maybe, she would have a talk with the children's father. She wondered what she could say that would make any difference. Go on day shift? Stay home with your children? Get a girlfriend who likes your kids?

Might as well command him to be rich.

Chapter 24

Jane locked up her room and stepped back into the courtyard. The children were no longer in the window. Fine. She wanted to look around, and she didn't want an audience.

The sidewalk on her wing lay in darkness, due to the second floor breezeway overhang and the lack of bulbs in the sockets on this side of the courtyard. She stayed in the shadows and kept the flashlight off to avoid attracting attention. At the arched entrance to the courtyard stood two deep red planters. Somebody had put a palm tree in one of them, but it needed a trip back to Florida if it expected to live.

Beyond the arch, concrete steps on her right led up to a tiny office in a corner turret. It had windows all around like a lighthouse and overlooked the intersection of Sylvan and Fort Worth Avenues. It could wait. The "ghost" digging at the cabins down the hill held her interest. As described by the boy, the ghost sounded like Burr Cartledge, the uncle of that kid—Carl Ray—who knocked over Willie's casket last night. At the wake, she'd heard whispers about Carl Ray's father and some bank robbery money.

A steep sidewalk ran northward downhill along Sylvan. Two distant streetlights gave enough light to see by, so she tucked the flashlight into her waist. If a car came by here, she didn't want the occupant to notice her. Past the hotel, a vine-covered stone wall began at the cliff and continued down the hill's slope for two or three hundred yards, seemingly without a break.

She felt her way along the wall as she descended the steep hill. Where was the gate the boy had mentioned? She proceeded slowly, feeling the wall for a break in the foliage. Halfway down, the stone quit, to be replaced by cool iron and leafy tangle. She tore at the vines covering the gate. After five or six minutes, she got them cleared off enough to reach the trip latch.

The entry opened after metallic protests onto a darkness not touched by the streetlight. She flicked on the flash. Brick steps led downward into a deep hollow—the "bowl" the boy had spoken of.

She balanced the flashlight in the elbow of her injured arm and grabbed an iron handrail on her left. It was cold and rusty but gave her something to hold as she stepped onto each level, mindful of nocturnal animals and broken ankles. One plaster of Paris cast was enough.

As her eyes adjusted to the area, she picked out pink shapes in the distance. The pink cottages the boy had mentioned. She guessed the hollow itself spanned three or four acres. The cottages sat in two rows of opposing semi-circles, facing some center stage like old amphitheater ruins. From her vantage point, she counted sixteen of the tiny buildings.

She listened for digging sounds. Burr Cartledge surely would not be down here now. He should be at Willie's, paying respects after the funeral.

She took a deep breath and walked down the steps toward the cabins. Red-eyed rodents ran from her light as she picked her way along the crumbling sidewalk toward the property's dark center, where she found the abandoned pool. The flashlight revealed seahorses in blue tiles on the inner rim, marred by jagged rust stains pointing into black gunk in the pool bottom. An ancient icebox, a bent stroller, and the rusted hulk of a Model T on its side, shared the pool's deep end.

This must have been an old dumping ground for someone too lazy to find a creek bed. Frog chirps and furry rustlings announced a battle in progress.

She looked at the terrain surrounding the pool. The cottages appeared uninhabitable—some roofless, all windowless. She walked over to one, hearing her heels click loudly on the sidewalk, signaling Burr Cartledge to her location, inviting him to come bash her on the head with a shovel. Her scalp tingled and dread slowed her movements.

Get on with it, she told herself.

She shone the light into one of the cottages. Long trenches flanked dirt mounds where the floor should have been. The boy had been right; this was excavation, not burial.

She shivered inside the sweater. The main hotel loomed high above her on the cliff to the south. Down here was a separate little world, invisible from the street, derelict and fascinating. She wished she had time to explore all of it, but thought she should just get the lay of the land and get out of there before Albert and Jill returned. Before Burr Cartledge showed up with his staring eyes, indignant at her intrusion.

The boy had mentioned a warehouse by the cliff.

She looked between two cabins and spotted it, a hulking shadow against the white cliff.

An overgrown path, muddy but passable, meandered through rocks and brush to the building's eastern end. Jane picked her way along 'til she reached it. All the windows in the large openings were broken out, making the place look more like a parking garage than a commercial building. She walked around to the cliff side, curious that a structure this size stood outside her own kitchenette window and she'd never noticed. Not something to confess to her boss at the paper.

She walked to the foot of the steep cliff, to see how they connected. Building and cliff stood maybe ten feet apart, with a crumbled concrete sidewalk running between them. She shone the flashlight upward. The warehouse stood three stories high, its roof-line probably level with the first floor of the hotel, high on the cliff.

To her surprise, a wooden ladder spanned the gap from the building's upper floor to the outer edge of the hotel's north wing.

Her wing. She did some mental measurements and pin-pointed her room. The ladder was one room over. It led to the back side of the vacant room next to hers.

Surely it belonged to the padlocked boy, a leftover from his free-roaming days.

She stepped across a low sill into the warehouse. Broken glass crunched underfoot and glittered in the flashlight beam. Brick support pillars divided the long room into thirds. In the middle, what looked like a chicken-wire pen set off an empty ten-foot square space on the floor. She moved closer. The pen was actually four separate screens hanging from chains in the ceiling.

"A platform elevator," she said aloud. She'd seen this type as a child when she'd gone home from school with a friend whose family operated a furniture warehouse. Unlike modern elevators, the platform elevator wasn't a traveling box in a covered shaft, but a flat bed that moved through a hole in each floor. Workmen operating a wheel and pulley assembly would crank the platform to the desired floor, remove the screens, shove cargo onto the bed, then work the pulley to raise or lower the freight. Her friend's father had forbidden them to go near the pens on the upper floors, so of course they had gone. She remembered the loose protection of the hanging screens, and inside them the gaping holes that went for what seemed like miles below. Not a place for children to play.

Maybe that father who padlocked his kids inside was right. She directed the flashlight upward. The second floor had the hole; further up, the third floor contained the platform. The lifting mechanism was bolted to a brick pillar next to the pen. She went over to it and forced the wheel a quarter turn. The contraption whined and protested, but lowered the platform a couple of feet.

Near the pillar, a set of wooden stairs led up to a landing, then turned again into darkness. The banisters were long gone, if there ever had been any. She took a tentative step onto a riser. The first step creaked mightily, but held. The higher she went, the more certain she became that her next step would send the structure down. At the landing, she wanted to turn back but forced herself to make the turn and take the second flight up. The stairs held, although most of them felt dry-rotted and insubstantial under her weight.

On the second floor, another chicken wire pen protected the hole. When she peered beyond the wire into the opening, the same dread she'd felt so long ago in her friend's warehouse swept over her.

"Oh, stop it," she admonished herself aloud, and looked around. The area contained old machinery and stacks of dusty plate glass, possibly windows that were never installed.

This floor could wait. She wanted a look at that horizontal ladder on the top floor.

Upward, then. The country had defeated Hitler. She could walk up a stupid set of stairs.

A riser between the second and third floor made splintering noises, which set her heart racing and convinced her to run the rest of the way up. The stairs ended abruptly like attic stairs, with no protective landing or railing to hold onto on the top floor. She reached out to the planking for support and knocked over a clay pot at the edge of the opening. Someone had lined up a series of pots around the sides and back, possibly to demarcate the dangerous spot. Overhead, pigeons fluttered from bare rafters.

She stood still until her heart slowed to a normal rhythm. The birds settled long before she did.

Not far from the stairwell, the platform elevator hung in its hole where she'd cranked it, a couple of feet below floor level. The screens that should have protected the area lay in a broken heap on the opposite side. Beyond the screens sat a grouping of crates and old furniture—couch, end table, armchair. An ashtray full of cigarette butts graced the small table. Empty potato chip cans and sandwich wrappers lay in a heap on the floor.

This was trash of recent origin.

Was this floor the boy's clubhouse? How recently had the father applied the padlock?

A lot of vines had grown back over the Sylvan gate since the kid had been through it, so this was probably not his trash.

The hotel was only a mile from the rail yards. Perhaps a hobo lived up here. Her heart picked up again.

Who else would know about this place?

Burr Cartledge. Maybe he came here to smoke and rest between diggings.

She went to the side nearest the cliff and looked out the window openings. Ten feet away, the pink outside of the hotel nestled into a low retaining wall. The ladder stretched from the warehouse ledge to the wall behind the room next to hers.

It was time to go back.

Below her, something metallic crashed, then footsteps thudded on the stairs. It couldn't be the kid, he was locked in.

The footsteps rose on the stairs.

Jane cut off her flashlight and looked uneasily at the ladder, then down into the space between warehouse and cliff face.

The broken step—the noisy one between the second and third floor—creaked under the weight of the newcomer.

Oh, hell! She tucked the flashlight into her blouse, climbed out onto the ladder, and started the slow crawl across. It must be an eighteen-, twenty-foot drop. The cast on her right arm made progress difficult. The ladder could slip from its mooring or break and send her plunging.

When she was halfway across, a clay pot sailed past her head and shattered on the side of the cliff.

No doubt about it, she'd been seen.

She increased her speed, made it to the other side and scrambled into a slim space between the hotel and the retaining wall just as another pot shattered on the wall. The pigeons cheered one of them on, she wasn't sure who. She ducked below the low wall and crawled east, past pipes and debris as pots continued to break above and behind her. At the hotel corner, the path turned and widened into a thick ivy patch. She turned the corner and got out of range of the artillery. The path ended at the Spanish arch, and she was on the Cliff Heights driveway again. She ran through it and across the empty courtyard and locked herself in her room, leaving the lights off in case the pot-thrower came looking for her. A peek out the kitchenette window revealed the dark warehouse, with ladder still attached. No one watched from the ledge. No figure moved in the darkness. No pots flew into the abyss. Even the pigeons were silent.

A double whiskey on rocks fixed her pulse and her perspective. Whoever was back there could have, might have, dislodged the ladder and killed her. The creep must have only wanted to scare her off. Okay, it worked. She would be no threat to the hobo in his retreat, or to mad digger Burr Cartledge, or to whomever else it may have been.

She lay on the bed in the dark and poured another whiskey.

Sometime later, noises in the courtyard stirred her. She pinched the window curtains apart and looked out. A taxi was letting the two evening-gowned girls out. They paid the driver, then went to the room opposite hers. One of them used a key to unlock the door. The cab drove away and Albert's gray Hudson purred into the courtyard. It stopped in the center. Using the Hudson's noise as a cover, Jane unlatched her window and raised it.

Nightlife at the Cliff Heights was about to begin.

Chapter 25

The two evening gown girls stood outside their room and waved at the Hudson.

Ronnie, Albert's cohort from the Star D, slid out from the back seat and held the door for someone.

An elderly man with a silk cravat and gold-topped cane unfolded from the car. For a moment, he stood in the Hudson's headlight glare. His face was covered in either liver spots or faded freckles; his gray hair retained copper glints from his youth. He looked familiar. Was he some Dallas oilman? Had she seen his picture in the paper?

The old man greeted the ladies by name—Sharon, Lavonne—while a fortyish, dark-haired man with a hawk face alighted from the front passenger seat. Jane had seen him at Willie's wake.

"Evening, Baron," Lavonne said.

The man called Baron went into the girls' room, wearing Sharon on one arm and Lavonne on the other like expensive furs. Lavonne peeled off him at the door and remained outside. Hawk-face joined her.

The Hudson made a U-turn and parked in front of the room next to Jane's, the room with the ladder behind it. Jane held the curtain taut as Albert got out and looked intently at her window. Could he see her? She wasn't sure. He stood for a few seconds, turned away, and walked toward the lit-up south wing and greeted Lavonne and the hawk-faced man at the open door. Then he went past them inside.

Lavonne and the hawk-faced man still did not go in. Lavonne pointed across the courtyard and whispered behind her hand to him. He looked over at her window.

They were watching her watching them. Jane waved. The girl waved back uncertainly. Inside the room, Albert was shoving the bed across the floor.

Now why would he move that bed?

She realized why. There was another room underneath.

This wasn't prostitution at all. The men were gamblers. Someone was running an illegal card game. Sharon and Lavonne were hostesses, dressed up in evening gowns and long gloves to make high stakes gamblers like the Baron feel like a million while losing thousands.

The game must be below, through a secret stairwell in the floor, inside the cliff itself. She'd known of many gambling hidey-holes in Chicago.

Francy would be proud. She had a scoop.

More cars arrived. Albert and Ronnie came out and acted as valets, apologizing more than once for the muddy conditions that prevented more private parking behind the hotel. Ronnie assured a nervous guest that the cops would not be a problem. After the guests were inside, Lavonne and Albert went in, but Ronnie brought a chair outside and sat by the door. She'd lost track of the hawk-faced man. The courtyard remained quiet for a few minutes until a Cadillac drove in and a stocky man she recognized got out. Macauley Porter. David's sister Resa was about to marry his son. She'd met him only once, when she was in the hospital. He and Troy had come to her room to pick up Resa, who'd been visiting her.

Ronnie leaped to his feet and yelled, "No." He pointed at Mac Porter the way an angry teacher points at a misbehaving student.

"Aw, Ron, let me in. I always pay my debts. I've done it for years."

Then a dark car, an Olds, rose up from the street and its driver stepped out. His hat low over his face, he stormed in the direction of Ronnie and the stocky man.

Too familiar with the Chicago method of settling disputes, Jane rolled off the bed, hoping to get to the bathroom and into the tub before the gunfire began.

"Dad, you come home with me." She recognized Troy Porter's voice outside and crawled back to the window instead.

"Now, son, don't go calling the old man out in front of his friends." Mac Porter's voice aimed for lightness, but the desperation cut right through.

"Dad, you promised."

"There's no game going on here anyway, Mr. Porter. You were misinformed." The hawk-faced man stepped out of the doorway of Sharon and Lavonne's room. He must have been watching from the window behind Ronnie. He held his palm up toward Mac's Cadillac—the way a maitre d' directs diners to a table. Within the mannerly gesture, though, there was an inhospitable finality that Jane hoped Mac wouldn't argue with.

"Aw, Cab," Mac Porter said.

The old gentleman came out of the room. He shook his head. "Go on home, Mac." His air of authority made Jane realize he was not a guest but the master of ceremonies.

Mac Porter continued to protest but the hawk-faced man moved closer and said something Jane couldn't hear, and Mac climbed into his Cadillac without another word and backed out through the arch. Troy Porter followed in his car.

The tall old man stared toward her window, and she realized where she had seen him. In St. Louis, with Albert as he came out of the office building. She backed away and sat on the floor, making sure her door was locked.

Footsteps clicked across the courtyard. Someone tried the knob. She stayed on the floor, not breathing. A head pushed through the open window. It was the hawk-faced man. He laughed a mean sort of laugh, the kind with evil in it.

"Miss, if we wanted you, that lock wouldn't stop us." He pulled his head out and laughed all the way back across the courtyard.

Jane shut the window and latched it with shaky hands. For some reason he scared her more than the "ghost" in the warehouse.

She wanted to call David and tell him what she'd seen. She wanted to hear his voice, and tell him she was terrified.

No. He would use her fear against her, to drag her out. She couldn't let him do that. Not yet. Too much was going on here.

Cab's laugh echoed in her ears far into the night. Who was he? Who was Baron? Maybe it was a name, Baron, or "the baron," like a title. Cab had not said *Mr.* Baron, so it must be a nickname, but for whom? Willie's gambling rival, Martin Hubert? Hubert was about the old man's age, she thought. She'd never seen Martin Hubert. She wasn't sure if she'd even seen a picture of him in the short time she'd been in Dallas. Francy would kill her for her ignorance.

After a while, she fell into a light sleep and in a dream saw the outer walls of her room dissolve into fog. At the back, where the kitchenette window had been, a shadowy figure watched her from the dark warehouse. Out in the courtyard, hawk-faced Cab grinned wickedly while she tried to tack a bedsheet up into the space where the wall had been. From the empty rooms overhead, she heard digging.

Chapter 26

It was way past his curfew, but Carl Ray figured Bonnie was knocked out and Burr was out on his new job for Laidlaw, wherever that was. Both of them were so happy about Martin Hubert leaving town that they wouldn't do too much to him about the curfew anyway. He still had on his suit from the funeral, so he might as well go out on the town, enjoy his freedom while he could.

Before the worm turned, as Willie would say. Something fluttered in his stomach and Carl Ray wished he hadn't thought about worms, not with Willie being fresh buried today.

He went out to the barn and got his bicycle. He hated to have to use it, but he couldn't very well steal Burr's Ford if Burr was off in it, now could he?

He rode the bike up to the main road and headed for Singleton. If he didn't get too tired, he might ride all the way downtown.

There weren't many cars out on Singleton. Carl Ray pedaled in the middle of the road and thought about Willie and how Willie tried to help him when he was alive, and how Willie had helped him after he was dead. Willie did woodworking on Sunday afternoons, just like an old man, and built those sawhorses himself.

Now Martin Hubert had to leave town over one of them sawhorses breaking.

Mama would have called it a sign.

Carl Ray surveyed Singleton's nightlife. Out here was hookers and hoodlums, and people Burr called chumps, businessmen who came to get drunk or look at peep shows or get laid. Underage kids could buy liquor, and old men who wanted a bigger kick than package booze could get shine. They even had dope out here, though he'd never seen any. Willie never got involved in that. Martin Hubert ran all the dope around town. Maybe Laidlaw would run it now.

It was a chilly night for April, and he wasn't staying warm, even on the bike. He itched to boost a car, but you do it to these people on Singleton and they would stick a knife in your gut and jerk it all around before they pulled it out. He could maybe pick up a car downtown, but he didn't want to push his luck. Burr might have bought off one cop, but he probably wouldn't do it a second time if Carl Ray got caught. He had to play his cards right with this Martin Hubert business, but wasn't sure how. He needed to keep Burr wanting that bank money, and believing he could lead him to it. But if Laidlaw let Burr help with the big card games, Burr might lose interest in the bank money and Carl Ray would lose what hold he had on him.

Burr being happy wasn't something he'd seen much of, so he didn't know quite how to manage it.

"Willie, tell me what to do." The minute he said it, he checked behind him. Talking to the dead gave him the creeps, made him think they were really around. He better stop daydreaming and pay attention, if he didn't want to wind up robbed or dead.

Singleton was pretty empty for a Saturday night. Maybe everybody was at Willie's house. Maybe they were all staying home in case Martin Hubert came back and shot up the town.

He rode toward downtown, away from the Singleton bars. When he got to the Sylvan intersection, he decided to ride on over to the spot where Willie got shot. He couldn't leave town without seeing that. He turned south on Sylvan.

Beyond the tracks it was flat for a ways, then he came to this big hill. Way up on it was that pink hotel Bonnie called the Pink Palace. Him and Mama lived there for a little while before Stevie was born, before Stevie's fat daddy found them and brought them back to Tyler where he could whup on her some more. He realized now his Mama had moved there to look for the bank money.

Carl Ray strained to get up the hill. It took all his air, but he got up it. He turned left on Colorado. Tired as he was, it took a while, but he finally got to the Claypoole. It was a big apartment hotel, made out of red brick. Red. Maybe Big Ray's bank money was buried under there somewhere. Maybe that was why Willie came here that night.

The back parking lot had one light bulb over a door in the corner, so he couldn't see much. He left the bike against the steps, and caught his breath for a while. Then he walked right up to a spot that seemed right. Somehow he knew this was it, like something was pushing him to this one spot. Could've been his imagination, or him being superstitious again, only he did find some little round chalk marks on the asphalt.

He stood there and just took it in for a while, thinking about old Willie.

Willie made sure he had a home.

Willie wanted the bank money, just like everybody else.

Willie let his daddy go to jail for robbery and murder, and didn't save him.

His own daddy was a bank robber and a murderer, and a stupid one at that.

His granddaddy, Elder Ray, was a drunk that let Tom Weather steal his oil leases.

His aunt was a pill fiend.

His cousin Laidlaw was taking over the gambling rackets in these parts.

His aunt was married to Burr Cartledge. Bledsoes couldn't do better than to take up with Cartledges.

Those were his people. No better than animals. No wonder David Weather looked down on him. Carl Ray's throat tightened.

He wiped his face and walked around. It was real quiet back here. Nobody drunk and screaming. Nobody slapping their wife bloody. Nobody throwing whiskey bottles off the balcony. Nice people lived here. Ladies with pearl necklaces, and men with nice suits that fit right. People with good families and good jobs. Not a one of them would ever have a body weighted down with concrete blocks out in the family lake. Not a one of them would let oil leases slip right out of their hands to try to buy off the D.A.

With Elder Ray dead, and Big Ray dead, he would've had the shares by now if Tom Weather hadn't gotten them. No, Bonnie, being Elder Ray's daughter, would've got them. Who had them now? Mrs. Weather? Mrs. Hill-yard, he meant, David Weather's mother. She was always in the newspapers, going to parties and charity events. Probably she had them. Or maybe David Weather had them. Carl Ray kicked at a tire. That son of a bitch at the visitation, looking down on his family, telling him to think about the kind of man he wanted to be. He wanted to be the kind that grew up with his birthright, his oil leases.

The people that lived in this building would look down on the likes of him, would think he had too much corn in his voice. He could a been one of them if he had them oil leases like he was supposed to. It was not fair.

The people that lived here needed some unfair in their life.

181

He wondered which apartment was David Weather's. He ought to pay him a visit.

He wondered how much ammonia nitric it would take to blow this whole place up.

Chapter 27

At midnight, Weather stood in his den, staring at a mess. Stuffing hung in thick cottony clumps from long slits in the red sofa's camel back; torn cushions and detritus from his desk littered the hardwood floor. Empty drawers sat atop the rifled desk.

He found his .38 in the bottom of the closet. Holding it in his left hand, he returned to his hall and kicked open the bedroom door, hoping for a burglar to shoot. Someone needed to pay for this. No one was there. The intruder had pulled the mattress off-center, and it now sagged onto the braided rug beside the bed. Clothes and linens from the closet and bureau lay in heaps in the small room. In the bathroom, the cupboard was bare, its contents a slithery mess on the white tiles. Broken bottles of shampoo and aftershave gave the room a barbershop smell. His eyes watered and he marveled that he hadn't caught even a whiff when he first passed the door before discovering the break-in, but now his skin felt drenched in it. He went back into the hall and flicked on lights. No one was in the kitchen, either. All the cabinets and drawers were open, and some were upended on the floor. At the front, where it all started, the sofa cushions were pulled out and unzipped, but not shredded. Maybe he had stopped a shredding in progress. No one was hiding behind the sofa. He checked his front door, and saw scratches on the outside. Someone had picked the lock.

Maybe the intruder lay in wait on his terrace. He walked

183

back down the hall and through the French doors in the den and checked outside. No one lurked in the shadows, no one hung off the fire escape on the building's brick facade. He returned to the den and called the police. As he held the phone, he felt the tremors in his hands.

"How may I route your call?" a pleasant-sounding dispatcher asked.

"Get me Detective Hadley, right away."

She put him on hold, then came on the line and told him Hadley only worked days.

"Then call him at home."

"The watch commander would make the decision to call a detective at home, sir. What is the nature of the problem?"

Weather told her and she promised to send an officer to the Claypoole.

A young uniformed cop arrived within minutes and took his statement in so offhand a manner that Weather thought the police were a waste of time and taxpayers' money. When the kid was gone, he phoned Hadley's house. To hell with the damned rules.

No one answered.

He called the station back and demanded they contact Hadley first thing in the morning and tell the son of a bitch to get over here. Not in those words, but in a terse voice that he knew would earn resentment and non-cooperation. All his prosecutor's training—the right tone, the persuasive voice —flew out the window in the face of this violation. He kicked at a wad of stuffing on the floor and then closed off the den without straightening it. He cleaned up the mess on the bathroom floor and opened the window to air out the room, then took a long shower. He sorted out the bedroom enough to sleep in it, but lay awake thinking about the break-in. After an hour, he took pillow and blankets up to the front room. He couldn't sleep there, either. He considered a hotel but did not want to miss Hadley in the morning, so he stayed and lay awake far into the night.

Roma Bain couldn't rest. Sleep was something she didn't necessarily want, because soon she would have all there was, but the visitors disturbed her rest, yes they did.

First it was her daddy. She was at home, a girl still, but more woman than they knew. Sneaking out to see that one they called the devil 'til the devil put her in a family way. Then Mama and Daddy knew. They prayed and spoke in tongues and asked God to cast the baby out of her, but it didn't work. Daddy went off somewhere, and Mama told her he was going to cut the baby out of her himself if God didn't take it. Mama told her she had to go away.

I put you some clothes in this bag, now come on, quick.

A bright light stabbed her eyes something fierce and she thought it was her daddy, come to gouge temptation right out of them, but it was Tom Weather instead.

Come with me, he said, and held out his hand.

She picked up the dinner bell, her signal for that girl from next door to come help her, but the greasy-haired boyfriend came instead and took the bell away. That boy never even saw Tom standing there.

Come, Tom said again, smiling, giving her pity. She pulled the sheets up around her and screamed, only nothing but croaking came out.

Our girl needs help, she managed to tell him. *I can't go 'til I know she's all right.*

Roma, you got to come away. You can't carry this world any longer. He sat on the footboard and gave her those loving, pitying eyes, the way he used to in the old days. Seeing him again, looking at her that way, it broke her heart so bad she

185

hid under the covers.

Mama, Mama, Belinda said. Roma threw back the sheet and there was Belinda, crying.

Roma held out her hand, but the girl wouldn't take it.

Girl, your hair is a mess, you look like you been drowned in the river. Never could tame that little girl's hair. Just had to tie it back and put a bonnet on it most of the time.

Roma beckoned her over. The girl didn't say a word but moved up a little.

Baby girl? I don't feel so good, come hold your poor old mama.

Roma reached for her, but the girl jumped back and disappeared. Superstitious, that girl. Afraid she'd catch the cancer from touching.

The room got all gray and fuzzy, then light. Then Miz Neighborwoman was there, turning her and fussing at the sheets like it would do some good. The dinner bell was back like it hadn't never been gone.

Chapter 28

Sunday, April 20

Hadley showed up to view Weather's burglarized home at six a.m., looking exactly like a man who'd been up most of the night. Ragged, spent, but pleased about it. Weather wondered who the woman was. There was no Mrs. Hadley that he knew of.

"Where's Jane?"

"I can't tell you." Detective Diablo gave out his infernal smile.

"She's going to die because of you." Antagonizing an ally. He couldn't help himself.

"She's safe, that's all you need to know." Hadley started going through the stuffing from the red sofa. "Somebody got wind of you having Margie Lunn's old sofa, is my guess."

"Like I told you before," Weather said, "if that bank money was ever in there, it's long gone."

"I know. Somebody thought it was here, though." Hadley waved a hand around Weather's torn-up den. "This is not a common burglary. He, they, were looking for something specific. Who do you think did this?"

Weather thought of Laidlaw and the odds of retaliation if he made an accusation. He thought of the Bledsoe kid, angry about his father's conviction, angry about the oil leases. The last time he sent cops out to talk to the boy, Burr Cartledge had given him a beating.

"I don't have any idea. The story of the bank money buried in something red is all over town. Who knows how many people know I have the sofa."

"Hmmph. Let's look at the rest of the damage. Anything actually missing?"

"Sure. Money. I kept a small amount of cash in a drawer, and it's gone. Some family letters were out of their envelopes, but the letters themselves are still here. I keep anything of real value in a safe deposit box at the bank, so it's not like I've lost much."

Hadley stayed awhile, taking notes. Watching the detective write, Weather missed Keller for the first time. The partner kept quiet so well his absence was almost as easy to overlook as his presence.

After Hadley left, Weather cleared up the mess. When he put a cigar box he used to store the letters back in the closet, he remembered the one he'd taken from Belinda. Dammit. It was in the Saratoga in the Holcombs' garage. He would have to get it soon.

Jane lay in bed, examining her latest dilemma in undercover work. Not the fellow named Cab sticking his head in the window. That was nothing compared to this. The latest problem, Albert, lay snoring beside her. He'd used a key and come in late last night, stumbling drunk, stripped down to his shorts and T-shirt, and crawled into bed with her. She'd pretended to be asleep, and he passed right out. Now with morning light coming in, she got an eyeful more of Albert Florentine than she wanted.

Big, hairy, masculine. Attractive and tempting, she acknowledged frankly. Connie Petro wasn't altogether the Catholic goody-goody Wild Jill Cody thought. But the bulge in his shorts, or her reaction to it, wasn't what disturbed her most. It was the tattoo on his right arm. The anchor with the busty girl swinging on it left no doubt. Albert Florentine was Christina's boyfriend, Robert Verdi, the man who had thrown Christina out the window. Jane had tailed the right guy after all. Trouble was, she did not want to believe it. Albert was, on the one hand, entirely too nice, and on the other hand, she dreaded being the cause of his arrest. A man like that had plenty of friends. Putting him in prison could put her name on a mob hit list. If Connie Petro put him away, Connie could disappear, but then Jane Alder could never write the story of her trip to the underworld. But if she didn't produce a top story out of all this, she would be writing obituaries for the rest of her life.

Across the courtyard, Wild Jill lay entwined in messy sheets, thinking about her lover and how good life was. Except for that new girl, that Connie. Something just wasn't right about her. Hadley wouldn't say why he'd taken her downtown. "Don't worry," he'd said. "We'll find that bank money, and don't worry about the girl. I'll deal with her when the time comes. She's nothing."

Nothing, ha. Little Miss Wounded could snoop around and mess things up bad. Jill would keep an eye on her.

Chapter 29

Charlotte Craft Weather Hilyard seemed to grow colder and prouder, even taller, the angrier she got, Weather thought, watching his mother tear into a dinner guest.

"Mac Porter, please, please, can't you all stop talking about that gangster? I will not have my home sullied with his name. David, you're welcome to be here and I'm glad you've come, but this is my house and I believe there are more interesting topics than Willie Peabody! This is family day, and we're going to have Sunday dinner without Willie."

Mac gave her a baleful look. "You women expect us men to spend half a Sunday afternoon waiting on food, you gotta let us talk men talk."

Charlotte's indignity rose with the color in her artfully made up cheeks.

"Dinner is on the way. Let me bring you some hors d'oeuvres to tide you over."

Mac waved aside the idea. He hated prissy food, he'd announced earlier when she'd offered.

"All right, Mother, we'll talk about something else. How about the Texas City fire?"

Charlotte rolled her eyes and crossed her half-acre living room to the group near the open hall. Poor Charlotte. Mac Porter's oil money beat Bill Hilyard's, and besides, Mac Porter was a rascal, and rascals didn't obey ladies. Even when they were in the lady's house. Weather and Mac had taken up residence on floral Queen Anne chairs at the piano-and-patio end of the long room to dodge the boring social chat that went on every Sunday that this crew got together. On the other end, his two carefully urbane blonde sisters talked wedding with the other ladies while their dreary husbands and Troy spoke oil and bank with Bill Hilyard. Also down at that end, a fleet of Mexican maids distributed canapés to the better part of four generations of Hilyards and Weathers, Craft cousins, spouses, in-laws of spouses, kids, grandkids, and the rest of the Porters—Troy, Sylvia, and some of Troy's younger siblings.

Resa's betrothal to the Porter oil wells had brought about this ungodly gathering, and Weather wished the happy couple would elope. He had obeyed his mother's summons to the "little get-together" in a moment of weakness that morning. He ought to consider himself lucky to be invited. His mother had never really forgiven him for being his father's favorite or for being the Tomcat's alibi to get out of the house so he could see other women. Walking out now would only add to the long list of sins his mother held against him.

From the sea of sofas, Troy Porter kept giving his father disgusted looks. Mac Porter appeared cowed by his son for some reason and Weather wondered what it was all about. A brother-in-law alluded to a golf game he would miss if dinner didn't arrive soon and a sister told him to behave.

"Oh, what is going on in that kitchen!" Charlotte stormed out to attack the cook.

"So let's talk about the explosion," Weather said with false jollity.

Mac curled a lip and took a cigar out of his jacket. "I had a word with Odell about this Willie business."

"Oh?"

"That Hadley fellow's gonna leave me alone now."

"I see." If Hadley wanted Mac Porter, Odell Orton would be the last person on earth to stop him, but Weather decided to leave Mac to his innocence.

Resa trotted over to Weather and whispered, "Well, brother of mine, Mother's hopping! If you're going to risk your lives talking about the verboten Willie, I hope you two at least solve the murder."

"Since no arrests have been made, and I'm a possible witness, I can't discuss it," Weather said. He'd learned a lot about keeping his mouth shut at the D.A.'s, and enjoyed the power of refusal.

Mac grinned and fished a lighter out of his pants pocket.

Charlotte, who had returned in time to hear, charged them, her pale curls sparring atop her usually groomed head. At the last moment, she stopped. "Mac, could you take that cigar out on the patio, please? And Resa, would you go round everybody up and send them to the dining room? Mr. Porter can finish his cigar, then we'll see to it that he gets his dinner." Regal Charlotte gave a falsely indulgent, go-to-hell smile and practically shoved Mac outside and pulled the patio doors shut. Resa herded the crowd into the formal dining room across the hall.

Weather and his mother were alone. She pulled the piano bench in front of him and sat down.

"David, you simply must give up these discussions about Willie Peabody." She spoke in a whisper, although the room had emptied and, outside, Mac had engaged Bill Hilyard's German shepherd in a game of stick and was chasing the dog out into the grass.

"You heard me decline to discuss him," Weather said mildly.

"And decline I hope you'll continue," she said. "I don't understand why you let that, that hoodlum through your doorway at all. Surely you knew something bad would come of it."

"I didn't know he'd get murdered." Weather matched her low tones and kept his voice even.

Charlotte sighed. "Oh, David, why are you so intent on throwing your life away? You betrayed a decent girl, you spend your evenings at seedy bars, you consort with gangsters. Rumors are going around town that you killed Willie."

"I did not kill Willie. But I intend to find out who did."

Charlotte arched her long back, and leaned toward him from her perch. "No. Don't try. You know it had to be other gangsters. Let them kill each other off and be done with it."

"That would be helpful, wouldn't it? Then no one would know that your girls went to finishing school on Willie Peabody's oil money."

"What?" Charlotte looked suspiciously around the room.

"Don't worry, no one can hear." Weather raised a soothing hand to her shoulder, but she ducked it. "I have to rattle some family bones, but I hope I do it only to you. Now, listen. Before he was D.A., when he was only a prosecutor, Tom Weather—my father, your husband—came into some oil leases. He got them from Willie through a series of third parties, so the deal couldn't be easily traced back to Willie. In return, Tom took care of whatever little legal problems Willie's people might encounter."

"David!"

"No, don't stop me. It's time you and I put this on the table. The arrangement worked fine until Willie's country cousin, Carl Ray Bledsoe, Senior, robbed a bank and killed a guard and a city cop. Crooked as he was, Tom drew a line. He couldn't condone murder. I'm proud he could at least draw that one line."

"How do you know this?" Charlotte's face had aged fifteen years while he spoke. The old woman she would become peeked through the carefully applied face powder.

"Willie told me."

"Willie."

"He said you knew about the leases, too."

She lowered her eyes. Her voice was a bare whisper. "I suspected they were ill-gotten. I avoided knowing how they were gotten."

"And I, Mother dear, have avoided telling this part to the police. At the risk of jail. But if I'm called on to testify in court, I won't cover it up. I won't commit perjury, not even for the family's reputation. That's why I need to find Willie's killer or killers and enough evidence to convict him, or them, without my testimony."

Charlotte crossed her arms over her chest. "Then you have to find them. That man must not ruin this family from the grave."

Weather wondered if she meant Willie or Tom Weather.

Chapter 30

Jane stood in the kitchenette arch and summoned her nerve. "Uh, Albert, I know nothing happened last night, but I don't think we ought to be sleeping together. Yet." She tried to put a little flirtation into her voice but it sounded prudish.

He looked up from the comic book he was reading on her bed across the room. "Yeah, I know. I just thought you might need a little protection, that's all. Cab told me you was hiding on the floor, scared. I expect you're scared of men in general right now, but you don't need to be of me. I know you're not in any shape to take me on." He grinned at her. "Any woman takes me on gotta be in peak physical condition."

"Who is Cab, anyway?" She dried the last dish and set it in the cabinet. The little Catholic goody-goody, changing the subject. Was that Connie or Jane?

Albert eyed her for a longish while. She couldn't guess whether he was thinking about her question or her diversion. He sat up and held her gaze. "Cab is somebody you don't want to toy with, that's all. You let old Albert take care of you and you'll be all right." He got off the bed and went to the door. "Stay here, I'll be right back. I got something for you in my room."

He returned in less than a minute with a woman's dress under his arm. "I picked this up day before yesterday. It looked like your size. Put it on and I'll take you to the picture show."

She took the dress into the bathroom. The outfit was dark

green, a demure Connie dress, not a flashy Christina one. It had big sleeves and opened with a series of buttons up the front, which made it easy to put on with her cast. Albert was so thoughtful. He killed Christina, she reminded herself, but didn't believe it.

In line at the Majestic, she recognized the receptionist from the *Beacon*, but the girl didn't see her. The thug on her arm as much as the bruises on her face made her invisible to decent people.

After the movie, he took her back to the hotel and made them some soup for dinner. Then they played cards, then listened to a radio program. He stayed all evening, so she couldn't go out and explore. If she ever had a free moment again, she would try to get in that room inside the cliff.

At dinner, Bonnie patted Carl Ray's arm and said she was glad the boys were with them. Burr said he was, too, though it sounded fake.

Burr confused the hell out of him, every time he acted nice. This morning while Burr was driving them all to church, Carl Ray had said he hated school. Said it just to be ornery, not out of any real reason.

And Burr said, "Okay, then you can drop out if you want to. I can sign for you and your probation will let you do it."

After dinner, Carl Ray sat in his room wondering if he ought to drop out. He hated school, but he hated that damn garden, too, and did not want to be digging, weeding, or planting in it every day for the rest of his life. School was better than that. Ought to at least try to learn something, at least get the corn out of his voice, so when he ran off, he could sound better than this, and start off higher in life. The new man he planned to be would sound good. He would have a new name, and get better clothes, too. Not hand-me-downs and Salvation Army stuff.

Stevie came clomping into the room. "Let's go fishing down at the lake."

Carl Ray remembered what was in that lake and couldn't make himself go. "Naw, I got homework. You go down to the Rinkers and play." Bonnie looked at him like he was crazy, and Burr just looked at him funny, like maybe he knew. Carl Ray wondered what he would do in the summer when Stevie wanted to go swimming in that lake. Carl Ray needed to be gone by then.

Burr drove Stevie down to the Rinkers and stayed gone the whole afternoon. Carl Ray got all his homework done and went to the kitchen where he told Bonnie about what David Weather said at the visitation.

"He wants to help you! Well la-di-dah." She cussed Mr. Weather for awhile, and they both laughed.

"You're not mad at me about that damn sawhorse, are you?"

She laughed. "I'll tell you a little secret about that." She whispered something to him, tears running down her face.

Later that afternoon, he worked Bonnie's secret into the poem.

Listen my children for I shall say
Of the Very Last Ride of mister Carl Ray.
On the eighteenth of April in forty-seven.
Twas a night old Willie didn't go to heaven.
His sawhorse bucked, oh, it did sway.
And out tumbled Willie. They blamed Carl Ray.
Later Martin Hubert got blamed, of course
But twas Willie all along, messed with that sawhorse,

Carl Ray knew, like he knew his own hand
Willie, mad Willie, had it all planned.

For Bonnie once saw him loosen a nail,
And split that wood so it would fail.
He left Laidlaw the message that if he should die
His coffin, it should be hoisted up high,
Not on a table, but on this man-made contraption.
The noise when it spilled, made newspaper captions.

Carl Ray smiled. You had to hand it to Willie. He knew how to go out in style.

Chapter 31

Monday, April 21

Chicken soup from the Shamrock sounded about right for somebody whose insides were already eaten out with cancer. Weather paid for a jar of it and drove Beady's truck into West Dallas to Roma's.

The teenage thugs were not out front. Must be in school. Oh, their poor teachers. Did Carl Ray Bledsoe go to the same school? Willie's old farm was out this way, west of town, but maybe in the same district.

Weather pulled onto the gravel patch, intending to park next to the side porch, but another black truck, more beat-up than Beady's, occupied the spot. He looked at it for a while, deciding what to do. He'd been expecting another poignant moment alone with the dying Roma, and here he was faced with something different altogether. He got out of his truck and steeled himself to meet Mrs. Lee, the charity lady.

Once inside, he called out, "Roma, it's me, David Weather." He made plenty of human noise, not wanting to be mistaken for the Angel of Death twice. Mrs. Lee might also like a little advance warning. He left the soup jar on the bow-front chest with the beveled mirror and went to the sickroom. The charity lady looked up from the edge of a wooden chair facing the door. Roma slept.

Weather went in and kissed the charity lady on the cheek.

" 'Mrs. Lee?' "

Charlotte Craft Weather Hilyard sighed. "You never
heard your grandmother call me Charlotte Lee?"

"I guess I did. I just didn't put it together with Roma's
'Mrs. Lee.' No reason to." His mother wore her gardening
clothes—a tan smock, lank corduroy skirt, scuffed loafers. An
old blue scarf covered her expensive haircut. She looked sur-
prisingly unlike Highland Park, and he was glad she'd
adopted a regular-gal disguise for this neighborhood. "That's
your chest out there." He pointed in the general direction of
the main room, aware that he was making small talk, and
seeing the value of it.

His mother waved her hand in the same direction. "My
mirror, too. I never did get around to having them refinished.
This place was nearly bare when I started coming. Belinda
had sold off most everything her mother had, to pay the
doctor when she got sick. I needed the storage room for
Resa's trousseau, so I brought a few things over. I hired a
Mexican boy to haul it; his family could use the money, and
you know I think the able-bodied should work, have pride in
their accomplishments, not feel they were being pitied.
Besides, I have so much, and some people have so little."

"She had a child by your husband," Weather said, barging
into the topic she was chattering madly to postpone. "She
embarrassed you and shamed your name. What are you doing
taking care of her?"

Charlotte hung her head and swallowed a few times. "Get
that chair from the corner and put it over here," she commanded. "I don't want to have to shout. It might wake her."

He got himself situated, and watched her inspect her fingers for a while and swallow a few more times. Another family
secret was on its way out.

"I have to take care of her," Charlotte finally whispered.

"And make sure she doesn't unburden herself to the wrong people about your father."

"Which is why you're paying neighbors to watch her instead of letting the County take her? Mother, she would be better off in a facility."

"No!" Charlotte the Imperial raised her hand, then dropped it in her lap, and stole a glance at Roma. The patient slept on. "Bill knows, of course, since I've taken over his fishing truck, but the girls can't know about this. Especially Resa. She was too young for most of this, and I'd like to protect her innocence."

"Listen, I've spent my life in courtrooms and I can tell when someone's holding back. Now tell me the real story. Why are you taking care of Roma Bain? She could have 'unburdened herself' about her affair with your husband anytime over the past twenty plus years. What are you hiding?"

Charlotte gave him a stricken look and lowered her eyes. "She saved my children's lives."

"How?"

She sighed. "I knew your father was taking bribes."

"From Willie Peabody."

"Yes, from Willie and others. I didn't want to know who, so I kept my ears shut. A wife finds ways to protect herself. Not long before your father died, I had decided to divorce him. Francy Cotton and other reporters were always on him, and I knew that his arrangement with Willie—and God knows who else—would come out."

She pulled a handkerchief out of her purse and touched it to her eyes. For show, he thought, since she wasn't crying. "He was about to be exposed and ruin all our names. I'd decided to leave him. Richmond was advising me, of course."

"Of course." Weather's hated uncle Richmond Craft had tried to "knock some sense" into him after Tom's plane crash. They'd both landed at the emergency room, and Weather had spent the rest of that summer with Tom's mother on her ranch.

"One night not long after I'd finally, finally, finally decided on the divorce, Roma Bain showed up at my back door. Like some beggar woman, going to the back door. Your father wasn't home, of course." The handkerchief came up again, but she remained dry-eyed.

"She said that Tom didn't know she was back in town, and not to let him know, and that somebody was going to throw one of the Weather girls down in a quarry to punish him for not honoring some deal he'd made, I don't know what. She said they were so mad they weren't giving him a chance to fix it with them, and I'd better get my children out of town if I wanted them to survive."

"I don't remember any of this."

"You were in Colorado, staying with his other family, his mistress, Mrs. Spencer, and her bastard son, at the time. Roma said it would be one of the girls killed, and I understood why. A dead little girl would scare the city more than a boy, unfair as that might sound."

"So Roma warned you. What happened next?"

"After she left, I called Richmond. We packed up the kids fast, and had your Aunt Margot take them on the train that night to her mother's in Alabama."

Margot Craft had been a Gillespie, of the Montgomery Gillespies, and had been the most genteel Southern lady Weather had ever met. He imagined her breathless Southern warble as she herded sleepy children onto the train. He was surprised not to have known of this night journey, but who would have told him? Resa probably did not remember it, and the other children would obey their mother and never discuss it if she instructed them not to. He'd made it clear which side

202

he was on, spending summers with Mrs. Spencer while Tom told the family he was at fishing camp. His mother knew, even then, but they'd never discussed it.

"Richmond and I got back from the train station," Charlotte continued, "and I was packing trunks when your father came home. I screamed and screamed at him. Richmond would have killed him on the spot to eradicate the threat, only Tom tore out of the house and went God knows where. To Colorado, I guess."

"Yeah," Weather said, remembering. Once a year he spent a month with his father's mistress, Elaine Spencer. The high-class one. She had a son, his half-brother. They'd cut off contact after the Tomcat died, but he'd heard they were in California. "Yeah, he did. He showed up at the Spencers and was pretty secretive about something. He'd been moodier than usual with all of us."

"Then, then," his mother checked Roma to make sure she was still asleep, "he got killed." Charlotte Weather Hilyard whispered so low he had to lip-read.

"Along with Red Holcomb," Weather added.

"It was ruled an accident," she said hopefully.

He looked his mother over in the low light. She dropped her eyes the way the guilty do.

"You think Richmond killed him?"

"I don't think about it at all. Not ever. My brother is dead, so if he did something, there's no one to punish."

"Richmond didn't kill Tom," Weather said. "Tom killed himself."

She stared. "How do you know that?"

"He left me a note."

"A note?" His mother's voice squeaked into audible range.

"A suicide note. It said, 'It turns out I'm a family man after all.' "

"A suicide note," Charlotte repeated, as if she were learning new words, rehearsing a fussy director's last minute rewrite of dialogue she'd memorized another way.

"You thought Richmond had him killed, didn't you, Mother? You thought your brother killed your husband to protect your children?"

She nodded, looking at her lap. "I guess that makes me an accessory to something, doesn't it?"

"They call it murder. But since there was no murder, you weren't guilty of anything, after all."

"But there was a murder, wasn't there? Red Holcomb was a passenger on that plane. Your father murdered him when he killed himself, didn't he?"

"Yes, I'm afraid he did. And the killer executed himself at the same time."

On the bed, Roma sighed and turned on her side. They watched her for a moment, but she did not wake. Charlotte shivered and stared into the darkness. Weather leaned forward and put his good hand on her shoulder. Aside from social obligations, he couldn't remember the last time he'd touched her before this day. She reached up and put her hand on top of his. They sat that way until his bad shoulder forced him to sit up straight.

After a while, she got up and heated the chicken soup in a pan she found in the kitchen. Roma did not wake, so they ate most of the soup themselves, while he described his dilemma in looking for Belinda Bain.

"If I draw too much attention to her, it could maybe get her killed. I don't know what to tell people if they ask why I'm looking for her."

Charlotte fixed her clear blue gaze on him and shook her head in dismay at his masculine idiocy. "Just tell them her mama's dying and wants to see her."

Chapter 32

Carl Ray was sitting on the back porch, resting from chopping in the damn garden, when Burr came up driving an old beat-up Dodge truck. Burr got out and when he made it up to the porch, slung a carton of cigarettes at him. Luckies. "Here, if you're gonna smoke, no point in hiding it. You want to stunt your growth and stay a runt all your life, do." He was smiling. Oh, God.

"You having some trouble, Uncle Burr?" Carl Ray undid the pack and lit a cigarette. He would hide the rest, for when the nutcase switched on him again.

"No, no trouble. We just ain't gonna have nothing to do with Laidlaw no more. Gonna farm. In case you're wondering, I got this truck especially for the farm. Gonna need you to drive it sometime, haul pigs and seedlings and what have you."

"I get to drive it?"

"Yeah, and you might even get to take it to town sometimes, long as you behave yourself."

Carl Ray sat there, stunned.

"Now help me unload it."

Carl Ray went around to the truckbed. A large piece of canvas covered whatever was in there. The skin on the back of his neck prickled up. Some parts of the family business Carl Ray did not want a part of.

He hopped over the wooden gate and lifted up the edge of the canvas.

It was just some bags of ammonia nitric. Carl Ray let out a sigh.

"Your Aunt Bonnie wants to grow vegetables, she's gonna grow enough to sell at the Farmer's Market." Burr lowered the gate and grabbed up a bag, but gave Carl Ray a funny look, like he was laughing at him on the inside.

"Yessir." Must be thirty bags of that stuff. He could put some of it aside and wouldn't anybody notice. It was almost like Burr *wanted* him to take some and blow something else up.

Chapter 33

Weather didn't know 'til he got there that the Star D dancers didn't perform on Monday nights. The regular bartender was there, serving the usual drinks to the same old customers, only this time they were all talking about Martin Hubert. Willie's old enemy killed Willie and tampered with the casket. He hired the killings of Martel Gines and her boyfriend. He blew up the old Krueger Pants place to destroy evidence.

Poor Willie, Weather thought. Martin Hubert was taking over Willie's spot as Public Enemy Number One. Willie ought to be turning over in his grave.

"Say, I know she's not expected tonight," Weather asked the bartender, "but do you know where I can find Belinda Bain? Her mama is my client, and she's dying. She wants to see Belinda before she goes." He sounded rehearsed and unnatural, but neither the bartender nor the bouncer who stood within earshot reacted oddly when he posed the question to them.

They had not seen her.

"Falvey might have fired her," the bouncer said. "She didn't show up last Friday or Saturday night, and we're short a girl anyway on account of Jill quitting." The bouncer, a large cowboy with a ranch twang that belonged in a rodeo, spoke of Jill's departure with a tone of regret befitting the demise of Cleopatra, the destruction of Pompeii, the last of the red hot mamas.

"Jill quit?"

"Yeah. Got tired, or too old or something. She'd been planning to do it for a while. I hate to see it happen, though. This place is gonna go downhill without her."

Weather stifled a smile. Downhill for the Star D had to mean the building sliding off its foundation into the riverbottoms, but he kept his mouth shut.

He left and drove over to Highland Park. His mother let him in without comment and brought him to the back den where she and her husband were having a quiet evening, listening to the radio. Resa was out somewhere with Troy. He sat for two hours, not speaking, enjoying the program.

"Glad to see you two making an effort again," Bill Hilyard said before he shuffled off to bed.

Weather told Charlotte about his search for Belinda.

"Maybe she did leave town," his mother said. "If they want to kill her, she's better off gone. Still, don't give up just yet. For my sake. If she's still around, getting her to Roma's deathbed would be my final way of paying Roma back for her help."

"I won't give up. I just don't know where to look for her. I guess I could go down to Singleton and ask around."

"And get yourself shot? I'd never forgive myself!"

"Well, I appreciate the sentiment."

Charlotte reached over and patted him on the cheek. It got to him so much he made excuses and got out of there.

On his drive home, he remembered Belinda's cigar box. For once he thought of it at a time when he could go get it.

The Holcomb house on Arcady was dark, just as it had been the night he left the Saratoga in the garage. The big brown auto was still in there, safe. The cigar box lay just where he'd stashed it. On his way out, he patted the Saratoga on her hood and promised her better days.

He stowed the box under the seat in Beady's truck and drove home.

At his desk in the den, now somewhat cleaned up from the break-in, he dumped the box's contents on the blotter. Ninety-eight dollars cash. Grammar school pictures of Belinda. A newspaper photo of Carl Ray Bledsoe, Senior, and a photo of Margie Lunn's fire.

The cutline on Bledsoe's picture quoted an unidentified witness saying he may have gone to the Peabody farm or to the Cliffside Arms Hotel before his capture outside Margie Lunn's.

Burr Cartledge and family lived on the farm now. He didn't recognize the hotel name. There was a Cliff Heights Hotel over on Sylvan. Maybe it went by the name Cliffside in 1930. The Cliff Heights was falling down now and housed poor whites, if it was still open at all. He set the clippings aside.

His mouth went dry at the next item from the box.

A birth certificate. He recognized the seal of the state of Texas. Belinda Thomas Bain, Caucasian girl. Birthplace, Travis County, Texas. Born October 9, 1922. Mother, Roma Bain, age 23. Father, Thomas V. Weather, age 34.

Well, that answered that. Belinda knew who her father was. Disgust at Belinda's frank behavior the night of Martel's shooting added to the melancholy that had been growing in him since Willie's visit. His own sister would have slept with him, out of malice. Tom Weather's shameful legacy wore ruts in one's soul.

He would find the bitch, reunite her with her cigar box and her mother, and be done with her. He looked over at the gouged sofa, now upright and back in place, thanks to Beady, and decided to get rid of it. He would purge himself of all his links to Willie and that bank robbery.

The rest of the cigar box contained postcards and letters. He started to light a match to them, but decided he didn't have the right. Sulking over the behavior of one of Tom Weather's bastards did not entitle him to destroy her property.

He read each letter. One in particular piqued his interest. The envelope was addressed to:

Mrs. Frederick Lucas
Box 47
Range, Texas

Not possible. Or shouldn't be. Tom's mother, Rosalita, had a ranch in the Davis Mountains, and used that post office box as her mailing address. But Lucas Weather and Frederick Weather were Tom's father and uncle. When Lucas went to prison, Tom claimed Frederick as his father and invented an Italian mother to explain his own dark looks. A man couldn't easily enter the ruling class in Texas with a white trash criminal father and a half-Mexican mother.

No one named Mrs. Frederick Lucas ever existed in the family history. Someone, Rosalita most likely, had taken the two names as an alias.

He pulled the letter out.

April 7, 1913
Dear Mrs. Lucas,
    My dear wife and I were so very thankful you were able to take in our girl in her Hour of need. If not for you, we Are sure she would have kilt herself, or else we would have put her in the Asylum. But the Lord works in mysterious ways, and we Believe you can find a

Mexican family that will take the baby. We Believe that
if you could keep our girl with you as well, She will be
better off. Maybe work in your kitchen. Our Family can
never overcome the Shame she put on us by getting
mixed up with that Devil and we cannot see to bring her
home. She is tainted now and no decent White boy will
ever have her. We have prayed and prayed over this,
and Believe this is the Lord's Answer.

Bless you Always for your Home. If the girl does not
Behave herself there, we will swear in court so she can
go to the Asylum.

> Yours Truly,
> Rev. Freemason Bain

Weather read the letter twice, and did some arithmetic.
Roma was twenty-three when Belinda was born in '22, which
made Roma thirteen or fourteen when this letter was written,
which meant Roma had carried another child before Belinda.

Was Tom Weather the Devil referred to in the letter?
When did he start hiding his Mexican lineage from the world?
Did he knock up a thirteen-year-old girl? Where was Roma's
first baby?

He rooted through the rest of the letters. A hand-drawn
Christmas card from Belinda, age six, to Mama. A store-
bought birthday card to Belinda, from Mama. A set of
unused state fair postcards, the year it opened at Fair Park.

Nothing else about the other child or its father.

Roma could tell him.

He went to bed, forgiving Belinda her anger. To carry a
letter like this around, in which her own grandfather dis-
owned her mother, she must have a perverse need to suffer.

Chapter 34

Tuesday, April 22

Roma slept through the night, according to the neighbor who met Weather at Roma's door late Tuesday morning. The woman bore a hammy resemblance to the girl he thought of as Juliet, and made a reference to a daughter named Luella, who was at school.

"She could sleep through to the end, or wake up and ask for a Coke, you just never know. There something I can tell her for you?"

"Do you know where I can find Belinda? Where she might go when she wanted to hide out?"

"Lord, no. That girl knows people all over town. She could be anywhere. I hear she might be in trouble, so it might not do for her to turn up."

"Hmm. Yeah, I've thought of that."

"She was pretty good friends with her boss, though."

"Falvey?"

"No, I mean Jill. Wild Jill Cody, at the club."

"Jill quit the Star D. Got any idea where she might be staying?"

"Uh, yeah. Jill stays at the Cliff Heights."

Weather drove Beady's truck into a courtyard at the Cliff Heights Hotel, got out, and walked around the enclosure.

The hotel appeared deserted and his footsteps on the bricks echoed mournfully. Red bricks paved the entire area, red Spanish tiles covered the rooftops, a red pot at the front held a dead tree. If Bledsoe buried his bank robbery loot "in, by, or near something red," somebody would have an awful lot of digging to do. He imagined a panicked Carl Ray, Senior, knowing he'd done murder, stashing the loot under one of these ten thousand bricks. Weather toed a couple of them up. Nothing under but concrete. He walked around the entire courtyard, knocking on all the doors. No one answered, although a curtain moved in a window on the south wing.

From the middle of the courtyard, he surveyed the building. Chains near the arch blocked the iron stairways to the decaying upper levels of the two long wings north and south of him. Some of the top-floor rooms lacked doors, and part of the north wing roof could go any day now. Had Carl Ray Bledsoe, Senior, ever run along that upper breezeway, or climbed out on that roof to tuck cash in under the Spanish tiles? What secrets might lie behind that padlocked door up the staircase at the western end? Had Bledsoe hidden the money in that turret in the southeast corner?

He walked over to the turret's base, taking up part of the entrance arch's facade, and discovered a narrow set of adobe stairs snaking halfway around the edifice. He climbed up to a tiny office maybe ten feet in diameter. Broken Venetian blinds hung in windows on all sides. The turret-like room would make a good lookout point for the fortress. A faded Closed sign hung in the glass of the door. Weather tried the door, which was locked, and peered inside. The busted furniture might have been used in the past year, and it might not.

From the landing he spied a second set of steps leading down to the sidewalk on Sylvan, but he didn't take them. Instead, he followed the winding stairs back to the courtyard.

"Carl Ray, what did you do that afternoon?" he asked the air. Nothing answered.

He decided to find out.

Two hours later, Weather sat in a Lakewood housewife bar removed from the downtown gossip mill, waiting for Creevy. Several of the ladies evil-eyed him. He couldn't blame them. He had invaded their territory. If one of these ladies, in her clean white gloves and lace-collared afternoon dress, showed up at the Star D, the regulars wouldn't be too happy either.

After another hour, Morson's chief investigator lumbered up to the table.

"Now how is it I owe you this favor?" Creevy, who'd shared many a beer with Weather at the Star D in recent weeks, and many a beer with many a companion over his lifetime, occasionally grumped like a wet gorilla at the zoo, a gorilla that was tired of the parade of onlookers and ready to do a little chest thumping. Stoop-shouldered, hunched over from carrying his large belly, the older man slapped a thick manila folder onto the table before he removed his coat and sat down. Weather imagined his knuckles dragging the floor.

"You're doing me this favor because you find my public peccadilloes and personal pickles so entertaining."

Creevy's lips attempted a snarl but delivered a grin, which dissolved into a wheezy series of guffaws. "Son, some day you gone push too far." Merry, sharp eyes peered from beneath a low forehead.

"I'll do your next divorce, free, how's that?"

"It ain't gonna happen, buddy."

Weather hoped that was true. Creevy had a bad habit of marrying the same woman. She had different names, different hairdos in different shades of bottled red, but she was always a skinny, boozy woman with a rump that liked bar stools better than the parlor sofa. Creevy was on his third wife now.

"Beer," Creevy said to the waitress.

"Make it a pitcher and two glasses."

"That file leaves with me. Soon." The wooden chair groaned as the investigator shifted.

"Absolutely," Weather agreed. If Creevy were so concerned about time, he shouldn't have taken all day to get here.

"What the hell you doing looking into the Bledsoe trial anyway? The kid got caught with a bag of money and the murder weapon on him."

"Don't know. It keeps coming up, that's all." He told Creevy about how Carl Ray, Senior's stolen loot had been on Willie's mind Willie's last night on earth, and how certain parties claimed the robber buried the money.

"Yeah, that story is all over town. Look, if you got something new on this case, I want to know about it." The beer arrived and Creevy relaxed into a glass.

"I don't know what I have. Questions, mostly. I mainly want to get a clear picture of that bank robbery." Weather opened the envelope and pulled the papers out.

The pile contained transcript, witness statements, newspaper clippings, crime scene photos and prosecutors' notes. Tom Weather's handwriting knocked Weather back fifteen years and a pang of something like nostalgia for a world that never quite existed waved through him. What if the Old Tomcat had been half as honorable a man as he was a successful prosecutor? Why couldn't he have been content with how far he'd risen, and not stepped up to the D.A.'s spot? Old Tom always saw opportunities and not dangers, as Roma would say.

"Ahem," Creevy said, pointing at his watch.

Weather tamped down his irritation with half a beer and picked up the transcript. Creevy made even faster headway into his. His girth let him drink all day with little effect other than adding more girth.

Weather flipped through papers while Creevy worked through the pitcher. The bank robbery unfolded in repetitious detail from on-the-scene statements to trial testimony. Carl Ray Bledsoe robbed the bank near the two p.m. closing time. He ordered the guard to put up the Closed sign and to lock the doors. Bledsoe herded his hostages into the vault— two ladies (one an elderly housewife, one, Lou Lattimore, a sales girl whom Weather recognized as now having her own dress shop), two local businessmen whose names Weather knew too well, three tellers, a bank auditor from Austin, the president himself, and the guard Carl Ray would later kill. The vault area had a main gate that led into an anteroom. Inside, a nook on the left housed safe-deposit boxes. The iron vault itself stood open directly behind the anteroom, out of view of the nook. The robber made everyone but the president lie face down on the floor beside the boxes, while he kept watch on both areas from the gate. The president, one Charles Arthur Curtis, loaded two pillowcases with cash from the vault. The elderly woman swooned in the deposit-box nook and told Lou Lattimore that she had a heart condition.

At one fifty-eight, Bledsoe left the vault with two bags and the guard as hostage. Bledsoe needed the guard to unlock the door, Bledsoe said. He, or perhaps the guard, neglected to latch the outer vault gate. Some of the hostages spilled out into the lobby. Lou Lattimore, a teller, and the two businessmen ran out into the lobby, thinking the robber had gone, but found him and the guard at the door, struggling over the pistol. Bledsoe called the guard a traitor, and shot him in the gut. Lou Lattimore ducked behind a counter as Bledsoe panicked, shooting at anything that moved. The robber let himself out with the guard's keys, then locked the hostages inside the bank. Lou Lattimore called the police and went to the dying guard. Bank president Curtis, the auditor, and two of the tellers did not see the shooting because they were tending the lady with the heart condition in the vault. The lady, who survived, did not testify. Elderly damsels in distress made great prosecution witnesses, but not if they dropped dead reliving their ordeal on the witness stand. The auditor, old Theophilus Oliver—Weather assumed anyone bearing such an ancient name must surely have been born way back in the last century—also did not testify. He would have had to travel from Austin, and had a business conflict anyway.

Carl Ray shot his second victim, the policeman, on the street. No one from the bank saw that shooting. The witness was a rookie cop learning the beat with his partner.

The rookie was Prescott Hadley. Out of habit, Weather wrote the name in his notes, but he knew he wouldn't forget it.

Carl Ray disappeared in the confusion, but at seven that night, the hapless robber was captured outside Margie Lunn's, just as it burned to the ground. Like Creevy said, he had one bag of money and the murder weapon on him.

Carl Ray Bledsoe was convicted of the bank robbery and the cop's killing, and sentenced to death. He was not tried for the guard's death, because the prosecution believed the guard was an accomplice.

Creevy drummed fingers on the table and checked his watch.

"Okay, okay. I'm reading as fast as I can."

After Creevy had finished off the pitcher, Weather pushed

the whole mess back into the envelope and sighed.

"What?"

"I don't know. Or rather, I know what, I just don't know why."

"You sound like Willie Peabody, talking like that."

Weather eyed Creevy, decided. "This," he thumped the file, "this is not *sub judice,* obviously, but I need you to treat it like it is. No point in starting any rumors up, any more than are flying around."

Creevy nodded. "Mouth shut, ears open. Best advice I ever give any of my investigators. You want to talk, talk. But I gotta get it, and me, back to the office."

Weather looked around, suspicious of the housewives, of secret two-way mirrors. Some of the former were having a savage gossip session at the expense of someone named Shirley, and the walls were solid pine panels. He moved his chair closer to Creevy anyway.

"That night Willie Peabody visited me, he said he didn't kill my father, but should have. He claimed he'd bought the trial—'influenced it,' were his exact words." Weather put his good left hand on the envelope like he was swearing on a Bible. "But Bledsoe left seven witnesses and damning evidence. If Willie paid my father a cent to throw the trial, he should have known early on he could not get his money's worth."

"Yeah, so? Willie was stupid. Willie was arrogant. Your daddy was stupid and arrogant to take his money."

"Yeah, they both were. But listen. Two local businessmen were in the bank. Red Holcomb and Macauley Porter. And the rookie cop who saw the second shooting was none other than Prescott Hadley."

"Yeah, I went through the whole file before I brought it out here, but what's that got to do with anything?"

"I don't know. After Carl Ray was hanged, Red Holcomb got killed along with my father in the plane crash. And this past week, I had Sunday dinner with Mac and he was all over me about Willie Peabody visiting me. 'What did Willie say, what did you say?' That sort of thing. But he never mentioned testifying at that trial."

Creevy stood. "Any reason he should? The Bledsoe trial wasn't about Willie Peabody. Just some dumb cluck from Tyler, trying to be a big bank robber."

"Who happened to be Willie Peabody's cousin. Mac Porter would, should have known that. Why wouldn't he mention that to me when he asked all those questions?"

"Well, ol' son, I guess you want to play investigator, that's what you got to find out."

Roma was awake, but not in 1947.

The sitter, Juliet/Luella, looked relieved at Weather's arrival. Her boyfriend had bailed out, leaving her to sit up with the dying woman by herself. She volunteered to take the carton of Cokes he'd brought to the icebox. He heard the icebox door shut, then a series of other doors shut. The girl did not return.

He didn't much relish sitting up all night with a dying woman either, but thought he could manage better than a fifteen-year-old. Some things were not for kids.

He pulled a chair near the bed and watched the skeleton shift between terror and sleep, fighting demons all night long.

One was the Reverend Freemason Bain.

Sometimes she woke up and gave lucid answers to his questions.

By three a.m., he'd pieced together her story. Thirteen-year-old Roma Bain defied her strict father and sneaked out to see a Mexican kid named Santos Delgado. She got pregnant. A man from their town, a law student over in Austin named Tom Weather, heard about it and kept the town from lynching the Mexican kid and throwing Roma in the nuthouse. Tom Weather knew of an unwed mother's home that accepted mixed-race babies. A lady named Mrs. Frederick Lucas ran it. The lady was Tom Weather's half-Mexican mother, Rosalita. Tom gave her a white woman's name, since the Reverend Bain was the kind of man who would have killed his daughter rather than let her live among Mexicans.

Chapter 35

Wednesday, April 23

At eight a.m., Weather left Roma in the care of Luella's mother and went back to the Claypoole for a nap. Roma's story, and Carl Ray's robbery, denied him sleep.

At the desk in his destroyed den he thumbed through his notes from Creevy's file, then found his city directory on the floor where the intruder had dumped it.

Bledsoe's bank hostages were much harder to round up in 1947 than they had been for the robber in 1930. The lady with the minor heart attack had a major one in '42 and was no longer available for comment, a son explained when Weather called the directory listing. Red Holcomb, of course, was dead. The two girl tellers were not listed, nor was the young ladies' boarding house they had occupied. The girls had both been twenty at the time of the robbery, and likely had married and changed names by now. He called Creevy.

"Oh, all right," the investigator agreed over the phone. "Yeah, I'm intrigued, though I don't know why."

They agreed to split the witness list. Creevy would track down the girls, the auditor, and the bank president. Weather would take the rest. Next week, Weather would purchase Creevy and the missus a steak dinner at the Log Cabin.

The witness Weather expected to be the easiest, Macauley Porter, had taken his company's Twin Beech out in the field, or maybe to Texas City; Sylvia Porter couldn't keep up. She thought he would be back this afternoon, but wasn't sure. She sounded a bit relieved that she didn't have to know.

The woman from the dress shop, Lou Lattimore, answered. "I've been wondering if anybody ever would ask the right questions," she said in response to his query. "Come by the store at ten."

Lou Lattimore herself greeted him at the door and ushered him past pastel-clad models showing the spring line. She owned the place, eponymously called "Lou Lattimore," and enjoyed a budding reputation for haute couture in Dallas. Weather's ex-fiancée Leslie had sometimes shopped there, even though she worked at Neiman's. Lou Lattimore was a blonde with the roses-and-cream complexion of a Nordic milkmaid and a merry look in her eye that said she didn't necessarily live all her life in women's fashions. Tempting, but off limits, Weather reminded himself, thinking of Jane and his general vow of reform where women were concerned. Lou's place was a mix of gray-beige carpet and mirrors and looked like his mother's boudoir, minus the makeup clutter. There were no dress racks anywhere. Models showed off the clothes best, she explained. She took him to a curtained viewing booth and directed him into a pale wingback chair, then sat on one of those cushion-and-curlicue metal things that must be the most uncomfortable seats on earth, short of hard rock or Old Sparky.

A slender model in a silver fox fur and evening gown brought them coffee.

"You're looking for the bank robbery money, aren't you?" Lou Lattimore's light blue eyes held a hint of sadness.

"What makes you think that?"

"Oh, it's all over town. That's why Willie was killed. Something to do with that stolen loot. I heard it last night at the Century Room." She sounded tired, as if her experience in the bank still weighed on her.

"Miss Lattimore, I'm not sure myself what I'm looking for, and I don't know if the robbery has any connection to Willie's murder. I will ask you, though, not to discuss our conversation at the Century Room or anywhere else."

"Of course not! I haven't discussed this case outside of court and lawyers in seventeen years, I'm not going to start now." She looked down at her shoes, then, making some resolution, met his eye. "That guard died in my arms, you know. That boy shot his own . . . partner."

"What exactly happened? Can you tell it as best you remember it?"

"I'll never forget it." She gave a brief description of the robbery. Of Bledsoe disarming the guard. Of the guard locking the door and lowering the blinds. Of hostages being herded into the safe deposit ell of the vault. It matched what he'd read in Creevy's purloined file.

"After he made us get on the floor, he forced the bank president into the main vault."

"Tell me about the shooting."

"The guard had a second pistol, a little bitty thing, in his boot. I didn't know he had it. He must have hidden it in his palm while we were all on the floor in that nook, the gun was that tiny. Bledsoe got the money fast, and told the guard, Hiram Spring, I think his name was, to come with him. Maybe to use as a hostage in case anyone had tripped an alarm, I don't know, because he already had the keys. I knew I shouldn't have come out, but Mrs. Greene had her heart attack, and I just had to get to a phone. I didn't imagine that anyone would shoot anyone. I was halfway across the lobby, looking for a phone on a desk or behind the teller cages, when I heard the guard say something like, 'this wasn't supposed to happen,' or 'this was supposed to be a little job.' Maybe both. I gather you've read up on it. What did I say at the trial? It's been so long."

"It doesn't matter. Just continue with your story."

"Hiram Spring raised his gun to Bledsoe. Bledsoe said 'traitor.' He shot Spring and Spring shot back. I hit the floor. One of the hostages crawled out from the gate—I think it was Macauley Porter, but it might have been Red Holcomb—and dragged me backward by the ankle, away from the gunfire. By that time, Bledsoe had gotten the door open and run off."

"Then what happened?"

"I kicked free of Porter. That's who it was, Mac Porter! I found a phone and called an ambulance. While I was making the call, we heard more shots out on the street. That was Bledsoe, killing the policeman."

She stopped and put her palms out with a shrug. "That's it. It sounds like a simple narrative. I had nightmares for almost a year."

"Miss Lattimore, on the phone earlier, you said you'd 'been wondering if anybody ever would ask the right questions.' What did you mean? Have I asked the right questions? What's unanswered in your mind?"

She scratched her eyebrow, checked out her nails, looked in her coffee cup. "Mr. Weather, the last thing I want to do is brand someone guilty who isn't. I hated it then and I still hate it if my testimony ruined someone's name. But I saw what I saw and I heard what I heard. Hiram Spring was branded as the inside man because of my testimony, but I've always had my doubts."

"Why?"

"He looked so surprised."

"A man gets shot in the chest, he might show some surprise."

"Of course, but he looked surprised before he got shot, surprised at being called traitor. I said that from the get-go. To the police that day, and later in court. No one, not the prosecutor or the defense attorney, followed up on it. His widow went wild for a while, trying to get me to change my statement. I understood her shame and her grief, but I wasn't going to alter my testimony to protect him. I wound up asking your father to get her to stop. I don't know what he did, but she stopped." She sipped coffee and shook her head.

"But it's bothered me all these years, the guard's surprise at being called a traitor. The last thing I want to do is be the ruin of somebody good, you understand?"

"I understand."

"But the poor man, if he wasn't the partner, who was?"

"Who do you think?"

"Oh, no. I will not be a party to idle speculation. Like I told you, I don't want to be the ruin of somebody good."

"You could be the ruin of somebody bad, though. If that guard was innocent, then someone else may have been guilty. Or, it could be Carl Ray did this on his own, and just made a mess of it."

"The guard was guilty. Why else would the robber say what he said?"

Beady's jalopy probably repelled customers from Lou Lattimore, so Weather drove to Denton Drive and watched planes take off from Love Field while he reviewed his notes.

He started with Hiram Spring, the dead guard. The transcript and trial notes had described him as new to town, from Kansas City, out of work like so many men of that day.

What had gotten him the job when so many locals needed the work?

Weather had brought his city directory with him, so he

225

looked up Mrs. Hiram Spring. She was listed as Mrs. Henrietta Spring, "widow of Hiram." She lived on Canada Drive in West Dallas. The listing had no tiny bell beside it to indicate a telephone, but then, West Dallas was one of the poorest neighborhoods anyway. On some streets, indoor plumbing and electric lights were luxuries. It was the sort of place where a bank robber's widow could live and the neighbors, rather than shunning her, would bring flowers to the funeral. Of course, the flowers would be stolen out of someone's yard.

He drove over the viaduct and turned onto Canada. Beady's jalopy worked with the neighborhood.

He found the house and stepped over a questionable set of wood steps onto a sagging porch much smaller than Roma Bain's. It was a windless day and a smoky haze hung over the area, trapping a sour smell close to the ground. A lead smelter not far away belched smoke and God knew what else, and a nearby animal rendering plant greased the air. Weather coughed a few times and a woman with no front teeth flung the door open and peered at him through the screen. She looked fifty going on seventy. A drooling baby added to a wet stain on her shoulder. A soiled diaper smell came through the screen to compete with the outside muck.

Without inviting him in, she opened the screen enough for him to slip his business card through.

"Weather, hmmph. D.A. by that name already ruined my name once. What is it you plan to do this time?"

"Clear it, if it should be cleared."

Mrs. Hiram Spring pushed the card back to him through a tear in the screen. "You can go straight to hell."

"Ma'am, I would like to right the injustice done to your husband, if that turns out to be the case." He sounded like a politician and hated himself for it. Likely Spring was guilty as sin and his interference now would only cause his widow renewed embarrassment.

By way of answer, she burped the baby.

"Could I come inside?"

"You may not! My husband wasn't no bank robber. He was a good man. He got railroaded after he was dead because he wasn't from around here and I didn't have no money or no clout to defend him. I put up plenty of squawk on my own, but . . ." She stopped cold and lowered her eyes.

"But?"

She unhooked the screen door. "I don't need nobody seeing you on my porch. Get in here. I got to speak my mind in private."

Weather stepped inside. She was having boiled cabbage and pork for lunch. It didn't work with the diapers at all. She handed the baby off to a young girl of maybe fifteen and told her to change him in the bedroom and stay back there while the grown-ups talked. The girl and the baby left. Hallelujah.

The woman never invited him to sit, which was fine with him. He preferred the fresh air near the door.

"I had four children at the time Hiram got killed. And I got six grandbabies now. Three of 'em stay with me."

"Yes, ma'am."

"I had to stop trying to clear Hiram because of them, you see."

"Yes, ma'am. Er, ma'am, I've been going over the trial records and I have a few questions."

"I ain't got no answers."

"You do know that Carl Ray Bledsoe called your husband a traitor before he shot him?"

"Yes, yes, yes." She lit a cigarette. "And Hiram was supposed to be the inside fella. He was the inside patsy, that's

227

what he was. The other guard, Atwood or Allgood or something 'A,' took sick and Hiram was the replacement. Wasn't supposed to have the job but for a week or two, while the other guard got well. That Lattimore woman testified that Hiram said, 'It wasn't supposed to be like this.' Everybody in that court thought he was acting surprised that his partner shot him. But he said it because he was a two-week fill-in for the real guard, and he was surprised to be dying when he didn't even really have the job."

"He was a substitute guard."

"That's what I already said. He was filling in for some guy took sick. Pneumonia. That was the guy who was the inside man." She sucked on the cigarette, and gave a deep rumbling cough that could have passed for pneumonia itself. Or emphysema.

"Mrs. Spring, I feel bad about your loss, but wouldn't it seem funny that Bledsoe would stage a bank robbery and not know his partner was out sick with pneumonia?"

"Yeah, it would. But I never heard anybody say the boy had any brains, now did they? Them two planned it in advance for a certain date and Carl Ray went ahead without checking in, is all I can figure."

"And you don't remember the original guard's name?"

"Atwood or Allgood, or something."

"Or Atterly," Weather said, thinking of Fred Atterly, one of Willie's henchmen from way back. He needed to get back to town, and find out if Atterly ever worked in that bank. He needed to find out how a man from St. Louis got picked for the temporary job.

Mrs. Hiram Spring shrugged. "Maybe Atterly. I don't know."

"Well, I thank you for your time." He turned toward the screen door.

"You wait just a minute! Your daddy was in on this, on ruining Hiram."

"Ma'am, he used your husband's own words against him, words that could have had two interpretations. I'm sure he—"

"He was in on the frame up. Answer me this. How come after I started to wail around the D.A.'s office about my Hiram being innocent, how come I get a visit from a man I don't know? How come he gives me five hundred dollars to keep my mouth shut? How come he says, 'you can have this money and keep your mouth shut, or keep yapping and find one of your kids down in the rock quarry?' Answer me that! And what's to stop any of 'em from coming after me or my grandkids now for talking to you, answer me that."

Weather couldn't answer that.

Weather drove away, confused. The rock quarry threat started seventeen years ago. Mrs. Hiram Spring and Charlotte Weather both received the same threat. Recently, Lascalle from the *Beacon* moved his family out of town after an identical threat. Jemison thought Lascalle's menace had come from the Chicago mob, but Lascalle had been investigating both local and outside gangsters. Lascalle's caller, despite his accent, must be allied with a local camp, Willie's or Martin Hubert's, somebody who went back seventeen years.

But with Willie gone, was there a threat at all? He mulled it over.

Had to be, he finally decided. Martel Gines and the boyfriend died at the old Krueger Pants place after Willie got shot, not before. What did Martel or the man know or do that demanded such a permanent silencing?

It was past lunchtime. He found a diner on Oak Lawn and

ordered a chicken-fried steak. While waiting, he called Creevy from a phone booth inside the restaurant. Luckily, the fat man was in.

"Hoo, boy, you popular with the ladies. Ina Rae told me to tell you that you don't work here any more, and she ain't going to be forwarding no more messages. Course, she did pass these particular messages on to me, knowing as how we're drinking buddies."

"Tell Ina Rae thanks. And what ladies are you talking about?"

"Miss Lou Lattimore, for one. Wants you to come by her shop at closing time. Six."

"All right."

"You know anyone named Connie?"

Weather's insides went cool. Jane. "Sort of." Maybe she was ready to quit this little undercover game. Maybe she was in trouble and needed his help. Maybe she found out who killed Willie.

"She said she would try to get in touch with you later."

"That's it?"

"How many women you expecting to hear from, son?"

"I meant, is that the whole message from Connie?"

"Far as I know. You sound like some schoolboy, wanting to know what else she said. 'Connie,' huh. Two weeks ago you were fretting over that reporter woman from Chicago. I guess you got over that one pretty fast, huh?"

"Connie's just a witness, Creevy, that's all." He wouldn't tell him about Jane's undercover. Hadley and Keller knowing was trouble enough. "Did you get anything on the bank tellers?"

"I got info, but no girls. They was New Orleans gals named Marie Chantilly and Celeste Care-ay. They lived at Wisteria House for Young Ladies on Live Oak, which was run by a woman named Mrs. Eric Sanderson, now deceased. I got feelers out in the neighborhood for other gals might have lived there, but it'll take a while. Most girls stay home with mama and daddy 'til they get married, so it would be out-of-town gals that stayed there anyway. But I ask you, names like Marie Chantilly and Celeste Care-ay, that ain't bank teller names! That's dancers or grifters, don't you think?"

"Not necessarily. Everybody from New Orleans has names like that."

"Shame to waste that much name on bank tellers, don't you think? Only thing worse would be librarians."

Weather laughed. He looked forward to the steak dinner he would have to buy Creevy.

"Now, I did get something on the other two. The auditor and the president."

"What did you get?"

"The auditor, Theophilus Oliver, retired in '39. He supposedly moved to Missouri to be with his old mother. Haven't been able to track him down."

"And the president, Curtis?"

"Seems that robbery took the starch out of him and he sold his part of the bank not long after. According to sources here, he took his family to Tulsa, which is where his people came from. Started up some other business, nobody knows what. I got calls in up in Oklahoma, but nobody's got back to me yet."

"All right, thanks." Over at his table, the waitress put a plate of food down and waved at him to come get it. "Wait. There's one other person I'd like you to locate."

"That's getting to be another sirloin, this keeps up. We ain't that good a friends."

"Creevy, I'll take you out once a month for a year if you help me out."

"You got a deal. Who you got?"

"The regular guard at the bank. Supposedly Hiram Spring was a replacement while the regular guy had pneumonia. Sick like that, the guy might've been a patient at Parkland during the robbery. Spring's widow thought the man's name was Atwood or Allwood. I'm thinking it might have been Fred Atterly. Son of a bitch keeps showing up. I want to see if it's just coincidence."

"Fred Atterly, Parkland Hospital. Will do. Anything else, while I'm saving on my grocery bill?"

"Not yet."

Weather hung up, telling himself that people missed work and weddings and high school graduations because of pneumonia. Why not bank robberies?

Chapter 36

After lunch, Weather went back to the phone booth to call Mac Porter, who was supposed to be flying in from somewhere in the company plane this afternoon. The receptionist told him Mac Porter was expected in at four, but would be leaving shortly thereafter.

"Tell him to wait. He needs to see me." Weather left his name with the girl and drove downtown. He figured he would drop in on Betty Gottschalk at the bank.

Pacific Avenue State Bank president Clayton Barton shook Weather's hand, inquired about the cast, his mother, and her husband (Bill Hilyard's money helped keep the bank healthy). What could he help him with this afternoon?

Just cashing a check, Weather said, not eager to tell the banker his business. Barton glad-handed him a little more, then went into his office in the back corner. Weather stepped into one of the two long lines. He didn't see Betty Gottschalk at her usual perch. The tellers, both young women, dispensed cash from oak counters he knew had been put in after the robbery. The bullet-marked originals had attracted too many tourists during Bledsoe's trial.

He caught the eye of one of the tellers. "Mrs. Gottschalk in?" He pointed to the vacant third window where the woman usually sat.

"She took the day off," one of the girls answered, looking pleased. "She had to take her husband to the doctor."

"Oh."

He decided he would actually cash a check so he could buy time to look around. The rectangular lobby was small, especially for the drama it had hosted seventeen years ago. Behind him, opposite the teller cages, the gate to the vault and the safe deposit boxes had hidden the frightened hostages. Out here, near the door, white tiles covered the spot where a younger Lou Lattimore crouched with the dying guard. A few feet left of Lou, on his right, a loan officer's desk sat behind a ribbed glass partition. Remodeling didn't always destroy ghosts.

His turn at the window came. He wrote a check and the girl gave him his money with a smile. "Why so sad, Mr. Weather? It's a beautiful day."

Portex Oil took up the second floor of the Santa Fe building, above Red Holcomb's old office. Weather had waited for over an hour in the lobby before Mac Porter came in.

"Mac," Weather said as he stood.

Mac nodded a greeting and headed down a hall. Weather stayed on his heels.

"Hey, Dave, I just dropped by to pick up some papers and I gotta leave in five minutes. Meeting some fellas about an oil deal. Can we talk some other time?"

"No, this can't wait. I need to know about the bank robbery you witnessed seventeen years ago. Punk named Carl Ray Bledsoe killed a guard. Why were you in the bank that particular day?"

Mac Porter's face went red when Weather got to the words "bank robbery," then continued to change hues, going through plum and purple before fading back to merely florid.

"I was in there to do regular banking, that's why people go to banks, ain't it?" Mac inhaled a ragged breath, like he'd been winded and could just now get his air. "Why are you asking about this?"

"Oh, I need to entertain myself, I guess. You see, Bledsoe was Willie's cousin, and it's all over town that Willie'd started looking for Bledsoe's bank robbery money again. Some say it's what got Willie killed."

Now Mac was paler than usual. "I don't know about that, but they got half the money back, and the other half burned up in Margie's fire. Rumors been flying around for years about that money. I wouldn't put any weight on it as to why Willie died."

"Willie died over something. The money was on his mind. It makes sense to look into it."

"No, it don't, not if it's why he died. Whoever killed Willie might not be done killing. I thought you said Sheriff Orton was investigating this. Why don't you let him?"

"I'm not stopping him. I'm just doing a little private investigating on my own."

Mac picked up a file from his desk, shoved it into a briefcase, shook his head, and walked out the door. Weather followed. At the elevator, the oilman said, "You ought to leave it up to Odell. You told me yourself it was his case. I hear he's after old Martin Hubert. Let him catch him and let it end there. Here, ride down with me. I need to tell you something, and I got to catch a cab." Mac gave the elevator operator a dollar and told him to take a break, then he and Weather stepped into the car.

"I really do have this meeting I can't miss, or I would spend more time with you, just to tell you to back off this thing," Mac said as he worked the levers to make the box descend. "If Willie got killed over that bank deal, and you bring it to light, you'll wind up in the riverbottoms yourself. I tend to exaggerate a lot of things, but I ain't joking about this. Your sister wants you in her wedding. I'm telling you, family to family, don't mess with this." The elevator bounced a couple of times at the bottom and Mac let them out. In the lobby, he sprang ahead and slipped into the revolving doors. Weather caught up with him outside, as he was hailing a taxi.

"What do you know, Mac?"

"Nothing. Just that you're playing with fire, son."

Weather put his hand on the older man's chest as he opened the taxi door. "What do you know, Mac? On Sunday you were all set to gab about Willie 'til doomsday. Now you're clamming up. What's changed?"

The oilman shook his head and shoved Weather out of his way.

A distinct advantage in working for Falvey Johnson, Jane thought, was getting time off anytime he didn't want you knowing what he was up to. With a pending purchase of another nightclub, Falvey suddenly decided "Connie Petro" was too much of an unknown to know the terms of the deal and so he gave her the afternoon off. Jane suspected he needed to go off and bribe somebody for a liquor license or maybe pay off a cop, but she didn't press. She'd seen her dear old dad do it enough back in Chicago to know that when men took that "No Girls Allowed" attitude, they were probably going to do something shady.

Well, let them. Albert had dropped her off at the Cliff Heights and headed off with Falvey and Ronnie, so now was a good time to try to get into the room inside the cliff. From the courtyard, she peered in Sharon and Lavonne's window, fearful of Cab's head popping up from behind the curtains. She'd already knocked, and gotten no answer, and tried the door, and found it locked.

Through a gap in the curtains, she saw a bed, a dresser,

and nothing else. While she was looking, Jill's door slammed shut.

"Just what in the hell do you think you're doing?" The dancer glared at her from the sidewalk. She wore a blue evening gown and high heels. A bit early in the day for them.

"Just looking for Sharon or Lavonne. I wanted some company." Not yours. Please, God, not yours.

Jill did not volunteer it. "You get out of here now. Go back in your room."

"Noo, I think I'll take a little walk." She bolted for the arch. Jill followed, but lost ground from the high heels. At the Sylvan Avenue gate to the village, Jane stopped and looked back. Jill stood at the top of the blacktop driveway. They stared each other down for a couple of seconds, then Jill disappeared into the courtyard.

Jane slipped through the Sylvan gate and traversed the sidewalks to the back of the cliff, wishing the whole time that she'd taken the Fort Worth Avenue gate. She gave the warehouse a wide berth in case the mysterious pot-thrower was in residence, choosing instead to cross the low acreage by way of the pool and cabins, heading uphill at the edge of some dense woods in the northwest quadrant of the property. As she flanked the thicket, she caught a glimpse of something metallic on her right. The woods were too overgrown with brush to get in there to see better. She walked south along the woods edge, hoping for a clearing.

The woods ended on the upward slope of a clearing large enough for maybe ten cars in the area behind the children's apartment. The automobile gate the padlocked boy had mentioned loomed on the southern edge of the area. Beyond it, Fort Worth Avenue traffic cut through the stillness. She examined the woods from this angle. Tire tracks led downhill into the trees.

She followed them in, and found a black Ford with Illinois plates deep in the woods. Someone had draped branches over it, but because of the steep decline in the terrain, it wasn't visible from the clearing anyway. Judging from the dust and grime on it, the car had been in the woods a few days, at least. What happened to its owner?

She pushed some clawing branches aside and opened the driver's door, expecting dead bodies to fall out or someone to jump out at her, but the vehicle was empty.

The car registration named Clancy Burrows, 1111 W. Taylor St., Chicago, as the owner. She knew the area. A tough neighborhood, not far from her dad's bar.

A wadded handkerchief lay on the floorboard. She scooped it up and laid it flat on the seat. It was monogrammed with the initials C. B. and contained car keys.

She opened the trunk, found no bodies there, either, closed it, and returned the keys in the handkerchief to the floorboard where she'd found them.

While inside, she heard the big gates on Fort Worth Avenue open and a car drive in. Someone got out, crunched gravel back to the gate, shut it, crunched back to the car, shut the door.

She lay down on the seat and listened. Certain that her pounding blood echoed across the county, she lay there for much longer than necessary, fearing Burr Cartledge with his shovel and his staring eyes.

Picturing herself explaining to Francy Cotton why she failed to investigate, she summoned her nerve and crept up the rutted trail to the woods edge, where she hid in the foliage. Another Ford, this one newer, and gray instead of black, was parked beside the cliff.

A man knelt at a door in the cliff, picking the lock.

Detective Hadley.

He got the door open and disappeared into the cliff. This must be a second entrance to the underground rooms. She scanned the cliff wall and noted two widely-spaced windows in the hotel, about thirty feet up. The back windows to the children's apartment. They were open, but no one sat in them. The windows had no bars, but that didn't matter. It was too far to drop, and not an escape route for the children.

She waited, frozen at the edge of the woods, but Hadley didn't come out. She wanted to tell him about the Ford. He knew she was undercover, so it ought to be all right to approach him. The hidden car might mean nothing, and it might mean everything. So what if a gambler hid his car? But this car had been there a while. Hadley should know about it.

She walked into the clearing and went to the door in the cliff and pushed. It led to a dank storage room. Dusty jars without lids occupied a few plank shelves. Spider webs laced rusted rakes to a broken hoe on the wall. The place must have been a tool shed for groundsmen. Hadley was not here, nor was there an inside door leading anyplace else.

He had disappeared into the cliff.

No, wait. One of the shelves along the right wall stuck out at an odd angle. Could he be hiding behind that, expecting her to be a gangster? Would he shoot first and ask questions later?

"Hadley?" Her whisper, already hampered by the wires in her jaw, came out a low croak. She stepped closer to the shelf. "Hadley?"

No answer. Trembling, Jane went around the shelf, whispering, "Hadley, don't shoot."

He wasn't on the other side. Instead, the space revealed a short passage. She followed it to a kitchen. One dim fluorescent bulb over a sink lit the room. Bottles of booze filled the counters. This was the bar for the gambling hall. At the opposite end of the kitchen, a door hung half open. Voices came from the other side.

"Baby dancer, we will find that bank money," Hadley was saying. "Now don't fret about it. Just play it cool and do what I say and pretty soon we'll be sitting pretty."

"But what if it did burn up?" Wild Jill Cody's distinctive twang jarred Jane like an electric short.

"Then I have another plan."

"What's that, hon?"

Hadley wouldn't reveal that plan, but gave reassurances, made soothing noises, until the conversation turned to a more primitive language, one whose grunts and moans needed no interpretation. Jane backed into the passage, counting on Wild Jill's moans of pleasure to drown out her thumping heart.

She pulled the door shut and ran out a pedestrian gate beside the big gate onto Fort Worth Avenue, then walked to the corner onto Sylvan. Breathless, she arrived in the courtyard, where she met Burr Cartledge, carrying what looked like a bag of cement. He stared as she ran into her room. He cussed in her direction, then put the bag back in his truck and drove off.

Bonnie had her head twisted down in the kitchen sink when Carl Ray got home from school. She was running water on her face. When she came up, he could see she'd been crying.

"What's the matter, Aunt Bonnie?"

"It's Burr. He's so mad."

"He hit you?"

"Of course he did not hit me."

"Been messing around with another woman?" Hated to ask it, but it might be about time she knew.

"Hell, no! He knows I'd kill him."

"Then what?"

She shook her head and took her time answering. Looked him over a couple of times, the way grownups do when they're deciding if your little ears could hear whatever it was they were about to say. "The sheriff took him off in his car this morning."

"What for?"

"Burr wouldn't say."

"Is he in jail?"

"Naw. Sheriff let him go. Brought him back here."

"You think it was about Willie?"

"Hell, yes, it was about Willie. I think Laidlaw accused him of the killing and Odell had to question him about it. Course Laidlaw didn't have no reason on earth to do it, and the sheriff knows that. Burr's been screaming at me for the last hour about how he wished he'd never had nothing to do with anybody named Bledsoe or Peabody either. How he hated being mixed in with this family."

"Do you think he'll leave?" Carl Ray tried to make his voice plain, but could hear the hope in it himself.

"He can't leave." Her face went puffy and ugly. "We can't do without him, don't you see? I had an operation. I can't dance no more and I can't work in no factory no more."

At nearly six, Weather parked the jalopy in front of Lou Lattimore and went into the store. Lou Lattimore, the lady, not the store, said goodbye to a model and ushered him into an office. It had the same boudoir feel as the rest of the place.

"Brandy?"

"No, thanks. Whiskey or beer. My ex-fiancée always said I have no real romance."

She pulled a bottle of Black Jack off a tray and poured

them both drinks. "Two fingers, neat. I'm guessing that fits with your no-nonsense D.A. way."

"You'd be exactly right." Weather took the proffered glass. "Now what can I do for you, Miss Lattimore?"

"Well." She rolled the barrel glass in her palms for a second. "I said this morning I don't want to cause good people any harm. So I've given this a lot of thought. This could hurt innocent people. This could mean nothing. I have to trust your discretion."

"You've got it."

"That day. The day of the robbery."

"Yes?"

"When I did my banking, I generally went to Mrs. Gottschalk's window so we could have a chat. The poor thing has a crippled husband, you know, and she's the sole support of the both of them."

"Yes, I knew that." He always avoided Betty Gottschalk's window for the same reason. The woman was entirely too willing to list her troubles in detail, and entirely too willing to dismiss everybody else's, since hers were far worse. He liked to get his business done and get out.

"Well, that day, the day of the robbery, she was distracted. Snappy, in fact." Lou Lattimore took a sip of whiskey. "She said she'd had to postpone taking her husband to the doctor because one of the tellers was embezzling."

"Marie Chantilly or Celeste Carré."

"Yes, what lovely names for such unlovely actions, if that was actually the case. Anyway, a customer thought his deposits were being under-recorded and had asked for a special audit."

"What customer?"

"You know, she didn't say, but I suspected it was Mac Porter. You know Mac, how gregarious he is, how—"

"Careless with money?" Mac claimed he'd been in the bank doing ordinary banking. This was the same guy who told him to drop the investigation. Yeah, he knew Mac.

"Yes. Well, you understand my dilemma. I never mentioned this because Betty had a habit of accusing her help, and I didn't want those girls ruined. It never came up in court anyway. Your father never asked about it and neither did the defense. I expected the auditor would testify, but he didn't. I suppose with all the other evidence, an auditor being at the bank wasn't the main issue anyway. I liked those two girls. I didn't know them well, but I liked them. They're probably married with kids in school by now. A thing like that could ruin them if they're innocent."

"Or if they're guilty."

Weather had dinner with Beady in the old man's tiny kitchen. The Claypoole's building manager inquired if Weather would be returning the jalopy this century.

"Nope."

"Then how about lending me your car? I do have to run errands every now and then."

Weather reached for the keys, then remembered the reason he had hidden the Saratoga in the first place. Martel's killers had seen it. "Tell you what. You take cabs wherever you want to go, and I'll reimburse you." Might as well put his trust fund money to good use.

"Cab drivers don't always want to load up pipe fittings in their trunk."

"Beady, I can't give you the Saratoga. Let's just say it's in quarantine until Willie's killing gets solved."

"Hmmph."

Someday he was going to push that old man too far.

After dinner, he returned to his apartment and phoned Betty Gottschalk.

"Lou Lattimore called me and told me you would be calling." A long grievous sigh came over the phone line. "Come by at eight-thirty, after I get my husband to bed."

Weather wished Lou had not called Mrs. Gottschalk. He wanted to assess her raw reactions to his questions. Oh, well.

At eight-fifteen, he drove over to a dollhouse of a Swiss chalet on La Vista.

"I can't imagine why you are asking anything about that robbery now unless you really believe that stolen money is still around, and honestly, Mr. Weather, I would have given you more credit, you being a former prosecutor. Some silly rumor about Willie Peabody looking for it, my word, you should know better." Mrs. Betty Gottschalk nodded curtly as she poured hot tea into china cups. Limoges, she made a point of telling him. The immaculate floral parlor where this ritual took place was jammed with furniture. The dining room had been converted to a sickroom for the crippled husband, Mrs. Gottschalk had explained when Weather first arrived. The undersized arm chair he now occupied fit in a corner maybe eight inches from the coffee table, forcing him to sit with his knees in his chin. Mrs. Gottschalk appeared indifferent to his discomfort. She wore a black dress with white lace collar, had dark hair streaked with gray, and a mean scrunch in her tiny features.

"So where do you think the stolen bank money is, Mr. Weather?" She assessed him with darting eyes.

"I don't necessarily think the money is anywhere. In fact, I believe it burned up in the fire. I just wanted to ask you about the two girls who worked for you. Marie Chantilly and Celeste Carré."

She stiffened. "I wouldn't put anything past those girls. Little things, living with Mama and Daddy until they got married, spending all their money on hats and dresses, as if the country wasn't in the biggest financial mess it had ever seen. And there I was, having to support a crippled husband." She broadcast the last sentence toward the sickroom.

"Ma'am, these girls were from New Orleans. They didn't live with parents. They paid rent at a boarding house."

"Why, of course. I had them confused with some other girls who were there before. Locals. I remember the little French girls now; they stayed someplace near downtown. Well, what about them?"

"You told Lou Lattimore you thought either Marie or Celeste was embezzling. A separate crime. I wanted to hear why you thought that."

"Embezzling! I never told her that. Lou doesn't remember right. I've always thought the girls were partners in the armed robbery. Both of them left immediately after the trial, just didn't show up for work. We chalked it up to jitters from the robbery. Didn't either one of them do half their jobs before, and after, they didn't do even half of the half. We had to keep them on so they could testify, but I tell you, I was tired of doing their work!"

"We?"

"What?"

"You said, 'We chalked it up to jitters.' "

"Oh, yes, 'we.' Mr. Curtis and I. But privately I wondered. That guard's widow made such a stink about her husband's 'innocence.' Ha! He had guilt written all over him, shifty-eyed, surly to me. To me! And I was the head teller!"

"Er, ma'am, let's go back to Marie Chantilly and Celeste Carré for a minute." Just treat her like a derailed witness and get her back on the track.

"What about them?" Betty Gottschalk stared into her teacup.

"If they were so incompetent, or untrustworthy, why did you hire them?"

She stood, tray in hand. "I didn't. Mr. Curtis did."

"Instead of locals? In the Depression? And why girls, instead of men? Women didn't always work back then, yourself excluded due to special circumstances, of course."

"Well, he had an eye for the ladies, I guess. Local parents knew and wouldn't let their girls work there. And as for girls instead of men, that was partly me. Most men won't report to a woman, and I wasn't about to encourage Charles to hire someone who might go after my job. A little bit of womanizing didn't bother me. Those girls weren't innocents, if you know what I mean." She gave him a challenging look. "I suppose you think that awful of me."

"No, ma'am, I don't." He hadn't thought much at all about how a woman like her held on to a job. Her machinations, although not admirable, were no worse than any he'd seen among men. "Tell me about Mr. Curtis."

She shrugged. "I don't know what I can tell you about him. He left. Sold out and moved away. I had quite a time keeping my job after, but I did."

"Where did Mr. Curtis go?"

"Tulsa, I believe. He started up a new business, a shipping company that took him all over the Midwest, but around '33 or '34, he and his whole family got into a bad wreck. All of them except him got killed. It broke him, I heard. Mentally and physically. Put him in a wheelchair. Don't I know how trying that can be. He came to Dallas during the war, dropped by the bank to see me. He looked terrible. Shriveled and haggard. Kept a lap rug over his legs, poor man. He said he'd left Tulsa, but I don't remember if he said where he'd moved to. I gathered it was a rest home. If he's still alive, I'd be surprised." She pointed toward her husband's room. "It's time for his pills. I think I've told you about everything I know about that robbery. If there's nothing else?" Betty Gottschalk took Weather's cup and saucer off his knee without asking.

Weather rose. "One last, quick question, ma'am. Who was the other guard? The one who was out sick with pneumonia when the substitute got killed."

"The other guard?" She put her fingers on her throat. "I don't recall another guard at all. Only Hiram."

At the Claypoole, Weather jotted down notes about his meeting and compared them to his earlier notes from Creevy's file. An auditor had been at the bank. Maybe for a routine review, maybe for a special investigation. Mrs. Gottschalk was a compulsive gossip, the sort that used lies and truth equally to hurt others or aggrandize themselves. Probably Lou Lattimore remembered correctly, and Betty Gottschalk did accuse the girls of embezzlement back in 1930. Tonight she'd claimed locals were working there at the time, then she acknowledged the New Orleans girls and said she'd always believed they were in on the robbery. Was she feigning bad memory to cover up something else?

At her job, Betty Gottschalk milked dry her martyred breadwinner image, but tonight she looked expensive, too expensive for a home where medical bills ate up the budget.

Maybe she had family money. Or grown children to help out.

Or another source of funds.

Maybe she was the embezzler, and she hired out-of-towners to keep suspicion off her.

But Curtis hired the girls.

Wait. Betty Gottschalk *said* Curtis hired the girls.

One thing was clear. He needed to talk to those girls, to the auditor, and to Curtis, the bank president, who was probably dead by now.

Or so said Betty Gottschalk. Maybe she wanted to keep Weather from searching the man out.

If the injured Mr. Curtis were alive, what would he say about his former head teller?

Weather telephoned Creevy from his busted den. Ought to get the place cleaned up.

"Hey, old son," Creevy said. "I found your pneumonia-sick guard. You were right; he was in Parkland when young Bledsoe took that bank. Wasn't Fred Atterly, though. Man by the name of Cecil Allgood, you might not have heard of him, he made his name around the courts while you was off at law school."

"I don't know him."

"Worked for Martin Hubert and Willie both. Switched back and forth between, 'til didn't neither one of them trust him. Did a couple of years for burglary, '34 and '35. Didn't neither Willie or Hubert try to get him off. Once Allgood got out of prison, he broke his parole and supposedly went up north. I got feelers out, but these things take time."

"Is this 'up north' Chicago, by any chance?"

"I just don't know. Like I said, I got feelers out. They just ain't felt nothing yet." Creevy chuckled at his own wit. The noise started low, like throat clearing, but revved 'til it idled high at a rolling growl.

Weather grinned. "We gotta do that dinner soon, fat man."

"On you, don't forget."

"On me. But listen, about this bank robbery." He told the investigator about his visits to witnesses, about Betty

Gottschalk's insistence on the young tellers' guilt.

"Son, you got too many loose threads. Now what I suggest is, you take all this investigating and postulating to them that has the right to investigate and postulate."

"Hadley."

"Hell no, Orton. Isn't Willie's killing his jurisdiction? If any of this has anything to do with Willie, he ought to know."

"Yeah, but Hadley's partner got killed in that old bank robbery, so I see Hadley as needing to know, too. Tell you what. I'll tell them both and let them slug it out. One more thing. Will you put out those feelers for a man named Santos Delgado? He was thirteen or a little older in Travis County in 1913."

"Thirteen in '13, would make him about forty-seven in '47, now, wouldn't it? Who's he and what does he have to do with this?"

Weather told him about Roma's first baby, and the probable father of the child. "He might want to know she's dying. He might not."

There was a silence on the line. Finally, Creevy said, "Yeah. I'll hunt the guy down. You not going soft on me now, are you? Messing around finding long-lost lovers, sounds like you losing your edge. You got to get over your daddy, son."

"Yeah, yeah," he said, but Creevy had already hung up.

Weather phoned his mother, to tell her about the search for Santos, and agreed to meet her at Roma's the next morning. Charlotte recommended he not mention the search unless Santos was located and wanted to make contact. He agreed. After he hung up, he started to phone Hadley and then the sheriff, but decided to wait 'til morning. He was exhausted and wasn't sure he could make sense of what he'd learned. And he'd promised the bank guard's widow that he would not send the cops out to visit her.

Chapter 37

Thursday, April 24

A long sleep might have been good for the body, but it did nothing for Weather's guilt regarding Roma Bain's dying wish to see her daughter. He still had not located Belinda, had not even tried too hard. At least he had given her Willie's warning. If she didn't act on it, it was her own fault. She was safer out of town. Far out of town. He looked at the clock. He'd told his mother he would meet her at Roma's at eight, and the clock on his night table said eight.

Skipping breakfast, he scooped up the morning papers and headed out.

Jane watched Hadley arrive at Jill's door. Jill had on jeans and a cowgirl shirt and greeted him with a familiar hug. The detective pushed her away and spoke to her. Jill's face fell. Hadley pushed her into her room and they shut the door. What were they talking about? What did this mean besides the obvious? Was Hadley on the take with these gangsters, or on some maverick personal hunt for that bank money everybody was talking about? She ought to call David and tell him, but she knew he would try to pull her out of the game. It had been a mistake to phone him at the D.A.'s yesterday. Besides, Hadley already knew she was here. If he meant her any harm, or considered her a danger to his plans, he would have blown her cover that night at the jail, wouldn't he? She didn't know. The only thing she knew for sure was she couldn't trust the detective. She needed to find out who killed Willie and get out. Albert had let it slip that a big game was on for that night. She needed to get into that card game.

Charlotte Craft Weather Hilyard put her finger to her lips when Weather slipped into the sickroom, but Roma opened her eyes.

"I haven't located Belinda yet, Miss Bain," Weather said.

Roma gave him a puzzled look. "Oh, but she was here last night. Came with Tom, stood right there by my bed." Roma pointed to a spot. "She looked just like a ragamuffin, my little girl. You remember how tangled her hair used to get, Tom?"

Weather and Charlotte exchanged glances.

"Tom? Don't you remember? Tom?" Roma grimaced in pain. Charlotte adjusted the IV drip and Roma's eyes soon lost their focus. After a while, in a low, feathery voice, she said, "I want to go outside and run in the bluebonnets."

"Of course, dear," Charlotte said. "Aren't they pretty? They're wildflowers, you know." His mother draped a damp cloth on Roma's forehead, and Weather turned away, swallowing hard. Watching the dying could knock a man down. How did women tend them for days, sometimes weeks, on end?

"Me and Belinda go out and run in the bluebonnets every April, you know."

"I know, darling. We'll go soon. When Belinda gets here. When Belinda gets here."

"She already come last night, maybe she won't come again."

Charlotte wiped a tear from her eye and smiled over at Weather.

Disturbed, Weather took his newspapers in the kitchen and poured himself a cup of Charlotte's coffee. He unfolded the *Beacon* and sat down at the rickety table.

Bank Teller, Husband Slain
Burglary Suspected

The bodies of a popular bank teller and her crippled husband were found in their home Thursday morning by a neighbor. George and Betty Gottschalk of 10931 La Vista were bludgeoned to death in an apparent burglary in this quiet Lakewood neighborhood.

Weather sat up fast. Were other witnesses from the old bank robbery lying dead in their homes, undiscovered? He ran to the sickroom. "Mother, I have to go now." He showed her the paper and left without explaining further.

Mrs. Hiram Spring came out on the porch of her house on Canada Drive as if she had been waiting for him.

"You lying son of a bitch, you send that blond reporter around yesterday after you swore you wouldn't talk to nobody, but I didn't give him a thing but the front end of my shotgun, which I ought to take out after you. You shoulda seen that jackrabbit run back to his car."

"Mrs. Spring, I didn't send him, and I have some bad news to tell you." He told her about Mrs. Gottschalk, and she cursed him even harder about danger to her family, but turned grand dame in a hurry when he offered to put her and her grandchildren up at the Stanley Hotel downtown.

"At least till I'm sure you're not in danger."

"I want my daughter to go, too. And her boyfriend."

Weather agreed, and as he helped load ragtag suitcases and smelly children into the truck, he wished he'd offered lesser lodgings, where the family could blend with their surroundings better. At the hotel, he told the clerk the group were witnesses in an important trial, and bribed the clerk twenty bucks to get keys to a suite. He left them with assurances that he would pay any room service tab they ran up, and ushered the family upstairs. He made the Springs promise not leave their room, in case the killers had scouts in the lobby.

From the hotel, he phoned Lou Lattimore. "I'm not worried," she said, sounding worried. After some argument, she promised him she would go stay with her sister in Waco for a few days. Before he hung up, she asked him what a reporter was doing asking her about the robbery after Weather had sworn her to secrecy. Jemison again. Had the reporter followed him to Betty Gottschalk's as well?

"Muckrakers need to rake muck," he replied.

From the phone booth, he called and left a message for Hadley at the police station. Back in Beady's truck, his nerves boiled over into bad driving and he almost ran a red light.

Someone besides Jemison must have followed him around yesterday. But if so, why not kill all the witnesses last night? Because they weren't the loose thread. Betty Gottschalk was.

Was all the killing done? Someone followed him yesterday. Maybe they were following him today, too. He checked his rear view mirror. Nothing suspicious.

Had anyone followed him to Roma's this morning?

He'd left his own mother over there, unprotected. She didn't even have a phone. Would the killers go after Roma, or Charlotte? Logic told him they would not, but he nevertheless drove into West Dallas at speeds Beady's truck threatened not to survive.

He found his mother sitting calmly at the sickbed, wiping Roma's face with a rag.

"Well, for gosh sake," Charlotte said after his brief explanation. "Lead me away then. Just let me get the woman from next door."

Roma Bain smiled up at him from the pillow. "You tell my gal she's got to stay longer next time, you hear?"

He promised her he would.

Chapter 38

He followed his mother as far as Wycliffe, then drove downtown, where he parked in his old parking garage and sprinted the two blocks over to the Criminal Courts Building. On the sixth floor, several eyebrows popped at the sight of the banished Rascal on the premises, D.A. Morson's most of all, when the fallen prosecutor burst past Ina Rae into the inner sanctum.

"Get Creevy," Weather said from the connecting doorway.

Ina Rae's iron coif rose in objection to being ordered about by the Ousted, but she nodded obediently enough when the D.A. flicked a finger.

Creevy arrived and shut the door.

"I hope this is important, Mr. Weather." At his oak desk, the D.A. put his long tapering fingers together in an outward V. A benign-looking gesture, but in Morson-ese, it was a pointed gun, and Weather was the target. Embarrassing the D.A. had long-term effects and would never be forgiven.

He poured out his story to the two men.

Morson did not move a muscle in that commanding face the whole time he listened, and when he spoke, his voice seemed to come from behind him, or outside of him, noncorporeal, unearthly, what you'd expect from the voice of God. In fact, his whole silvery appearance could have come right out of the heavens.

"You think someone followed you last night? Besides that

son of a bitch Jemison, I mean," God intoned.

"They must have. Someone knew Betty talked to me and it got her killed."

"Unless it was the other way around," God spoke.

"What do you mean?"

"Maybe Betty talked to somebody after you left, and that got her killed. It would explain why your other witnesses were unharmed. Creevy, how about you call the phone company and see if Mrs. Gottschalk made any calls."

After Creevy left, Weather sat uncomfortably in Morson's office while the D.A. reviewed papers and ignored him. Weather was still the Rascal, a mere visitor in the inner circle, no longer a tenant, his leave of absence an insubstantial sham designed for public perception. Weather had offered his resignation before, in the middle of a noisy scandal, and Morson had refused it then for the sake of his office's image. After the Willie Peabody mess passed by, Morson would likely accept it. Weather looked at the top of the D.A.'s head, at the thick silvery hair, and mourned. Working for the D.A. had been his life's goal and he'd thrown it away.

Fifteen minutes passed before Creevy returned. "My operator friend will get back to me about Betty Gottschalk's phone calls," the investigator said. "I miss anything?"

Morson looked up, now that someone legitimate was in the room. "Not a thing."

"Good. I got a couple lines on those bank tellers."

Weather shook off his misery. "Marie Chantilly and Celeste Carré! Where are they?"

"They don't seem to be nowhere, now, which is kind of strange. I found this Catholic orphanage in New Orleans where they grew up. No family to speak of, so nobody to miss them. Marie had a fiancé down there, but he said he got a letter breaking it off. He couldn't recollect exactly when, but it sounded like it was about the time of the bank robbery. Her letter said he wouldn't amount to much and she'd found somebody new in Dallas. Whoever the new somebody was, she didn't marry him, not in Dallas County. Nor in any county in a fifty-mile radius. Nor in New Orleans. No marriage record around here for the other one, either. Course, Marie and her new man might've busted up, and the girls could've both gone to Timbuktu together."

"Did Marie tell her fiancé the new boyfriend's name?"

"No, she didn't. The jilted lover said he would of killed the guy and she knew not to give out a name."

"So how might the girls' disappearance from the area tie in to the robbery?" Morson asked.

The three of them sat in the D.A.'s office for a long time, discussing possibilities. Mid-afternoon, Creevy's contact at the phone company called back.

After Creevy reported what she said, Weather didn't feel so bad about Betty Gottschalk getting murdered anymore.

Carl Ray finished tilling some more of that garden and went back to the barn. Gonna be dark soon. Burr was in the house yelling at Bonnie and Stevie both.

"You can't do that!" Bonnie was screaming.

"Woman, don't ever tell me what I can and can't do." Burr yelled so loud it made Stevie start howling; Carl Ray could hear him all the way out here. There was a big slap, and the kid howled some more, then Bonnie did some slapping, little bitty pops that he knew would just make Burr laugh. Carl Ray gripped the hoe handle and wondered what he could do. Go in and attack Burr? Ha! Then Bonnie would side with her husband and send him back to the juvenile farm and Stevie to the orphan home.

Still, he was supposed to at least take care of Stevie. He listened, trying to decide. Bonnie yelled some more and so did Burr and then there was some more slapping, Burr doing it this time, loud cracks and pained yells from Bonnie, nothing that sounded too bad from either one of them, and then one big hard sound, then it got quiet. Burr never really had to beat anybody up, 'cause when he got mad enough to slap anybody around, their own good sense made them shut up and give him his way and it never went any further.

The place stayed quiet a good ten minutes, so Carl Ray figured the argument was over and Burr won. He always did.

Burr came out the back door, smacking his hands back and forth together like he was dusting them off. "Hey, Carl Ray."

"Hey, Burr."

"Come on down to the cabin with me, bring your smokes."

Carl Ray didn't much want to go, but couldn't tell Burr no without setting him off. Burr was acting friendly, like nothing happened. Only he had that look in his eye. Carl Ray reached down in his overall pocket and opened up Big Ray's knife, one-handed, just in case.

Couldn't hear a thing out of the house.

They rode to the lake in Burr's new pickup truck, because Burr was too lazy to walk. Carl Ray shifted in the seat and eyed the canvas in the truckbed. What was this crazy man up to? They got to the cabin and Burr stopped.

"Let's go sit on the dock," Burr said. Still friendly, but still with that staring look. Pop-eyed.

After they got settled out there and got cigarettes lit, Burr spoke up.

"You and me. We hadn't always got along."

"Nossir." Carl Ray wanted to jump up and run, but he was on the lake side and he knew Burr would grab at his legs when he tried to get by. He could swim, but the lake would be cold, and besides, he knew what was in it. However, if he had to swim in it to save his own life, he would.

"You listening to me, son?"

"Oh, yessir."

"Didn't think you was. Looked like you was thinking about something else. Looked like you was ignoring me."

"Nossir."

"Well, like I was saying, you and me ain't always got along."

"I guess not."

"We ought to, though, being as how we're family."

"Yessir."

"Laidlaw is family, and he seems to want to shut me out. He accused me of killing Willie. Now why would he think I'd do a thing like that when Willie was my meal ticket?"

"Maybe he killed his own daddy, and he wants to throw off the scent. Or he can't face up to it, so he's casting blame all around." Carl Ray could barely breathe.

"You know, I never thought of that!" Burr's pop-eyed stare faded from storm gray to plain rain. He slapped his leg and laughed. "Now that makes it all right then. Makes it *all* all right."

Carl Ray looked out at the lake. Wasn't nothing all right.

Burr laughed some more, and then he said, "Course, your Aunt Bonnie don't see it that way. That's why I had to do what I done."

A tightness clawed at Carl Ray's throat. "What'd you do?"

Burr ignored his question. "Now you and me, we're going to go out tonight, and seek a little justice. Let's go." His uncle stood up.

"Burr? What'd you do to them?"

"Nothing they didn't have coming. Now let's go."

Back at the house, nobody was around. Carl Ray wanted to see Stevie sitting on the back steps, sniffling and feeling sorry for himself.

"Go put on some city clothes. You get a night out on the town, you can't look like no bumpkin."

Burr grabbed his arm and wrangled him up the steps and across the porch into the kitchen. Bonnie wasn't in there. Burr slung him into the hallway. The door to Carl Ray and Stevie's room was open, but Stevie wasn't in there. Burr and Bonnie's door was shut. Carl Ray heard a whimpering noise. Maybe it was that damn dog under the house.

"Where's Bonnie and Stevie?"

"Don't you worry about them, they're taking a nap." Burr shoved a thumb toward the closed door. The whimpering was coming out of the room. It sounded the same as what came out of that canvas roll the night Burr rowed out to the middle of the lake.

"Burr, what'd you do?"

"Go get showered and changed." Burr pushed Carl Ray toward the bathroom, then stood guard in front of his and Bonnie's door with his arms folded.

Carl Ray got his things together and took them in the bathroom. The shower was plenty hot, but never did take the chill off him. He finished up and dried off. After he dressed, he stuck Big Ray's open pocketknife up his shirt sleeve. When he got out in the hall, Burr was still standing there, leaning on the door.

"Let me see them."

"Naw."

"Then I ain't going with you."

Burr put on a gee-whiz look, like whatever he'd done was normal, and Carl Ray ought not be doubting his actions. "They ain't really hurt that bad."

"Let me see them!" Carl Ray must've sounded tougher than he felt, because Burr opened the door. "All right, but this is to let you know I'm serious. You do what I say and they'll be all right."

Stevie and Bonnie were tied up back-to-back on the floor. Stevie was attached to Bonnie's back like some Indian papoose, only the baby was so fat it pulled the mama down on the ground. Bonnie had blood all in one eye and her head rolled around like Burr had slapped her silly. They both had gags on. Stevie cried hard enough to choke himself.

"I had to knock their heads together and tie them up. I didn't want it to be this way, but she didn't leave me no choice."

"Burr, this ain't right." Carl Ray stepped over to Stevie and pulled the gag off. The kid made big gasping noises, then started bawling loud.

Burr went over to the kid and grabbed him by the hair. "Shut up. You can holler all you want once we're gone, but I don't want to hear another peep out of you while I'm here."

Stevie shut up.

"You wouldn't be tied up at all if your aunt didn't get on her high horse about men's business." Burr gave Stevie's hair one last long pull, then let go. Stevie stayed shut up.

"What business, Burr?" Carl Ray felt the knife in his sleeve.

"Gonna settle some scores. Once and for all, that's all. Take care of some business that's been a long time coming. After it's done, I'll come back and let them go."

Burr had that lying sound in his voice.

Carl Ray pushed Burr aside and bent over Bonnie. Sure was an awful lot of knots in them ropes. Blood oozed from her wrists and turned the rope pink in places. She gave him a pleading look, or maybe she was just woozy. He looked back at Burr, who was leaning in the doorway.

His uncle shrugged like you tied up your wife and step-kid every day. Men's business. "Well, don't just stand there. Faster we take care of this, faster they can get loose."

Carl Ray put his back to Burr and knelt down by the captives. "Burr's right, Aunt Bonnie, you gotta understand men's business." He made some smart-ass tsk-tsk sounds to fool Burr while he shook Big Ray's pocketknife out of his sleeve into Bonnie's hand, tucking it around back a little where Burr wouldn't see it unless he was really looking. If she could wake up enough, she should have enough sense to know what to do with it. She closed her fingers around it. Carl Ray pulled her gag off and put it in her hands, to help hide that knife some more. She breathed better but still just muttered and mumbled. He couldn't tell if she was awake or not. He bent closer and whispered. "Can't nobody help you anyway, not no lawmen. You remember what we talked about, about who owes you."

Her eyes just flicked up and down.

Burr kicked at the door frame. "Come on. Time's a'wasting."

Carl Ray followed Burr out to the truck. "Women sure can be stupid sometimes," he said, acting like he'd gone along with Burr.

"Don't you try to fool me, boy. I heard you whisper to her. What did you mean, 'who owes you'? What the hell were you talking about?"

Carl Ray froze. "She owes us. The right to be men, I mean."

Burr seemed too irritated to try to work out if he bought that explanation or not. What a dumb sucker he was, really. Attention span of a cow. Carl Ray got in the truck with him, wondering what kind of nutcase crap Burr'd come up with now.

A few minutes later, his uncle backed the truck up to the arch of the Cliff Heights courtyard, and wedged it in sort of sideways so nobody else could get through. Carl Ray followed him outside to around the back of the truck.

"You remember that bomb you built at Krueger Pants," Burr asked.

"Yeah."

"You gone make a bigger one now."

Carl Ray felt like he was going to puke. He'd just got control of himself again when a man with a stocking over his head came out from behind a big pot. The man held a shotgun.

"What's the matter, boy, you never seen a shotgun before?" The other guy snickered along with Burr, then Burr leaned into the pickup bed and pulled the canvas back. There was a Tommy gun lying across bags of ammonia nitric and sticks of dynamite. Burr handed the Tommy gun to the man in the stocking mask.

"Carl Ray, you climb up in there and hand me down that stuff. You yell or try to run off and we'll have to shoot. I don't want to see that happen, but it could if you don't behave. If I have to shoot you, I have to shoot your Aunt Bonnie, too, and your little brother."

Carl Ray looked over at the other man with the stocking pulled over his face. He thought he knew him, in spite of that stupid mask. Yep, it was a lawman he knew. Damn, every one of them was crooked.

Burr pointed Carl Ray toward the truckbed. "Now, get this thing unloaded so you can get to work on your little project."

"Hey, I lucked into that bomb, Burr. Don't remember what I did to make it go off." Said it offhand, like it wasn't his fault for being so dumb.

"You better luck up again, then," Burr said, and motioned toward the pickup bed. "I want a lot of bang for my buck."

Carl Ray looked around. If he ran, he'd be out on Sylvan with a lot of open road, an easy target for them Tommy guns. With a sigh, he climbed into the back of the truck. While he worked, he sneaked a look at the two of them standing by the planter whispering.

"Cartledge, I told you the boy was a bad risk," the other fellow said.

"I got the little bastard under control. Got me some insurance back at the house."

Carl Ray stacked bag after bag onto the sidewalk by that planter. When he was done, he'd laid out sixteen bags of ammonia nitric and forty-two sticks of dynamite. He wondered where Burr got the dynamite. Probably stole it off a construction site.

"Burr, you idiot. This is some kind of overkill. We need to grab and run, not hang around here setting this all up." The partner waved the shotgun at the stack.

"It's okay. I already been putting some of this nitrate up in them top rooms every day since Wednesday. And I got a big stack in the basement, hid under a tarpaulin." Burr tapped his foot on the courtyard, like that was where the tarpaulin was. "Must be a couple hundred or more all around already. I just got the dynamite today. I figure I can build me a chain reaction fuse somehow."

"Huh. You planning to explode the whole town, man?"

Carl Ray watched Burr's eyes get all big and satisfied.

"Uh, Burr," Carl Ray said. "If you got dynamite, you don't really need me. I mean, you can just light it and you got your explosion."

Burr trained them silver blue eyes on him. "No, son. I do need you. You got a special part to play tonight, a part can't nobody else play."

Carl Ray's blood chilled, all the way to his bones.

265

★ ★ ★ ★ ★

Jane sat in the evening gown Albert had bought her, a silk scarf draped over the cast, smiling, serving drinks when asked, being quiet so as not to distract the gamblers with her rasping voice. This afternoon she had told Albert she knew about the game, had sugar-talked him into letting her in. Albert had taken her out shopping for the dress. He'd been so sweet, picking out a scarf to wrap around the cast.

She almost wished she hadn't pressed Albert to let her down here. The place stank, like mold or fertilizer. One little electric fan buzzed with the power and annoyance of a housefly. Behind her, the cavernous room stretched into dark crevices in solid rock. Tarpaulins covered bags of something in the furthest recesses. Claustrophobia and nausea rolled over her in competing waves. She willed them both down, especially the nausea. With the wired jaw, she could not be sick. She put her face in the fan and begged her stomach to settle.

Lavonne sat with her on the divan, smoking cigarettes through a long holder, like she was Tallulah Bankhead. Miss Vamp kept her nose up and feigned indifference to Jane's presence. The other one, Sharon, had the night off, since "Connie" was there. Wild Jill Cody shot eye-daggers at her, to which Jane lifted her chin. If these women wanted a bitch war, they could have one. Just wait 'til their names showed up in the paper. Somehow that bit of resolve knocked the queasiness out of her. Jane smiled around at everyone, like she was the hostess.

Albert was the only one who smiled back. He and Cab watched the stairs from twin settees. Upstairs, Ronnie stood post in Sharon and Lavonne's room, over the open trap door. The tall man with the cane—the one Cab called Baron—sat at the round table with six other men. High rollers. Four

266

more tables behind her near the rock stood empty.

The game had been on for about an hour. It could go for four hours or twenty-four. Thousands of dollars lay on the table.

Ronnie's head appeared in the ceiling opening. "Guest." A pair of well-tailored pants legs appeared on the stairs. One hairy, ringed hand gripped the railing, the other held cash. Lots of it. The newcomer's head descended from the ceiling square. Oh, dear God. Mac Porter.

"Look here, Baron. Here's what I owe, and a stake for tonight's game," Troy's father said. Jane shrank, hoping he would not remember her. She'd been much more bruised, her head in bandages, her hair longer.

Mac Porter stopped at the foot of the stair, gaping at her. "What in the hell is that lady reporter doing here? That's Jane Alder from the *Beacon*!"

She guessed he remembered.

Chapter 39

Curious faces turned toward her. Cab craned his neck with the same menace he'd shown when he stuck his ugly face in her window. Albert went from dumbfounded to murderous in the time it takes to sneeze. Jill let out an I-knew-it snort and glanced warily at the baron. Lavonne stared with a silly grin on her face, like things were finally going to get interesting.

The baron drew an unlit cigar across his upper lip, sniffing and smiling.

"Aw, Mac, you always did like to joke around," the old man said with a chuckle. "Cab, Albert, take the lady on out of here and let the big boys play. You want in, Mac, you can't pull these dirty tricks trying to disturb your opponents, break their concentration." He sounded reasonable and affable, like Falvey, only a bit more patronizing, but after he spoke, he shot her a narrow-eyed look and jerked his head at Cab. In that single motion, Jane knew she'd seen her death sentence handed down.

As one, Cab and Albert grabbed her by the elbows and escorted her into a middle room. The kitchen she'd seen before lay through a doorway beyond.

Jill followed, her eyes big as silver dollars. "Honey, I'm sorry, I really am. You brought it on yourself, though."

Cab shut the door, but someone shoved at it from the game room. Mac Porter slipped in. He looked scared and sick. "Now come on, guys. I mistook her for somebody else. She ain't the one I was thinking of. I don't know this girl."

"Mac, we float you too many times for you to have any say here." Cab pushed Mac back out and closed the door.

Wild Jill went to Cab and curled herself onto his arm. "Now fellas," she said. "We can get this sorted out later. Just tie her up or something, and don't jinx the game. Those men in there are rich men, used to fine treatment. They ain't going to want no part of this." She lowered her voice to a whisper. "Not of murder."

Cab shrugged Jill off him. "Well maybe they don't got no choice no more, either. Got too many witnesses already. Might have to take care of them, too."

"You are not going to take care of them. Those men are the golden goose. This, this is too silly. Reporters try to sneak in to games all the time. It's not that big a deal."

"It is to the baron. He don't like witnesses. Now you better decide quick which side you on, witness."

Jill gave Jane a helpless look and stood by Cab. *I tried, but I'm not risking my life for yours,* her stance said.

Cab tucked his pistol into his waistband and pulled a switchblade out of his jacket. "Let's take her up into one of the rooms and have a little fun first."

Jane sought Jill's eye to regain her allegiance, but the dancer had turned away. Albert still looked stunned and angry. No one would or could save her here. To survive, she would have to get to that fake wall, find the lever if there was one, push it, slip through, shut it. All with two armed men beside her. All while wearing a billowing evening gown and high heels.

It wasn't possible.

But her death this night wasn't possible either. It couldn't be.

Could not, could not, could not. Her blood thumped hard in her veins. Her muscles tensed, denying the evening's likely outcome, willing her to run. She sprang for the kitchen, but Albert still held her arm. He tightened his grip, and shoved her down into a tangle of satin and fear at his feet. His thumb, almost in her armpit, pinched a nerve that made her whole arm go dead. A sign of the future. Everything that lived, that wanted to live, would die. How incredibly wrong. Her throat tightened, and the nausea returned. No, she was angry. Angry. Angry. The nausea waned. She shot up, aiming her plaster-cast arm at his head.

He intercepted her blow easily, rolled her bulky arm back out of his way. They struggled in an awkward tango, Albert towering above her, leaning over her, pushing her against the wall. She toed off her high heels, hoping for a chance to run. Cab moved closer, grinning dangerously. Then she couldn't see Cab for Albert's body, covering her. It was as if he were shielding her.

"Albert, please," she whimpered, not above begging for her life.

"Yes, Albert, please, listen to how she's begging for it," Cab said.

Albert squeezed her arm—a signal?—and shook his head toward Cab. "I'm the one she's been messing around with. It's my right to deal with her. And I'll do it so those guys out there don't know nothing and nothing will show up in the newspapers. No point in killing a golden goose over her." He nodded toward Jill, then flung Jane onto the floor. She hit the kitchen table with the plaster cast so hard it sent an electric spark along the bone break. Dropping to her knees, she crawled wildly toward the cabinets, feeling for a lever in the semi-darkness. The fluorescent bulb above the sink produced more shadows than light.

Cab came after her, but Albert put his body in the doorway and spread his arms across the frame, crucifix style.

Only crucifixes generally didn't carry .38's in their right hands. "No," he said to Cab. "Go back out and stand guard like you're supposed to."

Somewhere on these cabinets was a button or lever or crank. She told herself to breathe deeply, get calm, stay focused.

Cab and Albert kept arguing. Jill got in the act, wheedling Cab to calm down so the guests wouldn't hear. Light bathed the kitchen. From the main room, the baron opened the door and spoke in a low voice.

"Jill, Cab, get in here."

They obeyed, leaving Jane alone with Albert.

Frantic, Jane looked over the cabinets. How did the passage open from this side?

Albert turned from the doorway. He knelt beside her, pointing the pistol at her. Hurt ravaged his face. "You're a reporter."

"I'm Christina's cousin. That's why I followed you, not because of my job."

Albert's eyes flicked wide. The anger drained out of his face, to be replaced by a sad resignation. He ran a hand over his shaved head. "Christina's—"

An explosion in the main room tore at Jane's eardrums. Lavonne screamed. Men yelled. The door burst open and Cab flew through the middle room, backwards, landing face up on the kitchen floor. Albert shoved Jane flat and covered her. From the game room came gunfire, different from the first blast. A rapid clatter. Machine guns. Together, Jane and Albert looked over at Cab. A large, juicy hole took up most of his chest. All that menace, stopped by one shotgun blast. Jane knew her gunshot wounds. Francy would be proud.

Someone out there yelled for everybody to get on the

floor. Jane recognized the voice from Willie's wake. Burr Cartledge.

Taffeta rustles preceded Wild Jill into the kitchen. She scrambled over Cab's body and came to a halt next to Jane and Albert on the floor. "Robbers," she whispered. She held her abdomen with bloody fingers. A couple more of the card players had escaped as well.

"Jill, where's the spring to the secret passage? Jill? Jill?"

Jill slumped into a bloody heap on the cold floor.

Carl Ray watched Burr's partner blow that guy with the sharp face clean through the doorway into that other room, maybe further. With numbed fingers, Carl Ray loaded the money in the pillowcase like Burr said. This was what Big Ray had done in that bank, and it felt weird to be doing this again. Not "again" really, but sort of. Big Ray was around, somehow. His spirit—no, his influence. His stupid influence. Carl Ray knew he ought to have left town the day Willie died, and he didn't. Stupid. Now he was party to murder and wasn't nobody on this side of the grave going to do a damn thing to help him. And this stupid stocking on his head itched.

Big Ray, what do I do?

The gamblers down on the floor were all quiet, except this one fat guy with a red face. He kept wheezing and begging and was about to get himself shot.

"Shut up, mister." Carl Ray was surprised to hear himself say that to an adult, but he knew Burr's temper better than that old fart did.

"Just take the money and go," another old guy said. He waved a cane around like he was a king.

Burr pointed his Tommy gun at his majesty and let off a few rounds. The old guy dropped back in the chair, with most of his head gone, just like that. A girl on the sofa to the right screamed, and Burr sprayed her, too.

Carl Ray could barely move or breathe. Burr had pulled the stocking off his face, so everybody could see him plain as day. This one woman in the other room looked back for just a second, and Burr sprayed her. She had her hand on her stomach, like it hurt. It was that same black-haired woman he'd seen Burr with at the cabin. The dancing girl. Two of the gamblers followed her.

Burr pointed the machine gun at the pile of men jammed in the opening.

"Laidlaw Peabody, death comes calling," he yelled, and gave out that crazy-man laugh.

"Laidlaw ain't here," Carl Ray whispered. He looked around for Burr's partner. Maybe the guy could talk some sense into Burr, but he'd disappeared up the stairs.

Nobody here but himself and Burr and some scared people trying to get away. Hell and damnation. Burr was going to shoot everybody. And him, too, Carl Ray understood, then Bonnie and Stevie and Laidlaw after.

This was it. This was the Last Ride.

It was now, whether he was ready or not. It decided when, not Carl Ray. Now, now, now, went Burr's gun on the wall over the men's heads. Mean bastard was gonna scare them first, then kill them.

Now, now, now. Burr shot up near the ceiling. "Laidlaw, where the hell are you?" He shook his fists toward the ceiling. "Son of a bitch was supposed to be here. I told him to be here."

Carl Ray felt the Tommy gun in his own hands. He'd never killed a man before.

Big Ray had.

That was different. Big Ray had done a robbery. Big

Ray killed out of wrong.

He had to kill out of right.

Carl Ray raised his weapon up to Burr and pressed the trigger. Damn thing kicked him backwards onto that dead girl. He jumped up in a hurry.

His uncle stopped punching the air and came over. He gave a little head wag. "Son, you shooting blanks. You really think I'd trust you with live ammo?"

Carl Ray kicked Burr in the stomach and ran for the stairs. Halfway up, he met Burr's partner. The guy kicked him back down. Carl Ray landed on his tailbone and thought it might have cracked. Some of the card players were trying to get through the door to the other room. Burr turned his gun on them and pulled the trigger. They yelled and jerked and flopped, and then they were just a pile of dead men. Two seconds. Four maybe.

Burr motioned to the bodies. "Collect up their wallets. Rings and pocketknives, too." Burr grabbed up money off the floor where it had fallen when the table broke and stuffed it into a second pillowcase.

Carl Ray dug around in the dead guys' pockets, hating the blood slime that got on his hands, and put the loot into his pillowcase. He let one knife fall short of the bag, on the floor. Not that it would do any good, but he felt better, knowing it was there. He looked all around. No windows, this was some kind of basement. While he was rooting through pockets at that pile of dead men, he reached up and turned the door knob. It was locked. The other people done locked themselves in. He wished he could get in there with them, but wouldn't none of them be happy to see him anyway, him being one of the robbers.

"Go on in there if you want," Burr said. "Ain't but one way out, and it's about to be on fire." He pulled out some ammonia nitric bags from under the stairs and cut one open. He poured it out in little trails, like he was trying to get some birds to follow him, and then the partner handed him down a can of gasoline. Burr took that over to a tarpaulin back in the center of the cliff and lifted the tarp up and poured gas on the bags he had under there. He poured a gasoline trail to the divan, with the dead girl on it, and he soaked them both. He stepped behind the divan and struck a match to his gasoline trail and it went both ways at once, to the pile of bags, and to the divan with the dead girl on it. Burr hauled out from behind there and shinnied up the stairs like some zoo monkey with his tail on fire.

Last thing Burr did before he climbed up through that hole was to throw Carl Ray's Tommy gun down. "This is the weapon you used to kill all these people before your gun jammed. Then you went crazy and set the place on fire. You been over here every night, setting out bags of this nitrate. You killed your own brother and your aunt and your cousin Laidlaw, too. I always did say you was a crazy sumbitch. Cracked in the head like your mama."

The trap door slapped shut and some kind of bolt snapped. Up in that room, they dragged something heavy on top of it. Up there, he could hear Burr yell through the ceiling, "See you in hell, you dumb sucker."

Carl Ray pulled the stocking off his head and coughed. The gasoline trail had burned right over to that big pile of nitric in the middle of the cliff. He climbed over the bodies at the door to the other room. His eyes watered bad and there was an ammonia smell in the room.

"Hey, anybody! They're gone. The robbers are gone." He beat on the door and screamed but nobody answered. Probably figured he was lying to get them to open the door so he could shoot them.

He fell into a coughing fit that took a while to get control of. The smoke was still kind of thin. He got Burr's tarpaulin off of some rocks behind the divan and pulled it on top of the divan to try to smother the fire. The middle fire needed to be put out too, but this sofa seemed to be getting out of control the fastest.

Maybe the other people were better off back there for now. He ought not try to open that door or the fire might spread faster. The dead girl's legs stuck out underneath the tarpaulin and puffs of smoke came out from around them. His eyes watered bad. If he plugged up all the air in the room, would it put the fires out, or would it help it build up pressure like it did in the *Grandcamp*? He would try to smother it. He grabbed up dead gamblers and pulled off their suitcoats and spread them onto the bigger fires.

He looked wildly from the trapdoor in the ceiling to the side door where that dancing girl had gone. Open either one and he would be feeding the fire with air. He needed to get that trap door open, and get the people to come out quick so he could save them. He needed to do it all fast, before the fire cut through the clothes and the tarp. Wouldn't nobody get out once the fire popped out again.

He pounded on the door for the people to hear him.

Albert shook Jill and got moaning in return.

"I'm a doctor," one of the gamblers said. He tore Jill's dress to look at the wound, then took off his jacket and pressed it to her abdomen. Jill's eyes fluttered.

"The passage," she whispered, pointing toward the cabinets.

Jane followed the line of Jill's finger and picked out a spot. "Try there," Jane said, guiding Albert's arm to the area. He pushed. The cabinet didn't budge. From the middle room, thin wisps of orange smoke came from under the closed door. Albert pressed on several more places, then turned and pushed with his back. His boots squealed along the floor, leaving black marks on the linoleum. Jane felt along the masonry, hoping for a trip lever.

"Damn . . . thing . . . won't . . . move." Tendons flared in Albert's thick neck. In the half light, he looked like an angry demon, frustrated by a foiled escape from hell. The devil was playing another one of his tricks, giving them hope and a blocked exit.

"Hurry up," Mac Porter panted from the darkness. "They set the place on fire. And some of us are hit."

Jane dreaded the talk she would have to have with Resa and Troy and Troy's mother if Mac died. Of course, she would have to survive to have the talk. Nobody was safe yet, and Albert had not granted her a pardon either. Further back, acrid fumes seeped under the door. Someone was beating on the door and yelling for them to come out.

"That's one of the robbers," Mac said. "He must want to make sure we're dead."

"Don't go near that door," Albert commanded.

Albert pressed, kicked, pulled at the woodwork. Jane coughed. If her nose clogged and she panicked with her jaw wired shut, she could suffocate. If they didn't find the trip lever, they could all suffocate.

Chapter 40

"We'll call if we need you," Morson said, and Weather knew the D.A. wouldn't. Weather drove to the Claypoole to continue his independent investigation. Morson could exclude him from official channels, but he couldn't stop him from using his own den telephone. He called Pacific Avenue State Bank president Clayton Barton and got some background on the missing guard, Allgood. He phoned his mother and utilized the ladies' gossip circuit to locate a former tenant of the boarding house where Marie Chantilly and Celeste Carré had stayed. Amazing how fast the female telegraph worked in this town, and how long its memory. Creevy should take lessons. He reviewed Willie's cryptic warning about his killer, not exactly a businessman, and figured he had a good idea who killed Willie, Betty Gottschalk, and her hapless husband. He phoned Hadley, who was out, and he phoned the sheriff, who was also out. He wanted to bring them over here and lay out his theory to both at the same time, so neither one of them could accuse him of messing up the investigation. He would put the meat on the table and let the dogs tear into it equally.

He would show Morson he could solve this case without his approval.

He was about to call Creevy again and lay out what he'd learned when the phone rang. It was Bonnie Bledsoe Cartledge. She gasped out a hysterical tale of bombs and Burr Cartledge and the Cliff Heights Hotel. He hung up and hurried down to the parking lot to Beady's truck, wondering if he should still call Creevy, wondering if Bonnie Cartledge had set him up to avenge her brother.

Weather cursed the idiot who had blocked the arch to the Cliff Heights Hotel courtyard. That truck was worse than Beady's.

Distrusting Beady's brakes on the steep hill, he backed down onto Sylvan and maneuvered the old Chevy onto the sidewalk and against a stone wall so it wouldn't roll. He walked back up the hill, still cursing.

Bonnie Cartledge had claimed her husband tied her up and kidnapped her nephew. Not likely. Burr was going to blow up a card game in the basement of the Cliff Heights Hotel, she'd said. She didn't trust Weather, she'd said, but she didn't trust any lawmen either. She picked him because he'd stuck up for Carl Ray in the Red Cross, because he'd said he wanted to help him.

Her story, her motives, sounded preposterous, but then, criminal intentions often did.

He wasn't sure what his role ought to be in rescuing a juvenile delinquent who hated him, but he knew it would bother him forever if he didn't try. And he guessed the Peabody clan would have one last long laugh at the Weather family's expense if this were an ambush.

Chapter 41

"Try further down," Jill said in a weak voice. "I saw the baron . . . do it . . . once. Pull that drawer out; and push that one in." Her words tapered into a long gurgle.

Jane pointed to the new spot. Albert pushed, with doubt and anger playing in equal parts across his sweaty face.

The cabinets groaned backward, revealing a dark space beyond.

"Let's go, let's go." Albert sent Jane into the passage and motioned the others forward.

The passage ended in the storeroom Jane had discovered earlier. The outside door latch responded without secret handshakes. Those who could walk dragged those who couldn't.

The group spilled outside into darkness and mud and breathable air. Jane took deep ragged gulps. The orange smoke curled after them. A couple of the men flicked cigarette lighters to see by.

Weather stood at the Cliff Heights entrance. Bonnie said Willie's secret game room was here, which made him think Jane might be here as well. If she were worth her salt in her undercover role, she would be.

The uglier-than-Beady's truck took up most of the arch. He slipped behind its bed to get through to the courtyard. Whitish pellets of some chemical rolled underfoot, momentarily upsetting his balance. He picked one up and sniffed. Ammonium nitrate. Maybe Bonnie had been telling the truth. She'd said Burr had been planting bags out here for several days. If this was a set-up, it was a well-staged one.

A figure in black emerged from a room on the north wing. On the south, thin smoke filtered out from under the door of the room Bonnie said contained the secret stairs. He heard yelling, faint and far off, that seemed to come from underground. He slipped past the truckbed along the courtyard edge and crouched low next to the smoking door.

"We can't wait for an ambulance, we've got to go now," the doctor said. Jill's face matched Jane's plaster cast, white and chalky.

Jane pointed to the woods. "Take the black Ford back there. The key is on the floorboard, in a handkerchief."

One of the uninjured men ran for the car.

"I think this one needs you just as bad." Albert prodded the immobile figure of Mac Porter with his toe.

The doctor pivoted over to Mac, applied fingers to neck, barked instructions. One of the others took over holding pressure on Jill's wound.

The black Ford sliced up out of the muddy trail just as the doctor finished making a tourniquet for Mac's leg out of the hem of Jane's dress.

The men loaded the dancer and Mac into the big car and piled in.

"No room," the doctor said when Jane tried to follow. He pulled the door shut. The Ford took off, rammed open the heavy gates and disappeared in a squeal of tires, leaving her alone with Albert.

Christina's boyfriend took her by the elbow. "We still got some business to discuss, Jane Alder."

★ ★ ★ ★ ★

Weather felt the door—it was cool—then pushed into the smoky room. A body lay just inside. Burr Cartledge's welcome mat. He bent over the man to feel the neck for a pulse. His fingers came away bloody. His throat had been cut ear to ear. The man was Ronnie something, the thug who had roughed him up at the Star D. Ronnie stared intently at the afterlife, which, judging from the terror on his face, did not feature golden mansions and fluffy clouds.

"Help me, Willie," someone wheezed from under a lopsided bed in the center of the room.

Weather got on his knees and looked underneath. The Bledsoe kid hung half out of the floor, his bloody fingers stabbing the floor with a pocketknife, trying to pull himself along. One leg of the tilted bed pressed down on the trap door. Thicker orange smoke flowed out of the hole and enveloped the boy.

Aware that his shoulder would give out, Weather sat on the floor and used his legs to push the heavy bed off the trap and upend it.

Carl Ray Bledsoe, Junior, sprang up like some macabre jack-in-the-box, emerging out of the fires of hell. Weather helped him the rest of the way out, away from the smoke, hoping his wounded shoulder would hold. The trap door fell shut. Carl Ray gasped for air.

"What are you doing here, Mr. Weather?"

"Your aunt sent me. Is anyone else down there?"

"Yeah, there's people stuck down there, at the other end."

"Is one of them a brunette with her arm in a cast?"

"Dunno. There's a brunette. She got shot."

Weather's chest tightened.

"Burr and this other guy shot half of them," Carl Ray continued. "They're gonna burn the rest of them up. They, I

mean the others, are locked in behind a door straight ahead."
He gestured toward the middle room, one floor below. He
made an attempt to stand, but collapsed on the wood floor,
coughing hard.

"Where are Burr and the other guy?"

"Dunno. The other guy had a stocking on his face. It's a
lawman. A cop or a deputy or somebody."

"A cop, you say?" Weather had an idea who that might be.
He lifted the square door and looked down into the pit.
Smoke stung his eyes.

"He wants to blow the building," Carl Ray said from
behind him. "He put ammonia nitric in the basement and
he's got dynamite he said he was going to string around. I
think he took that up top."

"I expect that basement will work like a cargo hold, once
that fire gets hot enough. Go find a phone. Call the fire
department. And the police. Tell them two gunmen are still
on the premises."

"Naw, I gotta help get the people first. It's my Last Ride."

"What?"

"Never mind."

Despite Weather's protests, the kid followed him down
the stairs into the smoky pit.

In the subterranean room, pockets of fire formed little
trails around prone figures. A tarpaulin and several suit-
jackets covered a smoking divan and seemed to be holding a
fireburst at bay. Weather carefully folded the tarp back to reveal
the surprised, and dead, face of a reddish blonde chippie. He
replaced the tarp. At a door on the west wall, he pulled bodies
out of a crumpled huddle, looking for Jane's. A quick look at the
victims revealed them to be certainly dead, beyond any possible resurrection by the most talented sawbones, although
the kid insisted on shaking every one of them.

"Jane," he yelled over the crackling flames.

His cry broke up into a dry cough. If he and Carl Ray didn't get out fast, they would succumb to the smoke. The open trap door acted as a chimney. It would be hell climbing back up there to get out. It was probably too late already.

"Come on." Weather pulled Carl Ray off one corpse and kicked in the door to the second room. The air was better there. He dragged the kid through and pushed corpses out of the way to shut the door. A rectangle of smoke poured through the busted panel where he'd kicked. This room contained another divan, and a man's body stretched out on the floor in a doorway on the opposite side. A large red stain covered most of his shirtfront. They stepped over the body, into a kitchen. The air was better here.

Where the hell did the other people go? Had Carl Ray been mistaken about survivors? No, the kid said a brunette had been shot, and they had not found her body.

"Jane! Anybody! Where are you?"

"What's that?" Carl Ray's voice came as a froggy croak from under Weather's arm.

The kid pointed to the cabinets on the inside wall. Something was askew about them.

Maybe it had to do with the rooms being built inside hollowed rock.

No. The orange smoke streamed behind a cabinet. There was air flow back here.

He dragged the coughing boy into a storage room, expecting to find the group cowering in a dead end.

Instead, the moving smoke trail pointed them to an open door.

He and Carl Ray popped out together, and nearly knocked down Jane and her jarhead thug, sharing an intimate embrace.

★ ★ ★ ★ ★

Jane wondered what David was doing there. He had not been one of the gamblers. She broke away from Albert, laughing, and fell into Weather's arms. "I'll explain later."

Albert Florentine grinned shyly at him. "I gotta leave town now, so take care of her."

"My uncle and some other man are going to blow up the building," Carl Ray blurted through coughs. "Anybody else in the hotel?"

Jane stared at him for a second, then screamed. "Oh my God, the children!" She ran back from the cliff a few paces and pointed. "Four children and a baby. Their father keeps them padlocked in while he's at work. They're alone. The windows are barred. The front one, that is. Those are too far to drop."

The group clustered around her and shouted upward. No one came to the dark window. At least the children's wing wasn't burning yet.

"What's the quickest way to them?" Weather asked.

"Burr's done put out enough nitrate to take down the hotel and the hill with it," Carl Ray said.

"I know a way," Jane said. "Follow me." She ran north, down a set of stairs, and disappeared around the corner of the cliff. Weather, Albert, and Carl Ray followed. Weather's shoulder ached from dragging the kid earlier.

Jane and Albert had the lead. She looked back at Weather and Carl Ray, taking up the rear. She still wasn't sure about Albert, and didn't want to be alone with him. "Come on."

"What is this place, a warehouse?" Weather asked as he and the boy caught up. They mounted wooden stairs in the center of a rectangular building. On their way up, two steps broke off under Albert's weight and they had to step over. Other steps felt rotten underfoot and threatened to break.

285

The handrails were long gone. Overhead, pigeons fluttered at their approach.

"This was going to be a garment factory back in the twenties," Carl Ray answered between gulps. "The factory never got started, but the owner rented out some cabins back there for a while when my little brother was a baby."

"Watch out for the hole," Jane cautioned, explaining about the freight elevator next to the stairs. The elevator bed itself hung below the third floor where she had left it. "Here we are."

The third floor was alive with shrieking pigeons.

Jane led the rescue party to the ladder, then remembered the ghost, hobo, or madman who lurked here. It would be stupid to be killed by someone like that when the building next door was about to explode.

"You both have casts on," Albert said. "I'll go get the kids."

"I'm going, Albert," Jane said.

"Me, too," Weather said. "Carl Ray, you stay here." Weather looked back. The boy had slumped over a workbench, and now made heavy rasping sounds.

"I'm going, too," Carl Ray said.

"The hell you are."

"I gotta. It's my Ride."

Weather wondered what the hell the kid was talking about, but figured it had to do with atonement.

"You guys slug it out, I'm going," Albert said. He climbed onto the horizontal ladder and shimmied across with the grace of a squirrel. Jane followed, then Weather. Ignoring their protests, Carl Ray took up the rear. Fire engines clamored in the distance, and Weather considered letting the firemen take the kids out the back window, but saw that Albert was already on the other side, slipping into a window of the hotel. Weather wondered if the firemen could maneuver a big engine through that back gate to set up a ladder rescue. The firemen would be in danger, too, from the potential explosion. The *Grandcamp* had burned for maybe an hour before it blew, but he had no idea how similar or different Burr's handiwork was from the ship's condition. Surely the ship had more explosives. Carl Ray had said he had dynamite too. None of that had blown yet.

All four got across and through a window into a kitchenette. Albert was already in the bedroom, crouching under the window, checking out the courtyard.

"Wait," Weather said. "Burr Cartledge is out there somewhere. He has a partner. And dynamite."

"They have machine guns, too," Jane added.

"I got my own firepower." Albert drew a .38 from his belt.

"I hope you see them first," Weather said. "That's no match for a machine gun."

"It is with me holding it."

Weather hoped that wasn't hubris.

Chapter 42

The four of them slid silently out the door and along the north wing toward the rear of the courtyard.

Black smoke poured from the south wing as flames shot out. Much more than the nitrate was burning now. So far, the north side lay intact. A chemical smell lay pungent and menacing in the air. Burr had set more fires above ground, and fueled them with a faster agent of destruction. And what about the dynamite?

"Look," Jane pointed to the children's wing. Smoke poured out of the boiler room under the apartment, and thinner wisps of it floated lazily out of the children's open front window. The older boy, grim-faced and silent, chopped at the iron bars with a hammer, making no headway. Inside, the baby howled.

"Stay here," Albert commanded in a whisper. "If we all get shot, there's no way to save them." The big man ran into the courtyard, mounted the stairs, and kicked the padlocked door.

It gave way with a mighty crack.

"I don't care, I'm going." Jane bolted out of Weather's loose embrace. Weather followed. No one shot at them as they ascended the iron staircase. In the apartment, smoke seeped upward through the floorboards, but the fire had not yet broken through. The children cowered next to the window. Weather and Jane ushered the frightened children out. From the door, Albert covered them all with the .38.

Carl Ray stumbled into the courtyard.

"Take cover," Weather yelled. The kid lurched back toward the sidewalk.

Fire from the south wing warmed their faces. The north wing remained dark and untouched, waiting its turn. All the electricity had gone out. Beyond the courtyard out on Sylvan, far out from the sound of it, a fireman bullhorned directions to his men.

A barrage of gunfire blasted out of the turret office onto the street.

"Shots fired, get back," the fireman on the street broadcast.

"We can't go out through the arch, Burr or his partner is in the turret," Weather whispered.

A window on the south side blew out. Angry flames ate the night air. They leaped off the stairs and bolted toward the north wing.

"I'm scared." The little blonde girl looked up at them with frozen eyes.

"You'll be all right," the teenage girl said, irritated. She gave Carl Ray moon eyes. Carl Ray took heavy breaths and let the girl pull him along.

Weather led them along the north sidewalk to the vacant room with the escape ladder. The gunfire outside ceased. More sirens shrieked out on Sylvan and Fort Worth Avenue. Several bullhorns chattered now, warning each other to stay away from the hotel. Weather knew the firemen would pull back and give the police the scene.

They were on their own. Somehow they got all the children out the kitchenette window. Somehow they got everyone across the ladder. Their passage was slow, hampered by screaming children and pigeons flying out of the warehouse, but they made it. Carl Ray slumped to the warehouse floor. His breath rattled like a choked engine.

"The stairs won't hold us all," Jane yelled over the pigeons.

"Let's get everyone onto the elevator," Weather shouted.

"The crank is on the first floor."

"I'll go." Albert ran down the unsteady stairs.

Weather and the older boy from the padlocked apartment lowered Carl Ray onto the wooden platform while the older sister helped the two younger kids on board. Jane handed the baby down to her, then stepped on.

"There's a gate way down the hill, you'll see the brick path once you get past those two rows of huts," Jane said.

The brother and sister nodded somberly.

"Go," Weather yelled down the stairwell at Albert after the children were all situated.

The big pulleys groaned as Albert worked from below.

"David, are you coming?" Jane asked from the platform as it descended.

"Not yet. We got another survivor." A movement in the kitchenette window across the gap had caught Weather's eye.

"Weather!" A man hung his head out the kitchenette window.

Hadley.

"The building's going to blow. Ammonium nitrate and dynamite," Weather warned.

"I know. Hold that ladder, will you?"

Weather went over to the ladder and put an arm on it to steady it as Hadley started across. "Do the firemen know?"

"Yeah, they're staying back. They've got a shooter, so they've cordoned off the whole place." Hadley finished his journey and dropped effortlessly into the room. "Anybody else in the hotel?"

"We got the only residents out. Burr Cartledge is probably still in there. Or his partner, or both."

"Where's the dancer, Jill?"

"I don't know. There were some bodies in the cliff room," he said, but Hadley wasn't listening. The detective had jerked to alertness and pulled out a pistol.

A noise came from the stairwell. A wood creak, a heaviness. Burr Cartledge? If so, Weather was sandwiched between Burr and Hadley. He glanced uneasily at the detective. Hadley motioned Weather back into the shadows with him and pointed the gun at the stairwell. Carl Ray had said the partner was a lawman. Not Hadley, surely not Hadley.

Jane's head appeared in the opening. "David, come on. The children are on their way to the gate with Albert."

"Go back," Weather shouted, but Jane climbed out of the opening and came toward him. She stopped when she saw Hadley with the pistol.

"Where's the dancer, Jill?" Hadley used his too-calm voice. He wasn't pointing the pistol at them, but was looking all around. He edged over to the stairs. Weather and Jane edged toward the window opening near the horizontal ladder.

"She went to the hospital with the others," Jane said. "She got shot. I don't know how bad. She could still talk, so that's a good sign."

Hadley nodded at the floor. He seemed to be hearing something beyond the fire crackle and pigeon noises.

Jane dug her fingers into Weather's arm and stretched up to whisper in his ear. "It's Hadley. He's crooked. He's Burr's partner."

Chapter 43

Hadley wiped his brow with his sleeve and grinned. "I got good ears, Jane. I'm not your crooked cop. I've been working with an informant for months on this mob war to find out who's behind a lot of crimes, including Willie's shooting."

"Jill. Jill is your informant. So that's why she's scared of me," Jane said.

"Folks, there's a load of burning ammonium nitrate next door," Weather said. "And Carl Ray said Burr was stringing dynamite, too."

"Yeah, let's go." Hadley lowered his pistol even more and went to the edge of the stairway. "You're gonna have a hell of a newspaper story, I promise, Miss Janie."

"No story," someone spoke from the shadows to the east. Sheriff Odell Orton stepped out from behind a crate, gun drawn. Hadley jerked his pistol upward, but Orton shot him before he even got the barrel aimed. The detective fell face down on the plank flooring, hard. A creeping red pool spread from underneath him. The pigeons squalled their protest.

"What in hell is going on?" Weather looked down at Hadley by the stairs and over at Orton by the crates. On the floor, the detective garbled something about Odell, then went still.

"Weather, son, you should have left this alone." Odell shook his head and motioned with the pistol for them to stand over by the window. He stepped between them and Hadley's body near the stairs. He had a pillowcase slung over his shoulder.

"Should have left what alone?" Jane clutched Weather's arm.

"Tell the little muckraker. I want to know myself how much you know, before I let Burr have a go at you. We're gonna let Hadley take the blame, though. Crooked lawman, stole that money and set those fires. His lady friend, Wild Jill Cody, was supposed to die in the robbery. I wanted to get all the rats with one broom. Instead I'll have to get her in the hospital. Thank you for letting me know her whereabouts, Mrs. Alder. Some syndicate thug will get blamed. How the hell you people got out of that basement is beyond me."

"There's a door behind the kitchen," Jane said.

"Damn! Always another loose end."

"David?" Jane continued to cling to him. He wanted to signal her in some way to run for it, but he couldn't rotate his bad arm backward to push her, and she wouldn't break her grasp on him. Besides, she would trip over Hadley, and Orton now stood between them and the stairs. And the stairs were rotten. And Orton had a gun.

Orton sent a worried glance toward the hotel. Weather noticed a red glow flickering in a room on the north wing, nearest the back. Either the fire had worked its way around, or Burr had set new fires. Where was Burr, anyway? In the turret, or stringing his dynamite? A flame shot out of a window down on the corner and a hundred pigeons objected. Weather didn't much like it either.

Weather looked over to the window ledge. Twenty-plus feet, onto concrete. A survivable drop, but with no guarantees.

How he could get Jane over the edge before Orton got off a shot, now that was a bigger problem.

Time to buy time. "When Willie came to me," Weather said, "he told me someone of great power in Dallas was behind the mob activity, someone no one would suspect. His exact words were, 'Someone will be risen, as if from the dead, not exactly a businessman, not exactly not a businessman.' Willie meant you, Odell, but someone else as well. A former businessman, out of the game."

"Permanently out, this go-round."

"Who are you talking about," Jane said. "Mac Porter?"

"No," Weather said. "Mac is just a rich man with a gambling habit. Willie's surprise businessman is, was, the former president of Pacific Avenue State Bank, Mr. Charles Arthur Curtis."

"Charles Arthur Curtis?"

"Yes. Charles Arthur Curtis financed some of Willie's gambling operations, and used the bank's money to pay off his own debts to Willie. A lot of the money went out as regular loans, except the businesses receiving loans were fronts for the Peabody organization. Curtis could have kept his books clean if he hadn't gotten greedy and pilfered customer accounts. I expect the first targets were elderly widows who could barely read their bank statements. He hired young girl tellers from out of town to take the fall if any depositors cried foul. When the girls got wise, Curtis would threaten to ruin them. It was the Depression, a hard time for anybody to get another job, and an easy time for the bank to get more employees. He used orphans or up-from-dirt girls who could put on enough class to work in a bank, girls with no families to stick up for them. His head teller, Mrs. Betty Gottschalk, was in it with him. They were lovers for years. How'm I doing, Odell?"

Orton grinned. "You've done too much homework, boy."

"Too bad Betty Gottschalk tried to extort more money last

night. He sent Cecil Cab Allgood out to kill her," Weather said.

The sheriff shook his head in mock dismay. "That murder will never get solved."

Creevy would solve it, Weather knew, but kept his tongue. He didn't want to levy a death sentence on the investigator. "The nickel and dime pilfering wasn't enough for Curtis, though," Weather continued. "He staged his own bank's robbery. Willie volunteered Carl Ray Bledsoe, Senior, to do the job, expecting Curtis to supply a guard in on the heist. Curtis didn't count on his man Allgood getting pneumonia, and he didn't tell Willie. Or maybe he did, but Willie didn't get the word to Bledsoe in time. Maybe he figured Bledsoe could handle it alone, maybe he got busy because of an audit. Anyway, Bledsoe went in expecting an ally, and when the substitute guard shot at him, he shot back." Weather glanced over at the hotel. The fire must be twenty, thirty minutes old by now.

"Carl Ray thought the guard he killed was going to help with the robbery?" Jane asked.

Near the stairs, to Orton's right, Weather noticed Hadley's fingers moving.

"Yes, Bledsoe killed the guard, and then the beat cop who chased him." Weather squeezed Jane's arm. *Don't look now, but Hadley's still with us.*

She squeezed back. She must have seen the same thing.

"Why didn't Carl Ray's lawyer use Curtis' involvement to plea bargain?"

Hadley's hand slid underneath his chest. The pigeon tempest muted his movements. Weather thought he'd never cuss one of the birds again.

"Because Bledsoe didn't know of it," Orton said. "Idiot thought the guard he shot was the only insider."

"So what does this have to do with you killing Willie?" Jane asked.

Hadley brought his hand out, with the pistol in it.

"I didn't kill Willie," Orton said.

"Then who did?"

"The bank president, Charles Arthur Curtis," Weather answered.

"Actually, the baron—that's Curtis' new identity, 'Mr. Baron had it done.' The baron won't dirty his hands with grunt work." The sheriff threw an impatient glance at the hotel.

The north wing poured smoke, a lot of it toward them. The pigeons were clearing out by the dozens. Smart pigeons.

Hadley raised the gun, but it swayed in his hand, like it was too heavy.

"Cab Allgood and Ronnie Vincent did the actual killing," Orton continued. "Made it look like amateurs to throw the scent. Left him alive out in the riverbottoms, to let him think about the suffering he'd caused Curtis. It would've been all right with Curtis if Willie lived. In fact, he wanted him to live and suffer, but hell, Cab and Ronnie got a little carried away. But go on, tell your story, son."

"Willie's killing was revenge for Curtis' family. A few years after the robbery, Willie arranged for Curtis to be in a bad car wreck. Am I guessing right, Sheriff?"

"On the money. Willie tampered with the brakes. He was punishing Curtis for Bledsoe's conviction and execution, see, because the robbery could have succeeded if the real accomplice—Cab—had been there as planned.

"The day of the wreck," Weather continued, "Curtis had his family with him, and they died. He was badly injured, and spent years in convalescent homes, and had to learn to walk again." *Hadley, shoot.*

"He should've walked somewhere besides back into *my* county, bringing all these goons from Chicago in his wake," Orton thundered over fire crackle and bird flutter.

"So tonight's massacre was to drive off outsiders? Because Curtis was connected to the Chicago mob?" Weather had always thought Odell a bit clannish.

Hadley's hand relaxed and his pistol thudded to the floor.

"I decide who works and who doesn't in this town. Curtis threatened to go to the papers about my arrangement with Willie if I didn't step aside."

"Oh, God, look!" Jane tugged at Weather's arm.

Fire flared in the room opposite the ladder, and a figure climbed out the kitchenette window.

Burr Cartledge.

Chapter 44

"Hold up, Burr, I want to make sure that ladder's steady." Keeping his pistol on his prisoners, the sheriff set the pillowcase down, stepped over to the edge, and put his free hand on the ladder.

Weather looked back over at Hadley. The detective lay motionless, his pistol on the rough floor beside his limp hand.

"That damn Laidlaw was supposed to be here, and he wasn't," Burr said from the ladder. "I checked every nook and cranny of this damn place. Thought the sumbitch would be hiding."

"Burr." Orton tightened his grip on the top rung of the ladder.

"What?"

"I told Laidlaw to stay home."

"What?" Cartledge jerked his head up. He hung onto the center of the ladder, out over the long drop.

"I never had any beef with Laidlaw. Fact is, he's been torn up that this financier he brought in killed his daddy. He didn't know Baron and Curtis were the same guy until Willie was dead." Orton raised the pistol and shot Burr Cartledge, square in the forehead. The body dropped onto the ladder. Orton hoisted the ladder on its side and the body fell to the sidewalk below. A hollow bounce followed. Orton looked down at his handiwork and smiled.

Weather and Jane peered over. Burr lay face down. A starburst of blood stained the concrete around his cracked head.

"Another loose end, tied up," Orton said.

"You let him think he would get Laidlaw tonight?"

Orton shook his head. "No more questions. That hotel could blow any second, so if you would be so kind as to stay where you are." Keeping the pistol on them, he went over to Hadley, and removed the detective's gun from the floor. He tucked it into his belt and pointed his pistol at them. "Ladies first?"

"No!" Weather shoved Jane down. A shot flashed from the sheriff's direction.

Jane hit the floor by the windows. "David, duck."

"No need," Weather said, watching Orton.

The gun fell out of Orton's hand. The sheriff teetered, then went down on one knee. He pushed up with the other leg and turned toward the stairwell, but his leg wobbled and threw him off balance so that he was facing the elevator hole instead. He tried again to stand but fell forward. He put his hand out to break the fall but overreached the flooring and pitched headfirst into the elevator hole. They heard him hit the platform at the bottom where the kids had debarked. The landing had a different texture from Cartledge's, more bouncing, more cracking.

"Well come on, didn't you hear the man say the building's about to blow?" Albert Florentine's head showed from the steps. "Wondered what in hell was taking you folks so long." He waved his .38 around. "Anyone else need killing?"

"No, I think we've got the right quota already," Weather said as he helped Jane up. She was unhurt.

Jane rushed to Hadley and checked for a pulse. "He's still alive. Oh, I hate to move him, it might make things worse."

"I'll raise that elevator and we can carry him down that way," Albert said. He disappeared down the stairwell. A moment later the gears groaned.

The flatbed arrived, already occupied with its first bloody cargo. No one bothered to check Orton's pulse. His neck bent at an angle that did not allow for life. Albert and Weather laid Hadley beside the sheriff's body, then Albert ran to work the pulley.

Almost as an afterthought, Weather went back for the pillowcase with the gamblers' money. He tucked the bag into his waist and stepped onto the platform as it began its descent.

They left the sheriff's body where it lay and climbed through a window opening onto the ruins of a brick sidewalk leading downhill.

"Through there," Jane said. "It's too brushy to go overland. We have to take the path at the center. Follow me."

The hotel could blow any second and Carl Ray was going to miss it. He sat on the street behind the police barricade, trying to tell his story to a cop named Keller just to get the son of a bitch out of his hair. A doctor brought this bed thing on wheels out of an ambulance and told him to quit talking, they were going to the hospital. The doctor and this other guy lifted him up and put him on it. He punched at them. He felt sick to his stomach and couldn't breathe too good, but he would be damned if he was going to miss the show.

The cop, Keller, pulled one of the doctors away.

"Hadley, the police detective. Where is he?"

"I don't know where the hell he is," Carl Ray shouted over all the noise. The doctors were tying a mask to his face. He grabbed at it and tried to keep it off him. "Mr. Weather and this woman with her arm in a cast were back at the factory, last I knew." Whatever was in that mask smelled sweet. "They oughtta blow any second," he said from under the mask. There was too much noise and his words and his brain got garbled under that mask so he couldn't tell it straight.

The cop backed away.

"Hey, don't let them take me."

While the two doctors were strapping him onto the bed contraption, he looked back at the hotel. Smoke was boiling out of it and everybody said to get back even further, that they weren't far enough off. A thousand pigeons were flying around, squawking up a storm.

The group arrived in a clearing with a pool.

"This path leads to the gate onto Sylvan." Jane pointed to another crumbled brick path that headed east from the pool area.

A series of rumbles came from the hotel.

"Too late, it's going," Albert shouted.

"Into the pool, run for it!" Weather pushed Jane toward the steps.

Carl Ray's eyes watered, and when he blinked again, he saw Burr and the sheriff come running down the hill, coming right toward him. Burr would kill him now, and he couldn't even get up and run.

"Hey, Keller. Help. It was them," he yelled, pointing.

Keller looked at him funny, like he was seeing things. The cop talked into his walkie-talkie and looked toward the fire, right at Burr, right through him, in fact, and ignored him like he wasn't even there. Then Carl Ray understood. Burr couldn't hurt him no more.

Two other men came running right behind Burr. One was Willie and one was a guy that looked sort of like David Weather. Black-haired, with these long coattails like an old country preacher. Him and Willie were arguing.

"Our arrangement never included murder," the coattailed man said.

"Carl Ray panicked so it shouldn't've counted," Willie said.

"It counted," the other one said.

Keller and the medic people lifted his bed up and put Carl Ray in the ambulance. They didn't see, but Big Ray climbed right in with him.

"Well, son," Big Ray said. "I got to tell you where I hid that bank money." Big Ray leaned in and started whispering, only the hotel blew up and Carl Ray couldn't hear a thing.

The first explosion knocked Jane to her knees. Several more shock waves flung the group against the pool bottom. Seahorse tiles popped off the outer rim and a big crack opened in the pool's side nearest the hotel. The fire must have reached Burr's dynamite.

Weather glanced toward the cliff. "The factory's coming at us. Get down there." He pointed to the deep end. Large chunks of cliff, concrete, and iron thundered downhill, knocking out the back row of cabins in its flow. They lurched toward the sheltering debris in the pool.

Albert tucked Hadley into the Model T. Weather pushed Jane behind an old icebox that lay on its side and raised the door as a shield against shrapnel. He checked behind them at Albert, who was crawling into the old auto.

"Look!" Jane pointed at the pool's shallow end. A figure splashed toward them in the muck. The village madman. With quite a female figure.

"Owww," the visitor yelled, hopping on one foot.

Belinda Bain dodged flaming missiles and pushed her way under the icebox shelter.

"Uh, your mama's bad sick, and wants to see you," Weather stammered from the dark rectangle as the shower of rubble continued.

★ ★ ★ ★ ★

They huddled in the muck for a while until the explosions stopped and the rubble settled.

"It's over," Weather said. He unfolded from the icebox door and helped Belinda and Jane out. Both were slime-coated and shivering from cold, even though the furnace on the cliff roared on. Make that the furnace in the crater where the cliff had been, Weather amended.

Belinda and "Connie" chatted like old friends. Belinda said she didn't mean to scare Jane the other night, but wasn't sure she could trust her to not tell. She'd been hiding down here or in the hotel for over a week now, and didn't know who to trust.

Albert stuck his head out of the Model T. "We need an ambulance for this guy. How he could hold on through all this, I don't know, but he did." Albert had stripped his jacket and shirt off to stanch Hadley's wound and stood there in his undershirt. Weather noted the anchor tattoo.

Robert Verdi. Jane had been hugging him earlier. He would ask later.

"I got a car stashed in the woods," Belinda volunteered. "I don't know if we can get it out, though, with all this rubble."

"If you're talking about a black Ford with Illinois plates, I already lent it out," Jane replied sheepishly.

Weather looked questioningly at Belinda.

His half-sister shrugged. "That guy with Martel didn't need it anymore, and I did."

"What are you two talking about?"

"We'll tell you later."

Albert carried Hadley up from the broken pool.

The group found their way out onto Sylvan through a small gate. Outside, fire trucks lined the street and a melee of firemen and police manned a tangle of hoses. Across the road, Beady's jalopy rested upside down, a smashed iron tumbleweed.

Weather found Hadley's rubble-dusted partner, Keller, who summoned an ambulance.

"The gunmen are dead," Weather told him.

Hadley's ambulance came from a barricade at the bottom of the hill from which hundreds of spectators strained to see. Keller got in the ambulance with the wounded detective and the vehicle pulled away, siren wailing.

"I've got to get to the paper," Jane exclaimed, declining attention from a medic.

"I've got to get to my mama," Belinda said, waving off more medical personnel.

"Let's ask someone down here for a ride. Albert? Hey, Albert, come on!" Weather looked around, but Albert had disappeared.

In the *Beacon* newsroom, Weather gave the pillowcase full of money to the young police detective who'd driven Belinda to Roma's and then dropped him and Jane off at the newspaper. Weather filled the cop in on the night's events while Jane dictated her copy to conscripted typist Bradley Murph, the awkward student intern who enjoyed occasional bouts of fantastic timing. Murph begged for a byline. Journalism was a disease that struck the able and unable with equal fervor.

"Shut up and type faster," Jane said.

After the story was filed, Weather had the detective, Sloane, drive him and Jane to the hospital. Hadley and Wild Jill Cody were both in surgery. It looked good for Jill and bad for Hadley. Carl Ray had been treated, then arrested for his part in the robbery.

"He asked for you to be his lawyer," Bonnie Bledsoe Cartledge told Weather in the waiting room. Bandages ringed her wrists and plastered her bruised face. "He wants these charges dropped and to get out of his probation altogether. He says he has something big to trade. He says he can solve a murder."

Chapter 45

Saturday, April 26

Saturday morning, Weather stood on the lake's edge with a dozen people—Bonnie Cartledge, Carl Ray, Jane, Morson, the juvenile prosecutor, three cops, three deputies, and the acting sheriff, who, eager to mend fences with the city, had invited Keller to run the investigation. Weather hoped Carl Ray wasn't playing them all for suckers. If those skin divers found nothing, he'd warned, it was back to the juvenile farm, period. Carl Ray had agreed. Weather wondered if severing ties with the D.A. to take this kid on was the right idea, but Morson had accepted his resignation with relief, even a little glee. Hurt feelings about his former career aside, Weather hoped representing the kid would clear up his father's old debt to Willie and let everybody—living and dead—rest in peace.

The usually silent Keller bullhorned instructions out to the rowboat where the divers were about to slip into the water.

"It's the wrong place," Carl Ray insisted.

"Be patient," Weather told him. "They're going to drag the whole lake and they have to be systematic."

The divers weren't in long before one surfaced and yelled to shore that they had something.

"That's still the wrong place," the kid objected. "It

couldn't have floated over there, not with those concrete blocks."

The two divers rose out of the lake and walked ashore at a shallow spot. Between them they carried a steamer trunk.

"Maybe that's Big Ray's bank money," Carl Ray blurted out.

His aunt put her arms around him. "Shush."

Keller allowed a photographer to take pictures of the unopened trunk, and then knocked a padlock off the brass fittings. Black water and silt filled it. Keller ordered a clean canvas be spread out on the banks, then had the divers dump the contents on it.

A jumble of bones, two skulls, and the remains of a lady's silver hair comb tumbled out.

Cameras flashed, one from the police photographer and one from Jane.

Bonnie went off to cry and puke and Carl Ray stayed on the bank to get a better look at those bones. It was just bones and skulls, but he could see the faces of the girls they belonged to, too. Pretty girls with French names, he somehow knew, and when Mr. Weather said Marie Chantilly and Celeste Care-ay, he shouted that was them, that was them 'til they all looked at him funny and asked how he knew. The girls were killed when he was a baby.

Bonnie came back and told them he was big-dogging it, and he let it go.

An hour later the frogmen pulled a canvas roll out of the muck. Weather watched with the others as Keller had his guys untie it.

Bonnie Bledsoe Cartledge burst into fresh tears. "Aesop Gance! He was staying with us. He was following Willie around, trying to get up his nerve to ask to come back in. Willie called him here that last night. He told him to come by the Star D on Wednesday to talk."

Chapter 46

Sunday, April 27

Roma enjoyed all the visitors. Santos, her first love, came back after all these years. He wasn't mean about what she'd become, but Roma could tell he was sad about it. He had a wife and family now, and said he was sorry he'd been the cause of her having to leave home.

If it wasn't you it woulda been somebody else, I was so hell-bent to get out, she'd said. She cried a little and Santos cried a little and then Santos left.

Belinda held her hand the whole time. Belinda couldn't see, but Tom sat at the foot of the bed, holding Baby Victoria.

That baby woulda been so pretty, honey, if it would've lived.

Yes, Mama, Belinda said.

And best of all, late in the evening, while Belinda was asleep, Roma's own mama came by and asked forgiveness.

That made everything all right again.

It's dark and cold in here, Mama, she said.

I know, darling, her mama said, and her mama took her by the hand and led her outside into the bluebonnet fields, like when she was a little girl.

Epilogue

After Jane's story about the Cliff Heights ran, the five children padlocked into the Cliff Heights apartment went to live with an aunt, and their father was arrested for child abandonment. Jane had the panther look in her eyes when she told Weather about it, and he sensed her fury stemmed from her own past. When he asked, she wouldn't talk about it.

Hadley lived. On Monday the doctors upgraded him from critical to serious, and in the evening, the detective opened his eyes. On Tuesday, the nurses still wouldn't let Weather see him. The patient stood too much risk of infection, one said.

Wild Jill Cody lived as well, and took advantage of Weather's new status as a defense attorney to hire him from her hospital bed. It was she who had put the ladder across to the factory, so Belinda could escape from the hotel room she was hiding in if she needed to run away. Since that ladder helped get the kids out, it oughtta carry some weight at the D.A.'s about this organized crime charge. Hadley was in trouble because of her and couldn't help. Could Weather get her off?

"I don't think that bit of nobility with the ladder is enough. The D.A. needs somebody to take the fall for that poker game. A couple of innocent gamblers got killed in there, and most of the big fish are dead. Unless you can give them someone bigger to fry, it'll be you in the skillet."

Wild Jill stared out the window, considering. "Well I just might."

★ ★ ★ ★ ★

Wednesday morning's *Beacon* fried a bigger fish.

L. Peabody Arrested in Gines Slaying
Second Gunman is FW Gambler
by Jane Alder

Nightclub owner Laidlaw Peabody was arrested yesterday in the execution-style slaying of dancer Martel Gines and her companion, missing cab driver Clancy Burrows of Chicago. Convicted Fort Worth gambler Shorty Lamont was also charged in the shooting.

Acting on an anonymous tip, Dallas police detective Robert Keller recovered the murder weapons from a locker at Union Station. Fingerprints linked Peabody and Lamont to the weapons and ballistic matches linked the weapons to the crime.

A motive for the killing has not been established, although Willie Peabody was acquitted last year of the murder of Gines' brother.

Peabody is also being questioned in the murder-for-hire of ex-convict Aesop Gance. No motive has been established for that killing either.

Weather folded up the paper and smiled. He knew the motive. Jill had given the D.A. plenty. Laidlaw, in his grief, had accused several people besides Weather of killing Willie. Some, like Martin Hubert, left town. Other less fortunate ones, like Aesop Gance and Martel, paid with their lives.

That afternoon, Keller summoned Weather to the jailhouse at the request of another new client, one of Curtis' card dealers, a woman named Sharon St. Pierre. Keller had caught up to her in West Dallas, where she'd hidden out to get news

311

of her friends before she skipped town. Sharon, quite distressed over her friends' murders—and her arrest—told him an interesting tale.

Curtis—"Mr. Baron"—had pulled her out of a Dallas brothel when she was sixteen, and she had worked for him ever since. The night before the long-ago bank robbery, when Cab went to the hospital, Sharon heard Curtis telephone Willie's house to call off the heist. Willie wasn't home, but Laidlaw was. Laidlaw was a kid back then, seventeen or eighteen. Laidlaw promised to deliver the message. Laidlaw assured Curtis that poor old Carl Ray wouldn't go in that bank alone.

"I'm pretty sure Laidlaw never delivered the message," Sharon said. "He was always jealous of Willie helping Carl Ray."

Recently, not knowing his own father murdered Curtis' family over Bledsoe's conviction, Laidlaw brought in a financier from up north. He wanted to impress Willie with his own ability to forge mob ties. The unseen financier he summoned had been Mr. Baron.

"So Laidlaw kind of killed his own old man," he said to Sharon during their talk.

"That's about what I would make of it," she said.

Of course, Weather couldn't give these tidbits to Jane. Attorney-client privilege.

Tuesday evening, after he'd secured Sharon's release from jail—after all, Keller had no real evidence to hold her—there was a knock on Weather's apartment door. He laid the paper on his living room sofa and opened the door.

His half-sister, Belinda Bain, stood there, her face a defiant pose betrayed by swollen eyes.

"You know Roma passed Sunday night."

"My mother told me. I'm sorry."

"Me too." A stray tear ran down her face. The tough girl slapped it away. "Well, your mother is arranging the funeral. Paying for it. I guess I got to thank you for that."

"It's the least we could do."

"Yeah, well, thanks." She shuffled her feet. The tough girl obviously hated to be beholden to him. "At least Mama knew me before she went. I'd snuck by there a couple of times before the hotel blew up, but she was out of her head, and I wasn't sure she remembered. But this time I'm sure she did." The feet went into a bulldog stance. "You got my cigar box."

"Ah, yes. Follow me." He led her down the hall toward the den. He'd shut the room off, still planning to call the junk man to come cart off the shredded sofa.

Belinda didn't blink at the mess. In fact, she looked a little proud. Too proud.

"This was you, wasn't it?"

"You blame me? I needed my money to get out of town. Where'd you have it hid, anyway? I looked everywhere."

"It was in my car." He took the cigar box off the desk and handed it to her.

Belinda opened it.

"What's this?" She pulled out a check from the Pacific Avenue State Bank.

"A little present from me and my mother. Besides the funeral, I mean. We decided you should have a share of Tom's oil money, since you're kin."

Her mouth dropped open. In her unguarded surprise he saw a hint of Resa around the eyes, in the softness around the mouth. It didn't last. The face hardened into suspicion, then indifference, then practicality.

"I guess that's fair. Roma did keep one of you out of the

313

rock quarry." The swaggering West Dallas girl was back. She was going to be so hard to help in any real way.

She stared at him like she wanted to say something else but shoved the box under her arm and turned to leave instead.

"Wait."

"Yeah?"

"That night we left together from the Star D. When we went to your place. When Martel—"

She winced. "Yeah."

"At the Star D, you didn't meet me from backstage. You got out of a car."

"Yeah, so?"

"I thought you might be getting dope. I checked your arms at your place. I didn't see any marks. If I misread you, I'm sorry, but if you need help, you can use that money for a sanatorium."

"I was in the car with Jill, asking her if I ought to talk to you or not. She wanted me to find out what you knew, what you were after. I never got tangled up with any dope. Mama did, so I didn't."

"Oh. I didn't realize."

"Yeah. But she got clean before she went. I'm proud of her for that." She looked down at the floor, then up at him. "If you want to come to the funeral, seeing as how you're paying for it, you can. It's tomorrow."

"I'd be honored."

Belinda buried her mother at Fishtrap Cemetery. Weather stood between his half-sister and Charlotte as the women tossed wildflowers onto the casket. His mother's husband and Jane stood nearby. A smattering of Roma's neighbors attended, but not many could afford to take time off from jobs to go to any funeral not their own or their own kin's.

Belinda asked Weather to throw the first shovelful of dirt into the hole, and as he pitched it in, he sensed a lightness he hadn't felt in years. The past went into that hole, too. Tom Weather, his legacy of betrayal and deceit, gone. Weather's own isolation from the family, gone. His shame at Tom Weather's past, gone. He was free of Tom's ghost at last.

After the funeral, Bill Hilyard and Charlotte rode in the hearse back to their own car at the funeral home. Weather and Jane drove Belinda in the Saratoga to Union Station. Belinda was headed for California, to seek out the Tomcat's other family, the Spencers, whom Weather had told her about, and to see Hollywood. She might want to take some acting lessons, she said, and figured that was the best place to do to it. She allowed Weather to pay a porter to load up her luggage, but declined any poignant goodbyes. He figured that was her right, and allowed her the dignity of shrugging him off.

He sat at the station until the train pulled out, not sure if Belinda knew he'd waited or not.

Jane left him there to get back to the paper. At loose ends and unwilling to dwell too much on the day's events, he drove to the hospital to visit whomever he could. The nurses still wouldn't let him see Hadley. He went to Mac Porter's room, where Sylvia, Resa, and Troy sat by the oilman's bed.

"If you hadn't been gambling," Sylvia Porter was saying. Weather guessed from Mac's peeved expression that this was the five hundredth time she'd said it.

Mac greeted him like a past-due savior and asked everyone else to step out. He needed a word with David. They left and Mac motioned Weather closer.

"You did resign from the D.A.'s, for sure?"

"Yep."

"Good. Then I'm hiring you to hear this."

Before Weather could protest, Mac started talking. He had requested the audit the day of the bank robbery because he thought Curtis was stealing from the Portex Oil account. Red Holcomb and Curtis had assured him that the gambling debts he owed them required a certain amount of blindness where the bank account was concerned. If Mac didn't leave it alone, eight-year-old Troy might fall into a rock quarry.

Weather burst out laughing.

"What is so funny about a child being threatened like that?"

"Nothing. What is funny is I always felt bad about my father killing Red Holcomb, and now I don't, that's all. I didn't realize 'til now how he was involved. I always thought he was an innocent victim, that I should have stopped the plane crash somehow—"

"I don't know how you could expect to stop an accident, if that's all it was." Mac peered at him from the hospital bed and rubbed his beard stubble. "It wasn't just an accident, was it?"

Weather watched the older man and decided to keep the truth about the crash to himself.

Weather left the hospital free of Red Holcomb's ghost as well. He went by the Star D for a drink and to dirty himself up a bit. If he got any more squared up over any more of Tom's old debts, he would be too clean to live in this town, and now was a bad time to move away. There was a certain young lady reporter with an interesting past he wanted to explore.

"What I don't understand," Weather said to Jane later, as they engaged in some careful—injuries still a problem—necking on her den sofa, "is why you were kissing Albert. You went undercover to catch your cousin's killer, and you were kissing him."

"He was not my cousin's killer."

"Was, too. I saw the anchor tattoo on his arm. He was the guy the Chicago cops wanted, Robert Verdi. And you were kissing him."

"He was Robert, but Robert didn't kill Christina. He tried to save her. She was a dope fiend, and couldn't quit. She jumped."

"How do you know?"

"Because he paid for her trip to the asylum. He showed me the receipt he kept in his wallet. He tried to help her. 'I never killed a woman in my life, and I'm not gonna start with Christina's cousin,' he said. I was kissing him out of gratitude. For sparing my life and trying to save hers."

"And you believe that, unequivocally?"

"He did save us, didn't he?"

"Yeah, he did. But that doesn't mean he—"

"Hush," Jane said, and found a way to shut him up.

Thursday morning, Creevy called. Dental records verified that the skeletons in the lake were those of Marie Chantilly and Celeste Carré. Creevy also corroborated that Marie's mystery boyfriend had been Cab Allgood from the bank. Marie had possibly discovered his true nature and booked a train to go home. She and Celeste packed up in a hurry, but Cab must have caught them before they got out of town. Cab must have put the bodies in Willie's lake, in case Curtis ever needed any leverage.

"Helluva joke on Willie," Creevy said.

That afternoon, Weather opened his den to Biedermeier and two junk men. Jane had taken off work and had come over to fight over the fate of the shredded sofa.

"A sofa with this much history should be restored," she argued.

"A sofa with this much history should be burned at the stake," Weather countered, and ordered the workers to cart it off. He wanted his den back, and getting rid of the sofa seemed to be the only way to reclaim the room.

The junkmen upended the monstrosity and maneuvered one end through the doorway.

"No," Jane said playfully and tugged at a claw foot. It came off in her hand.

Cylinders of tightly rolled hundred dollar bills spilled onto the floor.

Additional acknowledgement information:

Other books that served as general references for Dallas history include:

Big D: Triumphs and Troubles of an American Supercity in the 20th Century, by Darwin Payne, Three Forks Press, Dallas, 1994.

Dallas, Public and Private: Aspects of an American City, by Warren Leslie, Grossman Publishers, New York, NY, 1964.

The Hidden City, Oak Cliff, Texas, by Bill Minutaglio and Holly Williams, Dallas: Elmwood Press and The Old Oak Cliff Conservation League, 1990.

The WPA Dallas Guide and History, Gerald D. Saxon, Maxine Holmes, eds., Dallas Public Library, Texas Center for the Book, University of North Texas Press, 1992.